LOVE LESSONS

"If I move in less than an inch and do what I've been aching to do all night, it won't stop with a kiss. . . ."

"I know," she whispered back, her voice full and husky.

"And if I walk you to your door, most likely I won't stop at the threshold. I'll carry you over it."

"I know."

"Two years is a long time . . . and two minutes can feel like two hundred years . . . and two days can feel like two seconds, when somebody makes you feel like this," he breathed, daring to reach out and trace the delicate line of her jaw. When she closed her eyes, his fingers caught on fire; and he felt the silken edges of the fine hair just behind her ear.

"Two years can feel like forever, and two days can feel like a lifetime . . . making patience so hard to come by, but I know that this is worth taking slowly," she murmured, touching his bottom lip till it quivered.

Other books by Leslie Esdaile

LOVE NOTES
SLOW BURN
SUNDANCE

Published by BET/Arabesque Books

LOVE LESSONS

Leslie Esdaile

BET Publications, LLC
www.bet.com
www.arabesquebooks.com

ARABESQUE BOOKS are published by

BET Publications, LLC
c/o BET BOOKS
One BET Plaza
1900 W Place NE
Washington, D.C. 20018-1211

First Printing: September 2001
10 9 8 7 6 5 4 3 2 1

Printed in the United States of America

This book is dedicated to all of those people in my life who have taught me the most profound lessons about loving another human being. . . .

To God, who loved and loves me when I sometimes didn't and don't love myself

To my loving husband, Aldine Jerome Banks, Jr.

To my children: Helena, Angelina, Crystal, and Michael

To my parents, William and Helen Peterson, and to my stepmother, Patricia Peterson

To my loving extended family: Mom and Dad Esdaile, Aunt Hetti and Uncle Harold, Aunt Jessie and Uncle Charlie (married for fifty years), Uncle Irvin and Aunt Doris, Aunt Amy, and Aunt Yvonne . . .

To those dearly departed souls, who are still with me and teaching me love: my mother—my best friend, Aunt Julia, Aunt Ruby, Nana Thornton, and Grandmom Pete

To my roadies, Tina and Andre, who always have my back

And to my other friends too numerous to name. . . .

I love you and thank you for all that you continue to teach.

One

Heathrow Airport, London

Trevor Winston looked down at his hands and rolled his shoulders as he waited for his flight back to the States to board. It seemed that he was always out of phase, jet-lagged, and too early or too late to make a difference. He was born too early, but late in the year—that's what Miss Cleo, their neighbor who read cards, had told his mother was his cross to bear. Destiny, she'd said.

Morose thoughts collided in his brain as he watched the comings and goings of passengers who linked up with loved ones in the airport before they went on their way. There had never been anyone to meet him at the other end of a journey that he could remember. In his experience, such emotional depth had been only on celluloid. Maybe that's why he had distanced himself after he'd been on the road when his father passed on. Odd, but he'd been away every time there was a critical family juncture . . . like when his mother closed her eyes, his wife overdosed, and even when his son took his first steps.

The goddess of fate seemed to have been conspiring and laughing at him as he'd come home feeling guilty and trying to fix everything after the fact. She seemed to know that he'd never forgive himself for where he'd been when the telephone call came in and went unanswered for days . . . and he was sure she relished the fact that his nerves were shot, and he couldn't even allow himself the simplest pleasures now without wondering what might be going wrong while he was off indulging his senses.

So, he'd stopped her laughter by stopping his own. He'd beat her at her own game by going celibate. He'd never miss a family-crisis telephone call again because he was untraceable, or spending the night absorbed in some woman's arms. The only card fate still had in her hand was that he had to travel to do his gig. One day, he'd find a way to best her hand in that game as well.

Sure, he'd always shouldered his responsibilities once he'd returned, but the fact that he'd always arrived just after each critical event now disturbed him. Somewhere between boarding calls, and between film shoots, and artists' conferences, and film festivals, and living, he was missing life.

His career had been clearly out of phase with his marriage from the beginning. Initially, he was out of step with the reality that his paramour wanted to be his wife, and had sealed their fate to be permanently connected by an unplanned-for child during the art-for-art's-sake years. So, he'd married her—again, making an obligatory move that was out of sync with that of his filmmaking contemporaries. Then, he'd been so distanced from her needs that heroin became her best friend, and he didn't even know it until it was too late. He just hoped he wasn't too late to hear his son's cry for attention.

Trevor looked out at the gray mist that pervaded London weather. Gray. His life was shades of gray, just like this environment, which he hated but to which he was repeatedly drawn. Why was all of this crashing in on his brain now? He knew how London was, and was used to traveling alone. In fact, he preferred it.

As he looked around, a strange awareness began taking shape in his head. London was like his ex-wife had been. Seductive to the intellect, but damning to the spirit, and filled with the clashing contrasts of gray business suits and underground black-leather punkers who sported neon hair. But why was she permeating his brain after all of these years? Memories of what transpired threaded their way through his soul and called him like sirens. He rubbed his face with his hands to remove the image, but like a dull, yellowed silent film, it ran through his mind to no avail.

Distanced from her family by their marriage and lifestyle, Jennifer had died seven years ago between those pallid shades. It was too late when he realized she'd been caught in the vise-like grip of being an artist herself and a new mother, and she'd allowed heroin to win, leaving him at another out-of-sync crossroads of being a traveling filmmaker with a year-old infant. Thank God for his own mother and sister then. Distance had first been his and Jennifer's ally, then soon had become their enemy. Then distance from everything had become his shield.

But, as all things do, that also changed. New York was too fast for his mother after his father had died, and his sister had already moved to Philadelphia to marry, then get divorced. At the time, moving his New York flat with them seemed to make sense, for where was home anyway? He'd thought he was making the right decision to buy the huge duplex on Springfield Avenue in the heart of a West Indian area in Philly. What did it matter; he was never there.

Plus, he no longer knew the people he called family back in Jamaica. That split had occurred when he was almost ten. He and his immediate family stayed in New York until he was thirty, but he was rarely there in his college years long enough to see a season change. He always had somewhere to go, places to be, people to see and capture on film.

London, where he met his son's mother, who soon became his ex-wife, repeatedly beckoned him and his cameras. Jennifer never did take to the States, so there was always the jockeying back and forth between London, New York, and California, but L.A. was her downfall. That was his fault, he reasoned, as he'd never had to bring her there for his first real significant gig.

Trevor tried to focus on the decisions he'd made and find peace. His choices had been logical. The rent for both intercontinental flats and the sublet on the West Coast was more than the mortgage on the grand old manor he'd purchased to house his sister and his mother and his son. Yes, that made sense. Just like it made sense to give up his sublet apartment in L.A. now, too. "Let it go, mon," he whispered, and shut his eyes, trying to get the headache that was forming to recede with the memories.

But, like the migraine, the images persisted until he could see them even with his eyes closed. He could see the duplex, which had big rooms, a nice front yard, and a garden in the back; it was near a park and solid public transportation. His mother could walk to the African and Caribbean markets on Baltimore Avenue, and his sister could ride the trolley to work at the VA hospital down the street, and Miquel could go to a charter school with children of every race and denomination. They'd loved the place, and loved his son, and that was all that mattered. Perhaps that was the only thing he did do right.

The wait for the flight felt interminable. Today, he just wanted to go home, and get into his own bed, and eat real food, and hold his son. He'd been on this junket for three months. Before that, he had only been home a couple of weeks before it was time to jet again. He needed time to think, to wash the travel out of his bones. He was sick of rock videos, rap videos, and of capturing shallow snippets of humanity on reels. What was the purpose? The thought of the entourages and excesses made him want to vomit, and he looked down at the small shopping bag filled with games and gadgets he'd brought for his son in exchange for his unending quest for artistic freedom. What the hell was the purpose?

They'd told him that he was too far ahead of even the avant-garde curve, and that his documentary films were too explosive and editorial, and on the bleeding edge, versus the cutting edge, of that insular industry. His movie concepts had been timed incorrectly from a developmental standpoint. The music videos had been lucrative because of his off-the-hook style, yet were a soul-dredging alternative to keep his hand in the business and his skills fresh. Yes, timing, he reminded himself. Time was running out to take a significant place in Miquel's life. The boy was eight, and it had come upon him like a time-space-continuum warp. One moment the boy was toddling around, the next moment, he was in grade school.

Trevor kicked the shopping bag with disgust, knowing that after each trip, his son showed more and more disinterest for the things he'd brought as a trade-off—because even the child had come to understand that the value of his father's time couldn't be replaced by toys. The trinkets no longer mattered. His son had challenged his world order. It was time to get real.

Fatigue crawled through Trevor's system like a virus, attacking every cell within him. If he felt this tired at thirty-eight, then what would forty, fifty, and sixty—if he made it that far—feel like, he wondered?

And what had happened to all of his dreams? It seemed like yesterday he was playing in the dirt in front of his home in Kingston, and like a flash, his parents had uprooted the entire brood of Winston children to play on the concrete in Brooklyn. In another sweeping, immediate time-space-differential, it seemed like he was transported to film school at NYU, then to Philadelphia to get his masters of fine arts at

Temple University, studying in London briefly under an exchange program fellowship, then married with a child on the way, and whisked into the music video scene—from which there had been no escape.

Trevor studied the lone silver bangle that his father had given him to remind him of his roots, and chuckled sadly to himself. "Golden handcuffs, brother," he murmured, then closed his eyes.

Music videos had not been his view of art, or what he'd wanted to contribute to the world. He'd wanted to create poignant views that exposed the issues of the people who had no power. He had wanted to tell the story that nobody had cared to hear. He'd wanted to be an advocate for the voiceless, and now he was making stars out of gangsters and drug addicts. Perhaps the worst part of it all for him was that he was so well paid for that type of work, whereas, if he'd gone back to documentaries, he'd have to scrape for grants and raise money to tell those stories that nobody seemed to want to hear these days.

At first, he'd convinced himself that there was a reasonable trade-off, and that he could save enough money to get back one day to his original intent. But, again, time was slipping by, just as his intentions were. Each substantial royalty check and payment always seemed to go to some operational expense—the mortgage, the charter school tuition, his sister's kids, a family member who required help—and to pay the high cost of his travels and lifestyle.

What would he do anyway? he wondered. If he stopped now, he'd never get back to his dream, and would never be able to finance it. But if he kept going the way he was going, he'd never remember how to hear the unheard voices, or have time to listen to them, much less film them—and would still never reach his dream. Yet, if he stopped now, perhaps he wouldn't lose his son's precious moments, and could capture them on the one format that never eroded—the celluloid construct of the heart.

Weariness collected itself between his shoulder blades and fanned out through his nervous system. One thing was for sure: he couldn't keep this up much longer. His mother had been right. Maybe it was time to take his son to Jamaica, where a bevy of cousins and aunties and family could watch out for the boy's welfare. But how do you re-enter a place that is more foreign to you now than London? And how do you just drop off your child to people who are now strangers with the hopes they will pick up where your deceased mother left off? No. That was just running from the problem. He had to face his demons and look them squarely in the eyes.

Trevor let his breath out on a long exhale. The life of an independent filmmaker was no life for a child—traipsing to every corner of the globe, keeping late hours, and maintaining a non-traditional lifestyle. Especially since his son had already been abandoned once, by the mother in London who didn't want the responsibility of raising an interracial child while the father of that child was out chasing his dreams, and capturing fictional images on reels.

Guilt clung to the fatigue within him like a spent lover. It was bad enough that he'd left his eight-year-old son in the care of a series of irresponsible sitters and caretakers after his mother died two years ago, while his sister had to work in a strange new town. But the fact that his sister or the sitters hadn't even had the diligence or presence of mind to follow up on the child's teacher's requests to come to the school had added insult to injury.

Yet, who was ultimately responsible for his child—him, or them? So there was no sense in getting all puffed up with righteous indignation, he reminded himself, especially when he was the one to blame.

Thankfully, his sister, Gretchen, had come up with

a temporary solution: inviting a cousin from Jamaica to come live with them for a while to watch both her children and Miquel. But their cousin was a mere child herself, studying at the university. When was his child-cousin, Samantha, supposed to have her youth? If his mother had still been alive, she would have asked him this same question without blinking. Only God knew how much he missed his mother. . . .

He'd once duped himself into believing that he could do this parenting thing without any wise counsel, and had lived like a monk for the past two years to prove it—focusing only on his craft to support his sister, then cousin, and always his son. Somehow, he now understood that all that he'd bought for his parents paled in comparison to the steady love and sense of grounding they'd given him. In the end, it was time that he couldn't buy back. The bills he'd paid for his parents, the cards he'd sent them, the house he bought for his mom . . . none of it gave them what they would have cherished most: their son.

Now, he was a father, and despite all that he materially lavished on Miquel during his absences, he hadn't given the boy what his own hardworking father had given him: a pat on the back while working under the hood of a car, a slap on the bottom when he'd done something wrong, a wide grin and a big hug at the very moment he'd accomplished something new. Constancy. The gift of consistent interaction that he'd taken for granted until that consistency was gone. The void was immeasurable.

So he'd cloistered himself. He wasn't quite sure why he'd taken such an extreme approach. Initially, he told himself it was grief. Then, he told himself that he was getting his head together. But the abstinence hadn't brought him home more.

Today, the images whispered to him until he understood that it was guilt, which seemed like another self-absorbed solution—which only made him feel even worse. He hadn't done it for them, if he were to be truly honest, he'd done it for himself—out of guilt. "God help me," he whispered, now staring out at the throng of people amongst whom he felt so insignificant.

He'd purged his system of wine, women, and song. He'd become absorbed in his work, which made him better at his craft, which in turn made him more sought after in his industry, which increased his profits from it, which now made it harder to leave it, which had taken him even farther away from his family, which resulted in his son not having a father around, which he knew was making his mother roll over in her grave. Catch-22.

Trevor leaned forward with his elbows on his knees and held his head between his hands to steady himself. He shut his eyes tightly to hold back the tears. At that time when he'd made his solemn vow to himself, it seemed as if it were the only private honor he could count on, the only way he could convince himself that all of his self-denial was for a worthy cause, and the only punishment that seemed adequate. For how could he justify being out until all hours, drinking and lounging in the arms of women, while the women in his family worked and cared for his son, receiving only his checks and notes and presents in the mail from some foreign land?

Plus, those women who wanted to be stars who hung around the sets, sat in the coffee houses and discussed rhetorical philosophies, then followed the subjects of his film shoots like zombies, were too reminiscent of Jennifer. Despite their outward beauty, there was a gray cast to their spirits, a lack of light to their beings, and something that he was now afraid to encounter—the loss of his soul.

So when his body ached for one of them, he reminded himself that they were vampires who only came out at night, and for money. He also reminded himself of the fact that he was bitten by one of them before, and was on the edge of turning into one of them forever. Sometimes the image made the ache to make love go away . . . sometimes the image stoked the need to a level of agony only comparable to drug withdrawal. Sometimes, the ache never came at all. Then, like today, it would start in his groin and move throughout his body disguised as fatigue, only to transform into loneliness, before it attacked him unaware.

Then his mind would play tricks on him, starting out the inner conversation about important things, and sad memories, as it was doing now, lulling him into a sense of safety before plunging him into the emotional void that made him ache for a woman's touch. The ache would then permeate his being, robbing him of sleep, distracting his thoughts, reminding him about things he didn't want to remember, and settling in his heart to accost him out of the blue—just to rekindle the awareness of just how lonely he was.

Trevor sat back and opened his eyes. "Not today, demon," he muttered under his breath. He had no right to focus on his own needs, despite what his mother's friend, Miss Cleo, had said. Such self-indulgence in his career had already led him to this juncture. He couldn't, and didn't want to, imagine what chaos paying attention to his inner spirit and his physical body might possibly bring to his family. Celibacy just made sense until he could sort it all out. He didn't need another Jennifer on his hands, or in his son's life.

Because, as his son age, the boy's needs seemed to change, and required more of him with each passing day. Why hadn't he seen this coming, and why hadn't he listened to the wise souls who had done this before?

When Miquel was a toddler, having someone available to simply love him, play with him, feed him, and keep him relatively safe had been enough. However, with each new school year, the developmental process of his son required more participation, and more involvement. It was basic. He knew it.

Trevor let his breath out hard as he stood in solitude and searched the flight board. He needed to get home and back to the place that contained his most precious creation—his son.

There seemed to be an ironic, inverse relationship to nurturing and raising another being, he mused. When the tiny person was very young, the focus had to be upon life support, safety, and basic survival. But, as that being got older, he became adept at independently making himself food, and selecting clothing, and even walking to school unescorted . . . yet his mind still required attention.

So many people had been right about this fact, and he'd been running from something indefinable for so long. Although he didn't know what it was, he did know that a change was eminent. He also prepared himself for the righteous indignation that he was sure would come from the old bat now in charge of teaching his son. That only gave him one day while in the air, and one night while he tried to sleep, to assess the damage of his travels for eight years, and to get immersed in the true raising of his son. This woman wanted to know his "plans." He didn't even know what he planned to do with his own life, much less his son's! She wanted to know if there was any way for him to restructure his life so that he could include more of Miquel in it, and he'd landed himself in the ironic position of having to explain it all to a teacher.

That left one friggin' day to figure out what he hadn't been able to figure out in all of this time, to plan his next move—when every move he'd made to date had been ill-timed from a cosmic perspective.

Watching the line slowly form, he gathered his carry-on luggage and his parcel, and moved like a robot behind a couple at the end of the line. He reasoned that after his sister had taken her normal passive-resistant approach, ignoring no less than five notes from the school by simply sending them directly to him overseas, his son's fifth-grade teacher would be sure to have transformed into a she-wolf—fangs out, hair growing on the backs of her knuckles, ears pressed back to her skull. But he was ready for all of that. He'd dealt with such authorities before, as well as people questioning how a bachelor could raise a little boy alone.

What he wasn't ready for was having to ask himself the question about what he'd done with all of his squandered time.

Two

Philadelphia, PA

Corey Hamilton looked out over her fifth-grade middle-school class and drew in a sigh. As much as she loved working with the children, and even though she'd been fortunate enough to land a coveted post at the brand-new Technology & Arts Charter School, this was not how she'd planned to live her life. And this was nowhere near where she'd thought she would be at age thirty-two.

Like her eager students, she'd once grasped knowledge and looked at the world through excited, anxious eyes. That's why it had never dawned on her that she might one day wind up like her mother had—teaching, instead of *doing* what she loved, which was to make images on celluloid. But life has a funny way of derailing dreams, she noted, casting her gaze out to her class and praying that none of the children in her charge would ever have to watch their dreams be deferred.

Corey didn't resent that her own sense of adventure and opportunities to travel had to be curtailed right after she'd finished graduate school because her mother got sick. Being the only child of a single parent—one who had doted on her, pushed her, and who always had her best interest at heart—had its requisite responsibilities.

There was no thicket of family to fall back on, or to carry the weight of intense chemotherapy treatments, or to count on during her mother's last days, she ruefully thought, then forced herself to recant the mental comment. Yes, there was. Her mother had had true-blue friends, because that's the type of person she had been—someone who inspired people.

There was a strong network of fellow teachers and her mother's senior girlfriends who were like angels in disguise, and whom Corey would never forget. If she were honest, coping with her mother's illness had not been a resentment-filled task that she'd begrudgingly complied to perform. Rather, it had been an awakening of a deeper bond between herself and the one person she loved so dearly. Theirs had been a love sublime, filled with unconditional caring, and mutual friendship borne out of mutual understanding and need. And, in the wake of her mother's passing, she was left feeling bewildered and alone . . . because those friends of her mother, and all of the activity that they brought into the house, seemed now to be quietly receding.

That was the part that people didn't seem to understand about the passing of a good soul. It left a void. All of the activity centered on the caring of that loved one while they were sick, then tending to the logistics of disposing assets after they were gone. But who tends to the remaining, after the prescribed period of mourning? Corey wondered. And yet, she couldn't fault her mother's friends. They were hurting and bewildered, too. That much she was sure of, and had determined on her many trips to their homes to check on them, to bring by a cake, and to deliver balm to their injured spirits. What she missed so badly was the person who'd always kissed her life's boo-boos, who understood that although she was young and seemed energy-filled with her future in front of her . . . most of the time she was also very afraid.

Corey surveyed her students, who were busily copying their activity assignments for the day from the blackboard. In that moment, she wished that she could turn back the hands of time and be like them, worrying about only the little things in life, and knowing that they had someone bigger and stronger to depend on. Then again, not all of the children had even that gift.

She cast her gaze over the one child in her class who she knew didn't, and she allowed her spirit to invisibly wrap itself around the boy, giving him an unseen mental kiss of encouragement and love. Who listened to his dreams? she wondered. Who heard his fears and kissed his boo-boos? If being without this type of support for only eighteen months had cut her so deeply as an adult, then what effect was the loss of parents having on that one small child?

Corey looked at the child's round forehead, which was partially lowered to his paper as he furiously scribbled. Admiring the quiet, handsome face and wide, brown eyes that still reflected innocence and trust, Corey wondered how people could throw such a gift away before they'd even opened the full package of potential? To be loved for no other reason than because you were here on the planet. To be loved because God had breathed into your soul. That's what children gave you for nothing, and each child deserved to be a child, and to know that no matter what, they were dearly loved.

Suddenly, her mother's sacrifice to be a teacher didn't seem to be a sacrifice at all. As she stood behind her desk gazing at all of the children, her mother's words came into her mind. "One day, Corey, you will realize that this is not a vocation, but an avocation. To do your craft fulfills your ego, but to teach it to someone else fulfills your soul. And, when one of your children excels and grasps all that you have to share, and takes what he has learned beyond what even you know, the sense of joy is greater than you can ever understand until you've been there."

How many times had an adult rushed up to her and her mother in the supermarket, or out on the street, and thrown her arms around her mother with tears in her eyes? Corey thought back on those days, and how she'd become impatient at the intrusion to their planned schedule. Yet, each time, her mother would stop and listen, and the seeming stranger would pull out baby pictures, or rattle off her résumé with a child's expression of expectation—appearing to hold her breath until Mrs. Hamilton told her she'd done well. That was true power. The power to make such a mark on someone's life that twenty years later, that person still cared about your opinion of her.

She remembered those days of standing by her mother's side fidgeting while some adult talked about his life's progression, which, for her, was replete with girlhood glee, frenetic activity, and a home filled with warmth and discipline. Every child should have that. Corey sighed. Her own mother was a single parent, and still there was love, structure, and hope . . . What was happening today with parents, and why was there such a void for the children?

Her own one-and-a-half-year-old void had been enough to send a ripple through the complex matrix of multiple dreams she'd once shared with her mother. Now, after the passing, shallow relationships based on sex alone were not substantial enough. She'd learned that much as her mother was dying, when those men around her proved scarce when all she wanted was a shoulder to lean on—which was why dating, intimacy, and all of the rigors of courtship had been abandoned for well over a year.

Having no family and no children now frightened her, for she herself was a motherless child. And her mother's passing also made Corey realize just how ephemeral time was, and how few promises it committed itself to. For now, every major life decision, every female rite of passage, everything would have to be done without the sage counsel of her best friend and the only parent she knew. So, then, how could children be expected to make wise choices when they didn't even have a memory bank of wisdom bestowed on them from which to draw?

Her mind plummeted into her New World Order, hypothetical though her imaginings were. There would be no squeals of joy from her excited mom when she finally fell in love and got an engagement ring . . . or to assist with the planning of a wedding, or to girl-talk in the kitchen about the progress of a baby growing within her womb . . . nor would there be someone special to still her fears and listen to her thoughts about career, marriage, or life's lessons. Indeed, her mother leaving the planet to become an angel derailed a lot of dreams Corey had hoped to accomplish and share. Her loss had landed her in the midst of an unshakeable depression, which only the children seemed to momentarily heal. Yes, teaching here was an indefinable gift, one that she would fiercely guard.

Tears filled her eyes as the children began to get restless, and she quickly dispatched them to break into their assigned activity groups. Corey collected herself as they tumbled into the four corners of her classroom and rushed about finding their section tables, and she continued to wonder why some of the parents of her charges took such a gift of promise for granted? She was especially concerned about little Miquel Winston—the shy, precocious boy of eight who sat in the back of her room, and whose large brown eyes looked like pools of unspoken hurt. They told a nonverbal story that she wanted to hear, but was not given his permission yet to fully learn.

Corey allowed rage and indignation at that child's possible circumstances to burn away the tears and set her upon a focused mission for the day. Her fingers found her curly Afro and dragged themselves through it until her brain ceased its collision course with despair. She had to pull herself together, if not for her own well-being, then for her class.

Trevor looked down at his watch and drew in a slow breath to steady his nerves. He hadn't even seen his son last night—because he'd gotten in from the airport so late, and his cousin had sent the boy off to school while he'd slept. The parcels he'd left for Miquel weren't even opened, and it disturbed him that his sister and his cousin hadn't allowed the boy to wake him. Then again, maybe Miquel had been the one to choose not to wake him, feeling that there was no use since his father was never around anyway when it mattered.

He shook off the eerie feeling of dread and reminded himself that he was ready for anything his family might throw his way. The elementary school was no different. It was almost three o'clock, and he could hear the students getting last-minute instructions through the door as he neared his son's classroom. He was ready for this old bat whose letters had become increasingly curt each time she'd sent one. That's right. He was ready for anything, except Corey Hamilton.

As he peeped through the door leading into her classroom, the sight of her took his breath. She stood five feet seven inches tall, he guessed, with smooth coffee-colored skin that made him immediately want to rush out to get his camera. Her form was lean and athletic, but not angular, and her back was held straight with unwavering dignity—just the way West Indian women seemed to carry themselves in full command of their universe.

Her petite breasts rose and fell beneath her lemon yellow cotton shirt, and her khaki slacks gave him an exhilarating silhouette of her firm, round behind. She was radiant, and seemed to give off her own light from an inner source that even made her short-cropped, curly hair naturally glisten as she moved her head and lulled the class to attention with the warmth of her saxophone-inspired, North American voice. She was art . . . but as she turned and smiled, her lush mouth and large, deep brown eyes became a stop-frame of stunning. This could not possibly be the she-wolf, or his son's teacher. Where was the old schoolmarm?

It took Corey a moment to process the image. Out of the blue a man was at her door and her class was all giggles. Not just a man, but a finely carved ebony statue of three-dimensional art . . . standing six-foot-four, if an inch, with limpid dark eyes like still ponds that belied themselves to hint at more intense depth. His regal mane of locks graced his well-defined shoulders and covered a portion of a cinderblock-inspired chest, contrasting the fusion of exotic colors echoing from his shirt.

All she could do for a second was stare at the man who donned a bright, tie-dyed T-shirt and black leather pants and boots. And Lord have mercy was he wearing those pants! The glint of silver from a bangle caught itself in the light and snapped back her focus well before she allowed herself to look like a fool in front of the man and the children gaping with her.

From the corner of her eye she saw one of her students immediately stand up. Then Miquel's always closed expression opened itself on the face that rarely smiled, his eyes lit anew, and his smile combusted into a full giggle as he ran to the door, yelling, "Dad!"

Instantly, her expression darkened—eclipsing curiosity and the momentary flutter of fresh attraction to give way to serious disdain. So, this was the god who shattered little boy's worlds . . . who never came to important school meetings and events . . . who was absent at the science fair, who was never around to pat the child on the back, and who was so self-absorbed that he couldn't take a moment to come to the school to see about the issues his son was having now!

Her heart broke for Miquel Winston as she looked at the man who soaked in adoration from her student. Her mind screamed at the man who clutched the boy to his waist. No one had the right to do that to a child, especially when that father was so adored on his infrequent visits in and out of that child's life! Oh, to be sure, she'd slay him.

Corey held her anger in check as the children poured out of the classroom, stopping along the way to surround Miquel's father and ask him about all of the music videos he'd produced. She was so furious that her vision momentarily blurred, but she remained silent, allowing her favorite student to bask in the rare awe of his classmates, while he recited off his father's accomplishments like a show-and-tell project.

"Okay, okay, guys," Trevor Winston said with a chuckle, giving his son another hug. "Yup, I worked with them all at one point or another, and they put their pants on the same way you and I do, one leg at a time. Go ahead, before your parents get worried, or you miss your bus. I promise to come in one day and tell you all about it."

Corey could feel pins and needles in her fingertips that now ached to strangle the man in her doorway, who, by the way the students flocked to him, could have signed autographs for every child in her class. The nerve! It was bad enough that he promised his son stuff and didn't deliver, but now he was promising other people's children a guest appearance? And what would happen to little Miquel when the great Houdini didn't show his face at the school for another year?

She watched as Miquel's father stooped and hugged

his son, and then had to pry the child away from his chest, promising to walk home with him, look at his three-month-old science project, and have dinner with the boy. Hot tears of rage made her look away. To be that adored and to take that adoration for granted . . . there were just no words. So she waited until the boy could be convinced to leave the side of his idol to run with the other children into the schoolyard.

With her back to Mr. Trevor Winston, she cast her gaze out the window to witness Miquel joining the group—for once having a circle of boys around him listening to his stories with real interest. She just hoped that this child's newfound voice would not be muted again by another one of his father's disappearing acts.

"You see that?" she asked with a near whisper through her teeth as Trevor Winston fully entered her room. When he didn't immediately respond, she spun on him and pointed toward the window, finding a new level of control in her voice. "Look out of that window, Mr. Winston, and tell me what you see."

Trevor Winston knew hardball negotiating when he saw it, and could feel a trap coming from a mile away. Opting for a defiant nonchalance until he could figure out this teacher's angle, he shrugged. "I see the boys all doing what children do after school—playing in the schoolyard."

"What you fail to see, Mr. Winston, is the fact that your son is in the middle of a circle of little boys, who earlier today have ignored him, called him a geek, or teased him unmercifully. Now," she exclaimed, her chest heaving with sudden rage, "because you've materialized and walked into this classroom unannounced, this child is a hero. His dad works at making videos of the stars. His dad is no longer a myth or an urban legend or a bold-faced lie. And you just validated everything Miquel tried to tell them about you, but they didn't believe—while invalidating him as an individual worthy of respect on his own merit in the process."

Her eyes burned with such intensity that he had to look away. He'd never even considered the impact he could have by just showing up at the school out of the blue. But what was he supposed to do? Not come? That she cared so much for a child who wasn't even hers simply floored him. It had been so long since he'd witnessed someone caring so much about a cause that had no personal gain in it for them. Not since he was doing documentaries. Not since he'd been to Kenya, or to some of the remote parts of his own land.

"So that's a bad thing now, is it?" he replied, moving toward the window to see better while trying to avoid her glare. He glimpsed her struggle to remain professional in the wake of her rage, and wondered where this conversation would take her voice next.

"It is the subject I wrote to you about time and time again," she said with disdain, suddenly sitting on the edge of her desk as though her inner struggle for calm had made her legs give out. "Mr. Winston, have you any idea what your absences in this child's life are doing to his social, emotional, and academic development?"

Her weary tone and question had caught him off guard, even though he'd been trying to prepare himself for it. It had been the same question that had plagued him for too long, and yet, he still had no answer. This time, he turned around, faced her, and looked her directly in her eyes.

"I know that I have not been there for the boy like I should, and that a boy needs his father."

His simple statement of truth momentarily stunned her. She was not prepared for him to acknowledge her accusations, and was braced to listen to a long litany of excuses. A basic confession was not anywhere near what she thought this arrogant man would have offered.

"Mr. Winston—"

"—Trevor," he corrected without blinking. "I am

fortunate as a parent to have my son's care and education guarded by such a fierce friend to him."

"Mr. Winston," she resumed, not moved by his sudden charm. "This child has been teased. Children in this school have set him apart, and a lot of it had to do with him bragging to fit in."

"I don't understand."

She watched his eyes search hers, truly seeming to want to grasp what had been occurring, and for the sake of the child, she went on in a less judgmental tone in order to make him understand.

"When he came to this school, his grandmother had just passed. I take it she was his primary caregiver?"

"Yes," Trevor Winston murmured, casting his gaze to the wall maps and books scattered about the room.

"And he kept talking about how his dad was doing all these wonderful things all around the world, and would show off by saying you were in London, Japan, Italy, Australia, Canada, Africa, wherever, and he obsessed about which stars you were doing a video for next. In trying so hard to fit in, and to downplay how devastated he was by losing his grandmother—then having this string of baby-sitters replace his aunt when her hospital shift changed—it impacted the way the other children felt about Miquel, because he always had to have the top story, to prove that his dad was doing things that were greater, or more important, than the other kids' parents. He was making you larger than life to fill up the hole left in his heart by your mother passing on . . . and to convince himself that you were immortal and wouldn't die, too, like his own mom did. This child has been so afraid that you might not come back—or that something could happen to his aunt Gretchen, and you wouldn't get there until after the funeral, or something like that. I started talking to Miquel when he began staying in at recess because of the boys picking on him, and he began hanging out here after school because there was nobody home . . . so I let him help me clean up."

He could not face this warrior angel whose voice was now soft and not accusatory, but whose eyes still burned with protective passion about his son's fate. What could he say? Trevor ran his palm over his locks and paced away from her, keeping his gaze now to the floor.

"Then," she went on, her voice breaking slightly with emotion, "because children can be cruel to one another, they started challenging his stories, saying that he was an orphan, that he didn't even know who his dad was, and that his parents were probably drug addicts—and that's why he made up the stories. Finally, fights started happening, always with Miquel in the center of the conflict. Soon, his work and class participation started deteriorating, but I couldn't seem to get anyone from your family to come in to discuss strategies to work with your son."

Tears had brimmed in his son's teacher's eyes, and she wiped them away without shame, which made his heart lurch with guilt. Her broken voice, the tone that showed how much she truly cared, the truth that she spoke, and those beautiful eyes that glistened with unspent moisture were all too much at once this soon. His gaze slid back to the window, and it took a moment for him to respond to the charges.

"I just got back from Japan and London, and my cousin is in school by day. My sister works. What the boy told the others about me traveling is true."

"There's no dispute about that, Mr. Winston," Corey said calmly, "but you haven't heard a word I've said."

"I've heard you," he whispered, feeling his throat close with emotion. "I'll fix it."

"You can't fix it on a pop-in basis, Mr. Winston. This child needs consistent interaction he can count on—the kind your mother used to give him until she passed. Did you see the way you had to pry him away from your body, as though you would disappear and be gone again for God only knows how long? Did you notice the way he begged you to look at his science project from months ago, in front of the others, and to just take him to McDonald's! I kept that project on the back table to reassure him that you'd see it when you came back—even after all the other kids' parents had come to collect theirs—his, I kept out."

Corey hopped off the edge of her desk and began walking in a circle. She'd seen these types of parents before, from all walks of life. From those with no jobs who prioritized street life over their children, to black urban professionals who couldn't detach themselves from a cell phone long enough to hear what their children were saying. Each one of them had an excuse. Each one of them promised to do better, to be more involved, to *fix it*—and each one of them eventually lapsed back into apathy, citing the stresses of daily life over the prioritization of their kids. But today, for all of those children who didn't have an advocate, she now had a parent with a bad rap sheet cornered in her class, and she was gonna give him what for.

"I said, I will handle my son!" Trevor said more loudly than intended, then inwardly cringed at the outburst.

"Don't you yell at me for caring about your child and making you address what nobody should have to tell you—and then have the audacity to tell me about a quick, just-add-water solution, Mr. Winston," she seethed. Oh, it was *on* now. Definitely.

This woman was digging at a fresh wound, and had no idea how tender it was. It had not been his objective to lose his cool; in fact, he rarely ever did. But there was something about the way her eyes bore through him that took away any inner place to hide. His mother used to study him like that. "I know what to do for him. I can fix this," he restated more calmly. "He'll be all right."

"I have watched this kind, extremely intelligent, gentle little boy go from being an outward braggart, to a social irritant, to now being so closed off from any participation in class that, if he were not in a charter school with a low teacher-to-student ratio, the administration might have missed what's really wrong and incorrectly labeled him ADD, drugged him with Ritalin, or slapped some other type of stereotypical designation in his school file—that would follow him all of his life. And you, of all people, should know what can happen to black male children if they get caught in the web of some system, with the wrong image and perception. You're a filmmaker. You know about image and perception, right?"

"I do, and I know—"

"This is downright neglect! I won't stand for it!" she bellowed, losing patience with her adversary's rhetorical responses. "Not when you are a parent with significant resources and education."

"Oh, so now you countin' me pockets and presupposing me education and résumé?" Guilt-dredged fury had broken his normally perfect, early British school system training down to a cross between cockney and patois. He held his tongue and jammed his hands into his pockets, knowing that if his speech had broken, he was on the verge of being so angry that anything might be said.

"That's right," Corey Hamilton went on, not the least intimidated by his response. "I don't care how humiliated you are, how embarrassed you are, how guilty you are, or how pissed off you are at this moment. All I care about is that you take the time to deal with this issue before you have no time left. Now, when you are interested in talking about some rational approaches and methodologies that might work, we can discuss this further. But right now, I don't know if I can have that civil conversation with you, Mr. Winston, and stay on the correct side of parent-teacher professionalism. Good afternoon."

She'd dismissed him? She'd literally walked over to her door after reading him the riot act, and flung it open until it banged, then dismissed him. She'd thrust her chin up in the air, rolled her eyes at him like she was going to call him into the street for an old-fashioned "fair one," slapped her hand on her hip, and given him the black woman's nonverbal warning to get out of her face. Where did she get the gall to speak to him, a parent paying hefty tuition, like that? And, what's more, she didn't blink or stutter when she'd read him. She didn't know jack about his life, his responsibilities, his pressures, or how much he loved his son! That presumptuous, bourgeois, know-it-all-without-knowing-the-facts . . .

He found himself pacing down the corridor and brushing by the concerned looks of the other teachers and parents helping out in the afterschool program. Then, as he approached the door leading to the schoolyard, he stopped, closed his eyes for a moment, drew a deep breath, and steadied himself. Miquel didn't need to see him like that, especially over his favorite teacher. Trevor let that reality sink in and ground him. He and Miquel would go get some dinner, tell some stories, laugh, and tonight, they'd do homework together.

"Damn!" Trevor yelled to the steel doors before opening them out to the yard. In all the fuss, he hadn't gone over to the back table to see his son's science project . . . which meant that tomorrow, for sure, he'd have to walk back into that classroom, face the she-devil, and give it the appraisal his son was waiting for. Why did that woman have to be so right?

Three

"You did what?" Corey's friend exclaimed between bites of lamb, breaking off a piece of spongy Ethiopian bread and shoving it into her mouth.

"I know, I know, Justine." Corey sighed, sipping her mango juice and shaking her head in disgust. "He'll probably never come back to talk to me about his kid. I literally lost it in there. I was so angry that I couldn't pull it together. I don't know why I was so upset in that moment. It was totally unprofessional, and worse, could have ruined the only chances that we had to encourage the father to participate."

"You need to call him," Justine said, sighing, "and fix this."

Corey's gaze slid away from her friend's, and she let out a long, sad breath. "Yeah. I do. I can't allow my personal opinion to get between this child's chance to have his father participate in his schooling, and I have no right to level a personal judgment about the way they run their family. I don't know what came over me, girl."

To Corey's surprise, her friend Justine chuckled.

"I do," Justine laughed slyly.

"What?" Corey asked in a whisper, becoming more depressed as her friend's mood shifted.

"Number one," Justine said brightly, counting off her points on gravy-stained fingers. "You are really, really attached to that student. Happens to all of us, at least once, if we're lucky as teachers. Miquel is going to be one of those children in your class that you will never forget, because the child touched you."

"And that's funny?" Corey remarked quizzically, now studying her friend's face.

"Let me finish." Justine chuckled again, now leaning her body forward. "Number two," she added with dramatic emphasis, "you were outraged because you know that boy comes from a solid family. His grandmother had been the salt of the earth, and his aunt used to come up there to the school in her hospital whites to pick him up, then a cousin, who is in college, now comes. Right?"

"Yeah, but—"

"And, threeeee," Justine said merrily, "you now know everything the boy said about his father was true, because he fell into your class like an African prince, and—"

"Wait. Hold it," Corey corrected, putting up her hand to stop her girlfriend's trajectory of thought before she finished. "This has nothing to do with—"

"Does too," Justine added with a wink, peeping past Corey's held-up palm. "The first thing you said to me was, 'Girl, you won't believe who had the gall and audacity to come into my classroom today, thinking he was *all that,* strutting in with some leather pants on and flashing a perfect smile, dropping the kids to their knees before him like he was some kinda god, and trying to be all nice, mesmerizing them with his baritone voice—after all he didn't do for his son. It was an outrage.' Didn't you tell me that?"

"Yeah, and, that's exactly what happened," Corey countered. "Then I read his butt and put him out."

"Look at you. Just look at you," her friend said, laughing. "And stop and listen to yourself. You didn't launch right into the discussion about what he said, or what you said to him about your student. Nope. You gave me a full description of the way this man's countenance nearly took your breath away, and you've been fired up, out of sorts, and angry beyond reason since the moment—"

"Oh, pulleeeze, gurl!" Corey scoffed, and snatched a hunk of bread, then scooped up a section of cabbage and vegetables with it and popped it into her mouth.

"How long have we been teaching together?" Justine asked as she pushed a silken strand of perfectly permed hair behind her diamond-studded ear, crossed her arms over her petite bosom, and thrust her chin in the air.

Corey glimpsed her friend from the corner of her eye and responded in the direction of her plate. "About two years. So?"

"And how far back do we go as friends?"

"Since grade school, where both our mothers taught. Why?"

"Then, since I know you both personally and professionally, I think I have a good sense of judgment about the way you respond to things. To date, even with the most outrageous parents, you have never lost your cool, or given them an ultimatum that could make them shrink away from participation, much less dismissed them."

"That's why I feel so badly about—"

"And I was not finished," her friend said, chuckling as she smoothed the front of her aqua-colored silk blouse after dabbing her fingers on her napkin. "The only time that I have ever seen you this passionate is when discussing politics, films, your students, or some man that you were interested in."

"Like I said," Corey hedged defensively, "I am very disturbed about what is happening to one of my students."

"You've had innumerable students, and we've discussed them like a social worker's caseload, right here in this same restaurant on Baltimore Avenue, and you've never once told me what any of their parents looked like—much less given me a description of their voice quality. Mesmerizing baritone. Hmmm . . ."

Corey let her breath out in an exasperated rush. "My concern is strictly—"

"It's all right," her friend said quietly, leaning closer so that their voices wouldn't be overheard. "Look, you're human . . . you care very much about the student—which is admirable—and you've taken him under your wing. You're angry that his father has been AWOL. You know that this family has the capacity to pull it together, unlike a lot of families, and you know that his father obviously is involved on some level. That's one of the reasons you're so pissed, because you don't want your special student to fall through the cracks, when the Winstons have the wherewithal to pull it together. You have higher expectations of them."

"Okay," Corey said, relaxing. "Now, you see my point. That's all I was trying to say."

"All right," Justine said with a wide grin. "To date, he's been no superdad, but he also didn't just up and leave the child with no support system, no roof over his head, and that brother did what a lot of single mothers and fathers have had to do for time immemorial—leave the children with the grandparents while they stabilized themselves economically. How many of us in our generation were sent down South or raised by an aunt or grandmother until Mom got out of school? But we were always loved, and had a base. Right?"

"Right," Corey conceded, trying to let her own value judgments about that option dissipate. Justine was making sense. A lot of folks were raised that way. Had it not been for her mother's fortitude after Corey's dad walked, she might very well have been raised by her grandmother until her own mother's career and finances stabilized. Until Justine laid it out on the table, she hadn't even considered that she still might be harboring latent resentment toward her own father for going AWOL on her and her mother all those years ago. Corey riffled her fingers through her hair and sighed.

"So, let's get this picture out of your mind that he just ran off to make videos and never interacted with that boy. He's not a deadbeat dad who doesn't care for the child's overall welfare, or you'll never be able to work with him on the child's behalf. Are you feeling me, Corey?"

"You're right . . . you're absolutely right." Corey shook her head and leaned back in her chair. "Mom would have said the same thing to me, and would have forced me to call that parent to apologize for my unprofessional—and unchristian, I might add—behavior."

"Given the circumstances that the grandmother and sister told you happened to the child's mother, what right do you have to judge the father—who both of them told you had switched residences, and has moved heaven and earth, to take care of that whole family? Gurl, the brother was scuffling, jetting, and doing what he knew how to do . . . maybe he doesn't have the type of touchy feely parenting skills you expect him to have, not because he's a slacker, but because he really doesn't know how. Ever thought about that?"

"I really hadn't," Corey admitted, suddenly feeling ashamed. "I used to talk to Miquel's grandmother, who said her husband always worked, and she took care of the kids . . . they were from that type of era, and—"

"And a lot of brothers think that their primary role is bringing home the bacon. Period. That's all they know. And you yourself know for a fact that when the female void is there, they don't necessarily know what to do. Usually a mother, aunt, sister, somebody steps in and that's what had happened here. Miquel's behavior didn't go awry until his grandmother passed and they changed his aunt's work shift."

"True."

"The man did surround his child with the best environment he could. Would you be as angry if he worked on the railroad, or was in the military, or worked on the Alaskan pipeline? What's up with that?"

"I know, I know, I know."

"Miquel was, and still is, a lucky little boy who is simply going through a family transition brought on by a crisis. The aunt is overwhelmed as a single mother, with teenagers herself and a tough job schedule, the cousin doesn't have the maturity to raise a child, and the father has to adopt some new skills and responsibilities. The family, with a little support in the form of discussing viable options, can pick up the baton from Grandmom Winston."

"If they're lucky, someone stable in that unit will pick up the baton." Guilt curled itself inside Corey's stomach, and suddenly she'd lost her appetite.

"In his mind, he probably started yelling because he's frustrated, cares, and doesn't know what to do," Justine implored. "So help him."

"Oh, girl, I really messed this communication thing up, didn't I? I didn't even give him a chance to explain, and don't know a thing about him, or what he and his family have been trying to do. I just jumped to conclusions, all out of pocket, and went off. Jesus."

"Yup," Justine said plainly, going back to their communal plate of assorted entrees. "But you do know that the man was divorced, his ex-wife died, and his mother died, leaving a terrible void in the child's life, and probably the father's life, too. And you ain't blind, as altruistic as you are. And you haven't had a date in like a year and a half—and have been living like a nun. And this tall, fine hunk just walked in off the street to make amends, and you couldn't process it. You overloaded and blew a fuse."

"That's not what happened at all," Corey argued, taking too deep a swig from her juice and almost choking.

"Admit it," Justine said, giggling and leaning in real close, "for a second he almost made you wet your panties, didn't he?"

"Justine!"

"Yeah, that's my name. Don't wear it out."

"For real, for real, that never even entered my—"

"Liar," her friend said amiably. "Then why is it so hard to call him and apologize?"

"Because . . . because . . . well, because, it was such a bad . . . because, there's now a professional breach of . . . oh, stop smiling like that! Cut it out, and get serious. I intend to call him and make amends. I'll deliver the olive branch."

"Tell the truth, gurl, since we go way back." Justine winked at her as she coolly sat back in her chair and tilted her head. "When you looked up and saw him standing at your classroom door, did you first say to yourself, 'Oh, whose parent is that?' Or, did you say, 'Oh, my God, *who is that?'* Be honest."

Corey looked away and closed her eyes for a moment.

"I thought so," Justine said, chuckling.

"Okay," Corey whispered. "The man is stop-your-heart gorgeous." She allowed the admission to mingle with the stomach acid now churning her meal.

"Pretty-boy fine, or rugged I'll-rock-your-world-like-a-real-man fine?" Justine inquired, giggling as she sipped her ginger ale.

"The latter," Corey admitted. "I don't want to talk about this. I want to talk about the rational, professional part of this conversation. None of that matters if this kid doesn't get some help."

"All right, party-pooper," Justine sighed, sounding dejected, even though mischief was still in her eyes. "We'll just talk about strategies to better communicate with this family. We won't talk about any potential animal magnetism or chemical reactions going on, and we'll keep the conversation focused."

"Thank you," Corey said on a rush of breath, allowing her shoulders to drop an inch as she did so.

"I'm your best friend, so I won't even bring up the fact that you have been so lonely lately that all you do is vacillate between tears and outbreaks of sudden fury. And we won't talk about the fact that the last time we went to the movies—last weekend, I believe—and saw that racy foreign film, you walked out of there like a junkie, all messed up, couldn't sleep for two days, and went on a cleaning spree until two A.M. to burn off that excess energy. And, because I've promised not to even discuss the subject, I'll keep to my word, and we won't talk about how when we went out clubbing, and that tall brother hemmed you up with a slow dance, you came back to the table with your hands shaking and told me to take your car keys. That was a month ago, right? Oh, yeah, it was."

"Justine, let it be. Leave me alone, girl."

"Oh, I promise. I'll behave myself in the context of this conversation. I told you I'd never bring up the situation that happened more than six months ago, when one of your ex-boyfriends called, said he was going to help you move some of your mother's furniture to one of her girlfriend's houses, and just being alone with him for an hour made you so horny that you came by my house so I could talk you out of going to bed with him. Naw, gurl, I'm your cutty. I would never bring up anything like that."

"I'ma kill you," Corey said, laughing and shaking her head. "Now, stop it! I cannot let my own personal circumstances bleed into this situation. For real, for real. It's dangerously tacky, unprofessional, unwarranted, and impossible. Plus, there is no sign of interest coming from the other side, and even if there were, I wouldn't react to it because it's not in the best interest of that kid. Okay? Case closed."

Justine shrugged and looked down at the plate.

"Okay. My bad. Well, you gonna eat any more of this, or can I polish it off?"

"Knock yourself out," Corey said, sighing.

Corey put the key in her mother's door, turned the lock, and slipped inside. The house was now an eclectic blend of her modern pieces and her mother's traditional belongings. Even though it had been more than a year since her mother had passed, it still felt strange to come home and not hear her voice. Suddenly, the place seemed too big for her. The small three-bedroom row house that she'd grown up in felt foreign, and Corey wrapped her arms around herself to stave off the immediate pang of loneliness.

Perhaps that was why she always liked to revel in the last vestiges of sunlight before having to turn on the lamp. Her mother always turned on the light. She, on the other hand, preferred the natural light, even twilight . . . maybe that was all that was left of her artistry in film—an appreciation of light.

God, how she needed a relaxing bath. What a day.

Moving upstairs swiftly, she entered her bedroom and turned on the radio. Music. Nice, smooth jazz . . . a bubble bath, a glass of wine, a good book . . . then she'd make that awful call.

Entering the bathroom, she adjusted the little plastic bowl under the tub pipe to catch the drip that was sure to come when she turned on the faucet. One day, she'd call in a plumber, she mused, swaying to the music. Yup, the house needed a lot of repair, and one day she'd call the different workmen required to fix the multiple problems that were a constant.

After adjusting the water temperature, she briskly walked down the steps, got her favorite wine and a long-stemmed glass, picked up her book, and returned to the bathroom to dump scented bath pearls in the water. Then she carefully arranged her wine, the glass, and the book next to the tub within her reach. Dropping her clothes in the middle of the floor, she slid into the warm suds, leaned back and looked out of the window to appreciate the sun going down in a rose-orange sky. Oh . . . yes . . . soft jazz, and this spectacle of beauty.

Why did things always have to be complicated, she wondered, when the world had such simple magnificence all around?

Taking a sip from her glass, she studied the way the dimming natural light reflected off the dark, ruby liquid. How could she blame a person for wanting to capture such beauty on film and put that to music, when that was what she herself wanted to do? She peered out the window and composed in her head, allowing the music to fuse with the image.

But music videos? At least the kind of music videos she had seen on cable. Where was the beauty in that? "Ugh," she scoffed, wrinkling her nose at the idea of it, then taking another deep sip of wine. "Perish the thought."

Corey closed her eyes and let the warmth of the water and the effects of the wine relax her. But instead of instant calm, her body tingled with a slowly creeping sensation that she couldn't ward off. She knew that soon her body would be under attack from acute frustration, and also knew that it had been getting harder and harder to ignore these unwanted episodes that came upon her with the stealth of a thief. It was also happening to her at the oddest times, not just when she was dreaming, or first thing in the morning, or in those quiet moments just before she was about to go to sleep.

Corey sat up, shaking off the ache that had settled between her thighs, and downed her glass of wine. Picking up her washcloth, she lathered it with soap and scrubbed her body hard, ignoring the stinging tips of her breasts. Nope, she was not giving in to this. She'd get out of the tub, busy herself with some chores around the house, read over her students' homework, make that important apology call, then get a good night's sleep. She was not going to think about the sensual scene from that movie she had foolishly allowed Justine to drag her to.

In fact, she argued internally, she was not going to read that book on the floor—which also had some graphic love scenes that were bound to make her crazy. Justine was insane. How was she supposed to read Colin Channer, with his fine Jamaican self, while celibate, and stay that way? The last scene she'd read had kept her tossing and turning for a week! Worst of all, she had begun waking up with her pillow between her legs.

Corey put down her glass, pulled herself angrily from the tub, snatched her towel, and gathered her clothes, leaving the wine and the book in the bathroom as she paced to her room. These feelings would subside, if she just got her mind off the wrong subject. But how in the world did her body just go there on its own, when she was just looking at a sunset, and not even thinking of anything in particular? Crazy. She was just wired from the day; that was all it was. Nervous energy was trying to convert itself into desire.

Roughly toweling herself dry, she flung the towel on the bed and grabbed the lotion. Nope. She was disciplined, and had been for almost two years. Some people could remain celibate—they did this every day. She pumped the lotion into her hands with fury and slapped it against her skin. People made firm choices about the quality of their lives, established their own value systems, and lived by them accordingly. She was not going to enter into any type of physical relationship with a man until they had become friends, and until a healthy foundation between them had been established. Doing any less had had emotionally devastating effects, and she for one was not about to continue a cycle of toxic relationships. And she was not going to have to masturbate all the time, either! Her life was full, challenging, and exciting. Sex was not a requirement to live, it was a want, not a need, and it could be curtailed through willpower.

Slathering on the lotion more slowly now, she sat in the twilight and steadied her breath, which she had been inhaling and exhaling too hard from the sudden burst of emotion. She closed her eyes and followed the shape of her legs with her hands, breathing deeply, and feeling herself become calm.

Okay. She could do this. She was in control. This was like going on a diet. No, it was a lifestyle shift like becoming a holistic eater had been. It was like giving up pork. Once you left it alone enough, you didn't even crave it when you smelled bacon. That's all that had happened today; she'd gotten a whiff of bacon, had salivated for a moment, her stomach had gurgled, and that moment had passed. . . .

When she moved her palms to her arms, smoothing on the lightly scented cream, she told herself that the goose bumps were from the sudden change in temperature. The water had been warm; the room was cool and airy. That's all it was, she told herself again, as she peered down at her taut nipples. Then why did they ache so . . . ?

Ignoring that part of her body, she added lotion to her thighs and tried to ignore the way they parted almost of their own volition as she applied cream to each one. And she also ignored the way her belly lurched and quivered when her hands found the tops of her thighs, feeling a heat emanating from the center of them that she dared not investigate. Moving away from that danger, she took her time to add lotion to her face, gently circling it with her fingertips with her eyes closed, and taking in her breath in short sips.

It seemed to help reduce the sting of her nipples

urgently throbbing in defiance, but with her eyes closed, her fingers found their way down her throat, across her collarbone, and to the underside of her now heavy breasts. Circling each aching globe, she promised herself that she would not touch the tender tips with the now warm lotion, for that sensation would surely be her undoing. But, to her dismay, when she reached for the bottle to replenish the dwindling amount of cream in her hands, her upper arms brushed the distended skin, which sent another quiver through her belly that connected with the swollen, angry heat between her legs.

In her haste to finish the task, she'd put too much cream in her hands, and somehow that excess found its way again to her breasts as her body fell back and her thighs parted once more of their own will. Telling herself no as the cream lapped against the hardened pebbles was futile, because her fingers had begun a gentle rhythm of circling, pulling, softly tugging to give way to lotion-filled palms that rubbed over the entire surface and backed away to yield to the interplay of her fingers. Rotating both tips between her forefingers and thumbs, she stifled a gasp as mounting desire throbbed in the region too aroused to immediately touch.

A shudder ran though her as one hand left her breast, slid down to her lower belly, and began its investigation in the moist private valley below. The rim of her opening burned and tightened, contracting and releasing itself in little spasms of need as she stroked the swollen lips that hid its entrance, and molten wetness met her fingers. Sliding her fingers up and down the slick outer seam, she chided herself each time her fingers went deeper on each pass they made. Unable to withstand the frustration of hovering just outside the angry nub hidden by folds, the tips of her fingers grazed past them to find the tiny secret petal that sat just inside their doors.

Somehow, her hands were not her own, and they defied her futile whispers to them to stop. *Two years,* became their reply as one fingertip pushed the petal back and forth to a hastened rhythm that matched the tugs at her nipple, which her other forefinger and thumb rolled between them. Then came the images in her mind, one in particular that she'd promised she wouldn't allow, and her legs parted wider, her hips rose and fell to meet it, and two fingers found their way into her depths.

Without mercy, her body replied in a hard staccato convulsion that jerked her head and shoulders and swept though her like a sudden, violent storm. Then she went still, and she lay in the middle of her bed, eyes tightly shut, breathing hard to regain her composure, while all of her promises to herself were momentarily forgotten.

Four

"Yo, Uncle T," Scott bellowed, jumping up from the kitchen table to thump his uncle's fist with his own, then embracing him with a macho hug as they laughed.

"Sight for sore eyes, dude." Trevor chuckled, holding the teen back, while accepting an additional series of squeezes from his eager teenage niece and cousin as both girls squealed with delight.

"Uncle Trevor!" Janelle exclaimed, nudging her way into the group hug that was forming around Trevor.

"Oh, me God," Samantha added, "I can't believe it! Uncle Trevor!"

"Did ya bring us anything from Europe?" Scott laughed, hitting Trevor's pockets.

"Gave your mom a whole bag of stuff," Trevor said, chuckling as he cast a concerned glance at his sister, who didn't acknowledge the comment.

"Yo, Ma, where's it at?" Scott whooped. "Brought us some promo videos, new releases?"

"Yeah, yeah, yeah . . . videos, CDs, coupla fly dresses for Janelle and Sam, some gadgets for Miquel, and for my sister—"

"Oooh!" Miquel yelled. "You didn't tell us you brought us stuff. Told you he always brings us cool stuff from being away! Aunt Gretchen, where'd you put Dad's stuff?"

"Yeah?" the two girls chimed in. "Dresses from Europe!"

"Auntie," Samantha said, giggling, "think I might have a date who could appreciate a new dress."

"Me, too," Janelle added, ignoring her mother's expression.

"Nobody is gettin' anythin' but dinner, so sit your butts down!" Trevor's sister exclaimed, becoming more peevish as the commotion continued.

"C'mon, y'all." Trevor chuckled hard. "Sit down before you get a whack-a-da-spoon."

Exchanging kisses and hugs with the children, Trevor laughed and teased them and pulled Miquel in, as the smallest child fought for a dominant position by his father's side.

"Told you he was coming, and he even came up to school," Miquel quipped, holding on to his father's waist as though Trevor were a prized possession that could get trampled in the melee. "He came to see me first, too."

Ignoring the scowl Miquel's comment put on his nephew and sister's face, Trevor ruffled his son's hair and dismissed the sudden undercurrent as he marshaled the bunch of kids to sit at the table. "Came to see everybody," he said. "Been too long between visits home."

"Glad to see you two could grace us with your presence," Gretchen said to Trevor with a huff as she heaped her son Scott's plate with food.

"Aw, Mom," the teenager complained, "curried chicken again?"

"Be glad you got food in yer belly, boy, and don' sass me 'bout what I make. Eat your vegetables, too," Gretchen fussed, putting a mound of rice and peas on the side of the meat, along with spicy cabbage. "I didn't waste my time on makin' all dis for decoration." She surveyed Trevor and Miquel, then sucked her teeth, making the age-old sound of black female disapproval. "A call would have been nice, especially since

I switched shifts to be home to cook for my brother. Hmmph!"

"My apologies," Trevor said with a wide smile, quickly standing and going over to his sister to hug her, ignoring the fact that she shooed him away. "You are still the best cook in town, even if we almost missed a Gretchen delicacy. Give us a light plate. We can squeeze a little room in our gullet for a taste." Wrapping his arms around her while she had her back to him, he pecked her cheek, then dipped a finger in her pots to sample the meal, receiving a quick slap followed by a pleased giggle from her.

"Me and Miquel had some catchin' up to do, Sis. Mano-y-mano. McDonald's seemed like a good waterin' hole for us to begin," Trevor replied with a sly wink in his son's direction.

"Yo, Uncle T," Scott barged in, obviously becoming impatient with the light social exchange, "you ever listen to my CD? Got any hot leads to get me up and outta this dump?"

"You gonna finish high school first," Gretchen snapped, spinning around fast and using a wooden spoon as a pointer so that everyone at the table ducked to avoid being splattered by pot juice. "And since when does your mother's house become a dump? Huh? Dis ain' no dump—as you call it, and don' be gettin' brand-new jus' 'cause your uncle flies all over da world unconcerned 'bout anything but his so-called art! I won't have such talk. Hanging out wit' your hoodlum friends, and making that awful noise you call music—wit' your grades sliding down the slope like an avalanche. Your poor granmodder and granfadder is rollin' in dere graves now as we speak!"

The room went still. Very, very still. Trevor's gaze slid from his sister's puffed-up countenance of battle, to her son's slouching defiance in the chair. He could tell by the way her words had begun to gradually transform back to patois that she was furious beyond a normal fussing routine. He glimpsed at his nephew again, who was now slumped in his chair with his face two inches above his plate. Then he looked at what the kid was wearing, and let his breath out slowly.

"Scott," Trevor said in a tone of authority, "what's up with school?"

"Aw, see now, Mom?" the teen protested. "You done got everybody in a big to-do about nuthin'—school's fine, Uncle T. Mom is just trippin'."

"Oh, so now I can't read the King's English?" Gretchen screeched. "Ds mean something different in today's world?"

Trevor glanced at his sister and gave her a look that told her to back off for a moment. "Yo, man," Trevor said in a less stern voice, "you gotta get your education, no matter what you do. That's the number one priority."

"Why?" Scott challenged. "What difference do it make? If I go to school and get my diploma, what? I'ma work at some bull job, killing myself like Pop—always scramblin' for Benjamins? Not me. I'ma get phat paid—just like you."

Serious concern threaded its way through Trevor's veins, and he took his time, assessing the quiet faces that waited for him to speak to this challenge. He looked at his fifteen-year-old niece's hoochie-momma outfit that was way too revealing for her age, but could have been in any of the recent videos he'd just shot. Then, he looked at his gorgeous cousin—who now sported a nylon wig and had damaged her natural nail beds with acrylic, dragon-lady tips . . . just as his niece had. Then his gaze went back to his nephew, who, if he didn't know better, appeared so gangster-hostile and ornery that, by the way he dressed, he could have just come back from robbing a bank. The teenager postured himself like he was packing a weapon, even though Trevor was pretty sure that the kid only carried bus fare. Dear God . . . what were the images he made doing, especially at the street level?

"Two things," Trevor finally said in a low, serious tone. "Number one, if you're going to make money in this industry, you must have a good mind. Stupid people get ripped off—I see it every day. A solid education ensures that you can read your contracts and you can count your money. Dig?"

When the teen looked up briefly and didn't argue, all Trevor could do was hope that some of what the boy's grandmother had probably said in the past might be in the back of that angry adolescent brain now.

"Two," Trevor went on cautiously, "I may have left home, but I never forgot home. And I never disrespected my mother. I got my education first, and didn't bring her no trouble. So the next time I hear you disrespect your mother, my sister, it's me and you—outside. Dig?"

Trevor watched his sister's countenance relax, and she began fixing more plates, pushing a heaping one in front of Trevor and Miquel, even though Trevor had told her that they'd already eaten. But the mood had irrevocably shifted. Now, the once-lively kitchen was somber, and his nephew, whose fragile new manhood had been disgraced before women, simply got up and walked out of the room. Then they all seemed to wait for the door to slam, which it ultimately did.

"He's like that all the time," Trevor's niece, Janelle, said with a casual shrug. "Serves his triflin' ass right."

Trevor blinked and turned his attention on the oh-so-nonchalant girl. "What did you say?"

"He's like that all the time," Janelle repeated, shrugging. "He's probably going down to his boy's jaun' to smoke a blunt, then he'll come back and crash and burn."

Drugs, too? Trevor's gaze instantly roved the room, first to his sister's dejected shoulders while she fixed more food, then to Samantha, who was eating, oblivious, then to Miquel—who seemed to be the only person in the room to catch the surprise in Trevor's voice. Then he stared at Janelle.

"I said, young lady, what did you say at your mother's table?" Trevor's gaze held the girl-child's in a constant, unspoken threat, which again had the effect of making the room pause.

"What?" Janelle exclaimed, becoming suddenly defensive.

"You curse at your mother's table now, and dress like this? When did this happen? And smokin' a blunt is just basic information one casually mentions at the dinner table? What? Have you lost your natural mind?"

The teenager nervously surveyed her own clothing, then glanced around the room as though looking for backup—which never came from the other children.

"Uncle Trevor, no disrespect, but you can't just roll in here and start breakin' on people like you so perfect and everything!" Janelle was now standing, hot tears from being crushed by her idol forming in her eyes. "Since when did you become our father?" Then, like her brother, she was gone in a storm of heavy teenage foot-stomps down the hall, followed by a slammed bedroom door.

"Did you do your homework yet?" Trevor asked Miquel in a softer tone.

"No," the boy whispered, casting a nervous glance to the remaining adults in the room. "But it's cool."

Trevor found his fingers smoothing back his locks. "No, it's not cool."

"Aw right, Dad. You startin' to sound like Miss Hamilton. I got it covered."

"Tell you what," Trevor said in a weary voice, "go get started, then take your bath, and we'll check it over together before you go to bed. It's almost nine-thirty."

"Nine-thirty?" Miquel protested. "I can stay up to eleven. Right, Aunt Gretchen? I always stay up late and watch videos with Scott and Janelle."

"Not anymore. That's dead. So is staying up past a reasonable time for somebody eight years old—no wonder your teacher's been concerned about your grades. What the hell is going on 'round here, Gretchen?"

Appearing shocked, Miquel glanced to the women in the room before he moved, and his unconscious gesture of checking the real authority in the house made Trevor's ears ring.

"Do as your father says," Gretchen muttered, letting her breath out hard. "Tonight, just do as he says, for me."

"Okaaaay," Miquel lamented, pulling himself away from the table with disgust. "Do I have to sleep in Scott's room, or can I go downstairs to me and Dad's house? I hate sleeping in his room after he comes back. He smells all stinky."

Trevor and Gretchen exchanged a look, and his sister leaned back on the sink and folded her arms without a word.

"Samantha," Trevor murmured, "I have a big favor to ask."

When his cousin nodded, her face open and innocent, despite the new U.S. culture that almost seemed to eclipse her naïveté, Trevor sighed before speaking. "Would you help Miquel move his clothes downstairs to our unit, and help him with his homework until I come down—and run a tub for him?"

"I don't need her to run no bath for me!" Miquel yelled, appalled at the suggestion.

"I didn't ask her to undress you, I only asked her to help you with your homework and to run a tub for you—which is a nice thing to have done for you at any age. Okay, dude? No challenge. Get going, and get on your homework. I need to talk to your aunt."

Miquel grudgingly followed his older cousin's lead out of the room, while Trevor stood and began collecting the array of abandoned plates. What had happened to his family, and since when did a father's word not count as martial law? He had never been so outdone in all his life. Women now ruled the roost when a man spoke?

"Some homecoming," his sister lamented, flinging her wooden spoon into the sink and turning her back to Trevor.

Sensing from the way her voice quavered that she was about to cry, he set down the plates and came to her stiffened back, embracing her from behind, nuzzling her cheek. "It's all right, sis," he whispered. "Everything will be all right. They're just kids."

"No, it won't," she said through a thick sniff, then snatched herself away so that she could look at him squarely. "Everything will not simply be all right because the Great Trevor Winston says so. And who are you to come into my kitchen making judgments about how I'm raising my children?"

"I wasn't making judgments—but since when does a man have to get a woman's nod of approval for children to move? Huh? Pop never ran his house like that, and you know it! Since when . . . What the hell is—"

"Since there has been no man around on any sort of steady basis *for years,* that's since when! Children respond to who feeds them, disciplines them, and is constantly around them—not to the occasional, fun Santa Claus, who is just having a snit. There's no teeth in your bite, Santa Trevor, and that's why I left all those gifts for all of them in the hallway closet!"

Not offended, and in that moment totally understanding where she was coming from, he made his sister unfold her arms, and he took her hand, then guided her to the table to sit across from him.

"Listen," he said quietly, "one person can't do this."

His sister's shoulders dropped about two inches, and two big tears formed in her eyes and fell.

"I don't know what to do," she confided softly. "Ever since Mom has been gone, these children have run amock."

"Remember how Mom and Pop used to correct our language at the table?" He chuckled, trying to use memories and humor as a balm.

"Trying to make us bilingual, so we would be able to finish school and get jobs," his sister said, laughing with him sadly. "Wouldn't listen to a word unless it was said in exact grammar."

"True, dat—even tho' dey spoke in de modder tongue, mon. It was not allowed for us. Remember?"

"Yes," his sister whispered with a sad smile.

"And remember when we could not bring a hat on our heads into de house, or speak the profane? Hmmm, darlin'?"

"Or hang out wit de wrong element." His sister chuckled again, looking toward the door with undisguised worry. Then her expression clouded over again. "Where's my son, Trevor? Where's my boy?"

"I'll find him tonight, and he and I will have us a little talk."

"Thank you," she whispered, considering the leftovers on the table. "I was so angry at you because you escaped."

When he didn't answer her, she looked up.

"I was angry, Trevor. Do you know what it's like to always be the dependable one, the one who is there?"

He had to admit that he didn't, and all he could do was cover his sister's hand with his own.

"When my husband walked out, Scott and Janelle were five and six—you know this. But Mom and Dad were there . . . then Dad went, but still, we was holdn' our own, until Mom went."

"I know, baby," he whispered, suddenly finding it difficult to swallow.

"No, you don't know," she said in a gravelly voice that brought tears to his eyes. "No, Trevor, you don't. It's not just the money needed for these kids; it's the structure around them. That's why I never went after anything for me, just for them . . . and this sad lot is all I have to show for the sacrifice."

"That's not true," he argued, trying to boost her self-esteem. "You have a lot—"

"No," she murmured, taking her hand from his and sweeping it down her torso. "I am almost forty years old, dear brother. But look at my figure, and be honest," she whispered beneath a new stream of tears that she quickly wiped away. "My middle is thick, my arms are flabby, and I have not been to the hairdresser in more months than I can count." Holding her hands out before her brother to survey, she went on. "Look at these cracked, old hands that look like a crone's from hospital work, and lifting the sick, and tending to the aged. I gave away my womanhood."

"No, sis, that's not—"

"I haven't been with a man since those children's father walked out the door ten years ago," she said plainly, and held his gaze so intently that it made him look away.

"You heard me," she said in a harsh whisper. "Can you imagine what it's like to be so afraid of what might happen to your children that you never accept a date, never go out with a person of the opposite sex, never take a lover, never get a kind word or touch, and must always work, take care of children and elderly sick parents on your own, while your brother gets to pursue his dreams? Money cannot buy back time, and it cannot fill an empty bed, now can it?"

He felt the shell of his body shrink at her truth, and all he could do was shake his head and stare at the linoleum before him.

"And, dear brother, money does not discipline children, or put values into their minds, or build a fortress against the bad elements that seduce them into the streets. Our parents worked so hard, and sacrificed so much, but now that is all a joke to my kids. Just like

I'm an old joke to them. Only Uncle Trevor's word carries weight. I find that so ironic and so very unfair."

"How can I fix this?" he asked, leaning his elbows forward and allowing his head to drop into his hands. "How can I make up any small measure of this to you—so it can be your turn?"

"I don't know if it's not too late," his sister said quietly. "If Mom were here, she would know. But I never got as smart as her."

Looking up at Gretchen, Trevor held her hands within his own, her face now blurry from the tears he fought to control. "You are a good woman, a beautiful, beautiful woman," he argued, seeing her for the first time as more than a sibling. This time, he looked at her from a man's perspective as he spoke, and he watched her gaze slide away from his. "You deserve happiness, beyond the children."

"And," she protested, "where would I find this happiness at this juncture? If I started seeing someone, it would upset the delicate apple cart around here—not that any man would want more than the obvious from a woman with four children under her wing . . . Miquel, Scott, Janelle, and Samantha. Oh," she said, laughing, "and where would such a woman find the time to prepare for such a mystery date? When would that time be that said woman would get all dolled up to go out without the scrutiny of the young people in her charge? And, heaven forbid—what if I decided to break my vow of celibacy to spend the night away? Hmmm? Don't be silly. There would be chaos, and one of my children would come home with a baby, and they'd tell me to my face that I did it, so I shouldn't preach to the choir."

"I'll be here," he found his mouth saying. "I'll guard the house and make sure everyone is where they are supposed to be so you can go out."

His sister studied him for a moment, then threw her head back and laughed again. "You? Oh, pulleeeze!"

"Why not me?" His tone had become more defensive than intended, and he tried to get her to answer him with a gentler question. "Why couldn't I give my sister a break?"

"Because for one," she said, gathering her arms about herself as she stared at him, "after about three weeks of being *involved* in raising these children, the videos will call to you. Then, all of my going out will be trashed in my face by these children that I will be left to raise—alone. My respect from them will be in shreds." She gave him a very far-off, sad smile. "That's why I never started the catering business. I knew that as soon as I really got it going, someone would get sick, someone would die . . . some child would have a crisis, and all that I invested would go by the wayside. So I kept what I could depend on—my job."

"Sis, I promise you," he murmured, "I'm not going to pull the rug out from under you and leave at the spur of the moment."

"Yes, you will, Trevor," she said quietly, shaking her head. "And I don't know if you are the sort of influence that I necessarily want for them, anyway."

Her comment made him sit back in his chair and stare at her.

"I've seen the types of people you make videos of," she said, shaking her head. "The language, the messages, the images . . . The kids imitate everything you have made, and I cannot say that I am proud of what you do."

Her words sliced through his conscience and dignity like a Wilkinson's stainless-steel blade, and he hung his head in shame. The fact that her tone was not accusatory, but simply honest, made him want to leave the room and get on the next plane to anywhere but there.

"So, how am I to trust that you've made this conversion to responsible parenthood?" she asked in a tone that sounded so reminiscent of his mother's.

"How, after all of these years, am I going to just up and do what I want to do, when I cannot be assured that the back door is guarded—when these children are all at critical ages. Besides, you're a man."

"What has that got to do with it?" he argued, now standing to pace the floor, and not addressing the first questions she'd asked.

"Face it, Trevor," she shot back, "how long will it be until you have to go out like a cat in the night to find a woman, or women?"

Her stare made him look away, and he felt himself becoming angry.

"I don't do that!" he found himself yelling.

"If you say so," his sister noted casually, studying her fingernails. "But I don't think you could go ten years."

The truth of that accusation made him take up pacing again.

"Just as I suspected," she stated flatly. "Now, how you gonna go a decade, by yourself, while I go paint up de town? Let's be honest, brother-of-mine, sooner or later—"

"Not true! I can take care of this family, and show these children a decent family life, without running the streets on my own accord. I have changed. I might even give up the music videos and work on some other stuff. I don't know. But I do know that I am willing to change, and that counts for something."

"It cannot be a whim," she remarked, again holding him with her stare. "And when it gets tough, you cannot cut and run on us."

"I won't."

"And you cannot make excuses, after we've all gotten used to you as a fixture in our lives."

"I said, I won't."

"And, if you give me a glimmer of freedom, and if I take it, have you any idea how hard it will be for me to go back?"

In all honesty, he hadn't considered that possibility, but when their eyes met, he knew that she understood that he didn't.

"Say I do as you ask, and I begin finding all that I've lost . . . and even fall in love with someone—as strange as that might be. And, say, after ten years of loneliness, I allow myself a man's touch," she whispered, as though the very concept of it was too delicious and dangerous to fathom, "and even start my little catering business? Then, all of a sudden, you find this too confining for you. Then what? How will I go back to being a cloistered woman, a woman without dreams and without—"

"Why can't a person have both?"

The pure frustration in his question left them silent for a moment.

"Because," she began slowly after a thought-filled pause, "it's not the having it that does the damage to the children, it's the finding it—the churning process that wreaks havoc."

His look of confusion seemed to spur her on, and he slowly returned to the table to sit down and listen as she continued.

Gretchen took her time to let the point sink in. "It's the finding of the person to be with, after going through a string of wrong choices, that messes up the children. I've seen this with me own eyes, and what's gone on with my girlfriends' children," she said seriously, pointing to her eyes as she spoke. "It's your emotional upheaval, and your own inattentiveness during your search, Trevor. It's the total focus required, if you are starting a new business, or following a career dream, that blocks them out, and leaves them without your attention. That's why it is an either-or choice, unless you are very, very good at balancing your priorities. I guess I never trusted myself that much, with so much at stake . . . and I guess that's why I've missed my window of opportunity. Such is life."

They sat at the table for a while, each absorbed in their own silent thoughts with their independent issues colliding and causing them unspoken fear. Both ignored the telephone when it rang, being far too consumed in developing a solution to pay it much note.

"I don't have the answers," he finally whispered. "I think there is a way, if we both work together. I'm not willing to let what I saw tonight go by unchecked, and I'm not willing to have my sister go through life without joy. That's unacceptable to me."

"I love you, too," she whispered as he stood to round the table and place a kiss on her forehead. "We won't solve this tonight. Just go find Scott."

"Uncle Trevor!" his still-angry niece hollered from the bedroom down the hall. "Telephone."

"Take a message," he yelled back. "I've gotta go out for a while."

Five

He was grateful that the spring evening had young men following the normal urban rite of passage of hanging out around the corner in front of the store. It had made it easy for him to roll up on his young nephew, exchange a series of high-fives with the teenager's buddies, then casually retrieve him from the group without incident. He also knew that his notoriety from working with their music icons had made his entry and acceptance into their conversation easy—an advantage that he used, but one that now deeply disturbed him.

And although the youngster who sat on the steps with him now seemed to hang on his every word, and no longer appeared upset about what happened in the house—only because his manhood had been restored by his favorite uncle's appearance in front of his "boyze" . . . there was still a lot of work to do.

"I know whatchu sayin', man," Scott argued. "Aw right, I'll give Mom a break. That's cool. But she don' understand what it's like out here. She ain't got no real pressure—she's paid, goes to work, comes home, don't know what's goin' on out here, and—"

"I'ma tell you the real pressure she's got, man," Trevor cut in, consciously keeping his voice judgment-free. "She's so worried about you and your sister that she hasn't even gone out on a date in ten years."

The casual way Trevor delivered the pronouncement made the teenager sitting next to him on the front steps just stare at him.

"Think about it, dude," Trevor went on in a nonchalant tone, looking out at the streetlights. It was an opportunity of a lifetime—and understanding that, he grasped the stun-advantage of telling the man-child beside him something he didn't already know. "Dig it. Your father left when you and your sister was about five or six, right? Which would have put my sister at about twenty-five or so . . . about the age of the women I film and you lust after, right?"

When the kid just stared at him, Trevor knew, for sure, that he had gained the upper hand.

"So your mom, my sister, had a choice. She could have dropped you all off on her mom, your grandmother, while she went and got her groove on, or she could have raised you guys herself—with a little help from her parents. What did she do? You tell me."

"She raised us," the youth murmured, "and only time Grandmom watched us was when she was at work."

"Right," Trevor agreed. "You ever get horny?"

"What?" Scott said with a laugh, looking sheepishly at his uncle and shaking his head in mock disgust.

"You heard me. I'm bein' real."

"Aw, Uncle T, you crazy . . ."

"But I'm real."

"Aw'ight, aw'ight . . . since we talkin' as men, den," Scott said, his street slang deepening to cover his obvious embarrassment, "yeah, who don't—less there's somethin' wrong wit 'em."

Trevor nodded, and allowed the long pause to settle between them for dramatic effect. Street traffic and far-off music from car radios punctuated the silence. Looking forward and not directly at his nephew, he could feel the young man hanging on his every word.

"I been with a lot of women." Trevor nodded, giving the point time to sink in.

"Know you have, dog," Scott said, laughing and punching his uncle's arm, then falling quiet again to hear every detail that he obviously hoped would come.

"Between men," Trevor said in a conspiratorial tone, designed to make the youth strain to listen.

"Yeah," Scott said quickly. "It's just me and you."

"All right," Trevor replied, repressing a smile. "Check it out. Your mother's a woman."

"What? Oh, c'mon, dude. Don't even go there . . . What's up, Uncle Trevor!"

It was all Trevor could do not to laugh. "This ain't no Jerry Springer stuff I'm about to tell you, so relax," he said with a chuckle that bubbled out on its own accord. "Chill."

He stared at the youth's face, which had momentarily gone ashen, and shook his head. "I'm not gay, either. This ain't what I'm getting at."

"Aw right, aw right," the kid said, visibly relaxing, and letting his breath out, hard, then wiping his face with his hands. "Dag, Uncle T."

"I'm trying to connect your brain with reality," Trevor said in a more serious tone. "Your mother is a woman—a woman who, for the love of her children, didn't run the streets, and who is now locked between a house and a job because she's afraid of what y'all might do. And, 'cause she's grown and human, there are times when she needs, just like you do, to go out. You followin' me?"

"Dag," Scott murmured, looking at the tops of his designer sneakers, "I hear you, but I don't even want to think about that stuff—not her like that."

"What son wants to believe that about his mom?"

Silence let the question hover in the air like a basketball over the hoop net before it fell.

"My mom, your grandmother, had a husband—so she didn't have to go out, per se."

"Grandmom . . . ? Aw, man, this convo is going—"

"To the truth, dig."

Scott let his breath out hard again and glimpsed Trevor with a sideways glance. "Why you tellin' me all-a dis now?"

" 'Cause, I can tell by the way you actin' that you ain't let the dog out yet. Have you?"

"Aw, man, dats not true, I get plenty of play, and I gots me some honeys," Scott protested, standing up quickly and promenading around the steps.

"Sit your virgin behind down so we can talk," Trevor commanded, speaking low so that his nephew didn't die of embarrassment on the porch steps.

"Uncle T, man, I ain't no virgin," Scott whispered, sitting down nonetheless, and looking at the cement between his feet.

"It's cool, man. Better that way, actually," Trevor said in a low tone, draping his arm around the kid's shoulders, hugging him briefly, then letting him go. "What I'm trying to tell you is a couple of things that your boys are too stupid yet to know. And, trust me, they have not been all around the globe to pick up this knowledge. Me and you, right?"

This time when Scott looked up, his young face held such curiosity mixed with awe and respect that Trevor almost laughed. But he didn't. Oddly, until he'd talked to his sister, he hadn't considered it, and he had thought he'd have years before having to have this discussion with anyone. Yet Scott looked up at Trevor with the expression of a student awaiting the mysteries of the universe from his Zen master. Trevor knew that whatever he said now could influence the immediate future, so he took his time.

"I don't care what you see on television, or hear," Trevor whispered, "a woman is a precious gift. But, as a man, you have to be selective. Some gifts look pretty on the outside, but inside, whew . . ."

"No doubt," his nephew said emphatically, bobbing his head in agreement.

"I messed up, and I wasn't selective. I could have died."

They held each other's gaze for a moment, until Trevor spoke again.

"Several of my boys are gone because of women. AIDS took 'em in every corner of the world. Being phat paid didn't help 'em on the way out, neither."

"Dag . . ." the kid murmured, still gaping at Trevor.

"And I hooked up with a honey that had my nose opened, and we had unprotected sex. That's how Miquel got here."

Scott exhaled and wiped his forehead again, but his line of vision remained on Trevor.

"Who you pick to lay down with is important, not just from on the outside, but from on the inside—because that person could be the mother of your baby."

"I ain't making no babies, Uncle T. I ain't goin' out like that."

"I hear you," Trevor said, looking away. "That's what we all say. I love my son. But I could have died making him. And he could have come into the world with AIDS or drugs in his system, or brain damaged, all because I was having fun with the wrong one—a woman with her head screwed on backward. See how serious this is?"

All Scott seemed to be able to do was nod.

"So now, I'm going to ask you again, on a for-real tip. Do you ever get horny?"

"Yeah, man, I told you that," the teenager whispered.

"And, sometimes, it gets so bad that you think you gonna go outta your mind, right?" Trevor waited as the teenager's gaze slid away from his.

Again, Scott just nodded and began kicking imaginary pebbles on the steps.

"Smoking blunts makes it crazy worse. Right?"

"Aw, man . . ." Scott whispered. "You don't know."

"Yes, I do, brother," Trevor said with a smile. "That's

why I don't mess with nothin' that could cloud my judgment."

His nephew studied him real hard.

"But you're in the scene . . . out in L.A., London, New York, around all them fine honeys, with all they stuff hanging out—filming them all day and night, how—"

"They are vampires, dude. Will suck anything, including your pockets dry, steal your life force, and mess up your family. Been there, seen it, done it," Trevor said with disgust. "So, when I see your sister dressing like them, and now Sam—who ain't even been in the States long enough to know, and I see you disrespecting your mother, it makes me nuts."

"But what has one thing got to do with—"

"Check it out," Trevor interrupted. "You think the music video scene is all that, and so you dress the part, walk the walk, and want the women who look like what you see, right?"

"Aw'ight. Yeah."

"But remember," Trevor cautioned. "I see what goes on behind the scenes. I'm the man behind the lens, and I drop tape on the cutting-room floor—I see what the public doesn't see." Once his street-stoop student nodded, he went on.

"I see the fine babes who gotta go get their AZT shot, I see the brothers who are so sick they can't hold up a lavalier microphone. I see people who gotta chase the dragon and smoke a blunt with heroin in it before they can brush their teeth in the morning. I've seen a lot of bad things, young brother. I've also seen how only like five to ten wannabes get on celluloid, and the rest crash and burn, and even those who are phat paid get beat out of their real money—because they're too dumb to read a contract. I also know about the thousands of off-camera jobs there are that can also make you phat paid, but we ain't in those jobs. But the worst . . . I see all these young people leaving babies at home for their mommas to raise, while they chase this bull. Then I see me."

"That's deep," Scott whispered, his jaw going slack while looking at Trevor.

"Do you know what would have happened to your mother, my sister, if I had swept her up into that scene with me? Or what might have happened to y'all if Grandmom and Grandpop didn't stay home and do those stupid mule jobs—as you called them at the table? Your butt might be dead right now, or you might be mentally retarded from having a crack mother starve you half to death while she tried to get on a video. Or your sister might have been raped by one of the men your mom brought in for the night, if your mother hadn't had the presence of mind not to have a high-traffic zone household. Am I making any sense?"

"Too much sense . . ." the kid whispered. "I just never thought of it like that."

"So, when your mom, my sister, flips about grades, and you smokin' reefer, and hanging with a bad crowd, is she stupid?"

"Naw, but they're my boys."

"Any of your boys get shot yet, or get sick?"

"Last year . . . Pookie's little brother found his gun and blew himself away. Man, it was deep. His mom and sister ain't been right since."

Trevor just nodded.

"If I had been in the joint, and just came home, and told you how bad it really was in there, would you listen to me?"

Again, his young nephew just stared at him.

"Well, I've been in the music video joint, and I just came home. And I'm telling you man to man, just me and you, I don't want to see you or Miquel get shot, I don't want y'all having no babies by no crazy women, and I don't want you to get played by The Man—who is only too happy to keep you illiterate and stupid. I also don't want any of your friends, or no grown men, looking at your sister and cousin like they're just some street tramps to screw and leave with a baby, or AIDS . . . and that's where everybody is headed. Down a dead-end street. So, for all of the days, for ten years, that your mother worked, and from before that when my mother worked, my father worked, and they denied themselves any pleasure, I want you to think about that the next time your boys pass you a blunt, and you go thinking about not using a condom."

His nephew didn't blink, and a rare glimmer of innocence shone past the fear that filled his young eyes.

"I don't want that for them neither," Scott said in a low, gravelly tone. "Dag. One time we showed Miquel a gun, and even let him hold it. But I tol' my boys to leave him alone—he ain't that kinda kid."

Anger and fear coiled itself inside Trevor's intestines, but he kept his gaze firm. "He's trying to be you, and you're trying to be me, but we've gotta get our acts together. We've got women to take care of, and a family to raise. Drug money just means trouble. Goes with that life."

"But my boys are gonna think I went soft. You know?"

"Half of 'em ain't got nobody at home who would lose their minds if something went wrong. Ask yourself, where are their mothers—then look around, and ask yourself where is yours? Then you decide. You a man. You got eyes. Tough choices have to be made, and you've gotta stand your ground—that's being a man. To hell with the crowd, dude. The other half of your partners are scared, just like you, and ain't doing all that they're claiming to do either—just like you. They're frontin'. You don't think my boys laugh at me?"

"At you?"

Trevor chuckled at the look of sheer gall that crossed Scott's face.

"I don't do drugs, number one. So I take a lot of

heat for dat. I don't chase women—anymore. So I get a lot of guff about dat, too. And I'm about to cut loose the golden handcuffs and go on the DL for a while to be here, in Philly—which ain't as excitin' as L.A. or New York. Trust me."

"Dag . . ." Scott whispered again. "How'd you just give it all up and take all that from your home boys?"

"Priorities. The drugs will make you stupid and susceptible to doin' things you wake up the next day and wished you hadn't done. In these days and times, you could wake up in the arms of death. Being in Philly is being with you, Miquel, and Janelle and Sam—and giving my sister a break. So, can't nobody argue with me about my blood."

"The women though, Uncle T. How'd you just turn off the tap on that, and give it up . . . did the drugs mess you up, and you can't . . . I mean, you know . . . you ain't sick or nothin', are you?"

This time Trevor laughed. "No, I was lucky, and I dodged a bullet," he said, shaking his head and forcing the fear of that reality out of his mind. "Miquel got made before my dead ex started using, and I was so angry with her, we fought most of the time she was pregnant—so wasn't nothin' going on, that much. Then, since she didn't trust me, and was carrying, she made me use something when we did . . . so God looks after children and fools. Having gone out like that, getting one woman pregnant—I was serious about keeping a layer of latex between me and anybody. Was so paranoid when I found out she was using, I came and got Miquel, brought him home to Mom, and got him and myself tested annually for the last eight years. Like I said, this ain't no joke."

"Dag," Scott repeated, letting his breath out in a rush, then looking up toward Trevor with a sideways glance. "But you left him off with your mom, right?"

"Yeah," Trevor said, sighing. "I was a punk about that. By rights, I should have been there to raise him, and probably to help my sister. My mother didn't make Miquel. I did."

As though sensing the morose thoughts battering Trevor, his nephew put his arm around his uncle's shoulders this time.

"Yeah, but Uncle T . . . you did more for all of us than my dad did. It's not like you just walked . . . I mean, you sent us stuff all the time, came home every holiday . . . always kept in touch, and you still send Mom and Grandmom money all the time . . . even bought the house we live in. We knew you was there, man."

"But being a father is more than sending gifts," Trevor whispered. "It's being present, not sending presents. It's being around to have your back—so your boyz ain't your only backup . . . you know, it's rappin' like we doin' now. Being real. I've seen stuff that you can't imagine. I'm just tryin' to keep it real for you so you ain't gotta go through all-a dis."

"Okay. That part I got. No drugs, no unprotected sex. Learn something. Stay away from guns. Give my mom her props—for all she gave up to get us this far. But, if we keepin' it real, you still ain't answer my question."

Trevor shrugged, and opened his hands. "What else can I tell you?"

"How'd you give it up?"

"I just told you," Trevor said, more defensively than he'd intended.

"I can see gettin' wrapped up in your work, and since you done been everywhere, a brother can take a break from traveling. I can see how bein' around junkies can make you give up da drugs—truth. I can see how watchin' people go out from the big disease with a little name can make you wear latex—no doubt . . . but I don't know if I could just go cold turkey on the babes. I mean, I'ma be honest with you . . . I ain't really had all you've had, and some days, that's all I can think about."

The two stared at each other until Scott's deep, penetrating gaze of honesty—the type of honesty that only young people and very elderly people seem to emit, made Trevor look away.

"Can we tell the truth?" Scott asked in a low whisper that forced Trevor to return his line of vision to his face.

"Yeah. Nothin' but truth."

"I ain't . . . I mean, almost, but . . . not all the way." Scott's expression became somber, then he began to study the tops of his sneakers again. "You know what I'm saying is . . . well . . . I coulda, but then her mom came home, and it blew the groove. She's scared she's gonna get pregnant like her sister and that I'ma talk about her to my boyz—drama. But, she sometimes lets me, almost, I mean, we be kissin' and stuff, but that's it. Then we broke up, and then we got back together, and almost . . . You feel me? And, it's the almost that drives you crazy . . . 'cause even though you try to shake it, it's like a monkey on your back—makes you think stupid, you know?"

Trevor cast his gaze to the steps, closed his eyes briefly and let his breath out slowly through his nose, and then looked back up to the young man-child next to him. It was a right of passage that all men knew too well. "I hear you."

Scott nodded, seeming to grow comfortable with his uncle's simple, nonverbal acknowledgment. "Then Miquel is always waiting up for me, and wantin' to talk—which is messin' with my head, and my mom is always yanging me, and my sister lives on the phone and in the bathroom, and some days, I wake up . . . well. You know. And, a brother can't get no space to shake the monkey off his back . . . then I go hang wit my boys, and the blunt is passin' around, and I get to thinkin' about her on the way home . . . and then, it's really bad."

Again, the silence cloaked them, and the sounds of

street traffic filled in the gaps. Trevor definitely knew how the kid felt. The problem was—how did one explain it without being as vulnerable as the question had suddenly made him? Here he'd been preaching all the basics, and in the final analysis, his sister and the kid had been right; he'd never make it ten more years like this.

"I don't know, man," Trevor said in a rush of honesty, then stood. Right now, even a menthol cigarette would have been good. A beer was definitely calling his name.

"It's on your back, too, ain't it?" Scott said with a quick smile.

"Like a mug." Trevor laughed, oddly feeling relieved to be able to admit it out in the open. "Been kickin' my butt for two years, dude. Don't know if you ever win that battle."

"Noooo. Are you serious?" Scott said in awe. "For real, for real?"

"Ever since my mother, your grandmother, closed her eyes."

"Stop lyin'," Scott howled, and fell back on the steps with laughter.

"Keep it down," Trevor said nervously. "I thought this was just between me and you—not the whole neighborhood?"

"It is, it is," Scott said, laughing. "Chill, man. Dag. We've got a lot more in common than I thought."

Trevor sat back down heavily and kept his gaze toward the streetlights.

"Whatchu gonna do?"

"Whatchu mean, what am I gonna do?"

"I mean, whatchu gonna do?"

"I'ma chill, get into some new work, and—"

"Start doin' your own laundry like I had to, if you keep this up," the youth said with a grin. "Man, how old are you?"

"If I hear 'bout dis in da street . . ." Trevor warned.

"I ain't gonna out you—not after what I jus' tol' you. C'mon, dude."

Both males looked at each other, then burst out laughing.

"See, it ain't easy, is it, waiting until everything is perfect?" Scott smirked, vindicated.

"No," Trevor grumbled, wondering in that moment who was the role model and who was the protégé. "It's driving me outta me natchel mind, boy, but I am determined." He laughed again, trying to wrest back his previous position as the mentor, and using a thick slathering of Jamaican accent to make the man-child next to him laugh. "Gonna wait for Miss Right to come along, and not be sifting in de dregs—no matter how tempting this starved dog may be, and gonna wear me Jimmy cap no mattry what, ain' goin' to die happy."

Both men slapped five, punched each other, and stood.

"Go inside and give your mother a break," Trevor said with a chuckle. "You know what's right—like the commercial says, just do it."

"Aw right, cool," Scott conceded with a laugh. "Whyn't you take Miquel downstairs with you, anyway? Then maybe a brother could get some space."

"Done," Trevor agreed. "I can dig it. Having a little cousin in your room all the time makes it hard for a man to discretely shake that monkey off his back, you know, you know."

Scott just shook his head and bounded up the steps. "Word!"

Six

He sat outside on the steps for a long while, just allowing the cool night air to talk to his senses. In the blue-black sky, thousand of twinkling stars seemed to laugh at his depressed condition, while the full moon cast a blue hue that met the sick-yellow tinge emitted by the streetlights. He wondered what their neighbor, Miss Cleo, would say if he threw back his head and just howled? Half wolf, half man, half father, half artist, half uncle, half friend, half brother, half boy, half breadwinner, half deadbeat, and half crazy—at the moment. In the city, who would care if he just let out a long, mournful howl like the street people often did?

But the one question still remained. How had he allowed so much to get screwed up in his life, which he could now see had a ripple effect on his entire family?

Remembering his promise to help Miquel with his homework, Trevor stood and slowly walked back up the steps to the house. His cousin Samantha smiled and looked up as he opened the door, and instead of bopping to loud music, she was curled up in the large easy chair, reading her college notes in the stark silence.

"He's asleep," she said with a quiet smile. "Did his homework, took a bath, and insisted he wasn't tired. So I read to him a little bit, and told him he could wait up for you. I left his night-light on so he'd know you were coming. Poor little thing was asleep before I even finished the story."

"What are you reading to him?" Trevor asked as he took a seat across from her on the sofa.

"Oh, the hottest new rage for all the kids, Harry Potter."

Not even knowing what was age appropriate for his son, or what the child was interested in, deeply penetrated his soul. But not half as much as the fact that he'd missed so many nights being able to read to the boy when it really mattered . . . like when Miquel was two, or three, or four. . . . Now Miquel was nearly past the point of being read to any longer, and the boy probably only allowed it because his glamorous cousin, with her soft Island lilt had sweetly begged him into such acquiescence.

A burrowing ache clawed at Trevor as he tried to smile and look at his young cousin. If his sister only knew how much he'd missed this window of opportunity, as she termed it, with his son. Maybe one day he'd explain to her just how she'd made the right choice after all.

"You've heard about it, right, Uncle Trevor?"

Trevor nodded, then stood and murmured, "thank you," then moved toward the small bedroom.

Creeping inside the room filled with toys and airplanes and maps, he saw his son sleeping peacefully and sprawled diagonally across the bed as though he hadn't a care in the world. What if that beautiful creation had been snuffed out by a teenage bullet, or marred by drugs? Trevor shook the dread from his bones and leaned over to touch the soft curls on the head of the sleeping innocent, then brushed the small forehead with a kiss. No. Life was too precious to squander. If he had to, this was worth ten years as a monk.

He left the night-light on, closing the door behind him, then went to relieve Samantha of her watch.

"Thanks, love," he whispered when he approached her, and gave her a brief kiss as she stood and stretched. "Don' know what I would do without you and Gretchen to watch over dat boy."

"Oh, it's nothing at all," she said with a smile, crossing the room and hovering by the door. "It's not so bad, you know," she added shyly. "He's a wonderful kid. Just like his dad."

Her comment shamed him, even though he knew it was her way of trying to encourage him. Looking at the floor, he nodded and waited to be alone.

"Oh," Samantha added. "I almost forgot. Here's a note from Miquel's teacher. Janelle took the message while you and Aunt Gretchen were talking."

Trevor sighed and accepted the piece of paper as Samantha scooted out of the doorway. The chicken scratch and misspellings that confronted him were appalling.

By age fifteen, he and his sister had mastered the language; little Miquel had been entered into school early and skipped a grade. He was definitely needed here. It was all he could do to make out the message on the badly crumpled paper, which said, *Miss Hamilton want to xten you an olev branch an talk. Didn't leave no number.*

Once the door shut behind Samantha, Trevor walked about the first-floor unit, thinking. Okay, he could be at home when Gretchen had to leave for work in the evenings. He could make sure that all the kids had their homework done. He could cook. He could go food shopping. He could go up to schools to see about wayward children. He could hold down the fort on the weekends so that his sister could go out with her girls—until she found someone special, someone whom she might want to date. He could continue to help her cover the bills, if she was serious about going into catering, and could probably make some calls to get her some of the finer catering jobs at the celeb parties in this area. But what was *he* going to do after the money ran out?

The question nagged at him and pulled him toward the back staircase, toward his inviolate sanctuary—his studio.

Flipping on the light, he slowly descended into the basement. A sense of comfort surrounded him as he surveyed the plastic-covered rows of digital equipment and Avid editing system he'd invested in so that he could make his own videos, edit his documentaries, and lay down sound. Peeping under the plastic draped over the Beta decks and CD-ROM burner, he sighed. No one had been in his temple, he noted, as every magazine was still in-place. The thick leather sofa even had a fine layer of dust on it, as did the brilliant blue butterfly chair, wrought-iron bench, and Ashanti stool. His world-scavenged art and carvings were all carrying that same archaeological silt of abandonment. Pacing across the thick Turkish rug that lay between the chrome-and-glass coffee table and petrified-wood end table, he went to inspect the closed-off portion of the basement that housed his darkroom.

Although bottled, the developing fluids could be faintly detected, and he switched on the red light just to remember what it felt like to work in still photography.

Trevor allowed his gaze to scan the room, noting how many photos of street scenes remained pinned to the wall and clipped to clothespins—each one that of a child. Then there were the groupings of the elderly, women gathering and talking . . . a cacophony of voices spoke to him from the images that he'd taken around the world.

He noted the way he had juxtaposed a woman from Kenya standing in tall grass against an American sister standing on an El platform in the same pose. Natural, unrehearsed, but captured in black-and-white . . . and the children, all the same, different only in skin tone—

not in their expressions of pure joy. He'd cataloged them at play in the dirt yards of some remote land, and in the concrete basketball frenzy of city-bound adolescents. Some of his favorites were the faces of the old, and the unseen beauty in their lines of wisdom.

Oh, god . . . he had to get back to his work . . . His gaze met with his cameras in metal cases on the floor. And his mind traveled to where he had been, and the tragedies fused with the beauty in the landscapes of war-torn worlds, and pivoted against the healing power of Mother Nature's excesses, and the way her courage defied even nuclear blasts—with one blade of grass growing green amidst the rubble, and his mind ricocheted to the way that same blade of grass could be seen growing up in crack-vial-strewn playgrounds, and his heart ached for his craft . . . until he finally wept.

How could he give up images, having formed them for so long? His fist clenched the badly scribbled phone message, and he wiped his nose on the back of his hand. Then he switched off the light and went upstairs, clicking off the main light and shutting the door behind him. It was over.

Going around the apartment in a frenzy, he switched off all the lights, walked blindly into his bedroom, sat on the bed, and stared at his still-packed suitcases and collection of cameras. He briefly considered the clock, and immediately decided it was too late to make a call—then again, how could he call back this teacher who had extended the olive branch of peace? The fool child, Janelle, had not even taken a number, which meant he had to return to the school, which he had to do anyway to make good on his promise to his son to take home the cherished science project. Everything was collapsing too quickly, like a universe imploding upon itself after a supernova.

Trevor flung the note in his hand across the room, stood, stripped, let his clothes fall where they did, and got into bed. Jet lag and emotional strain had wrung him out, and he knew better than to try to reengineer his life on no sleep. He'd go by the school the next day. Everything would be all right. He'd talk to his sister in the morning and review Miquel's homework before the boy went off to school. They'd eat breakfast together, and he'd collect the child at three o'clock, make a swift apology to the teacher, and they'd be gone. But she was so beautiful, and so very right. What had come over him? he wondered, drifting lazily on the thought. He'd yelled at her, when he should have been yelling at himself.

Everything she'd told him was being presented right before his eyes . . . those eyes. Worth capturing the fury and fire in them. Note to self. Passion. Rare, real passion. Set in a toffee frame. Natural. Natural hair, natural nails, no pretense, no acrylic. Smelled natural, not overdone, no heavy perfume . . . caring. Tears, because she was angry. Tears because she cared deeply. Not video-glossed sound bites of rehearsed phrases. No bourgeois restraint. Unvarnished . . . not professional . . . but real. She'd read him, all right. Royally. He could feel his face smile as he drifted off. God, she was beautiful.

Sleep mingled with the images, casting a short video in his brain. Sad smile . . . his mind floated on it. Saxophone smile. Open with long shot down hall, kids pouring out of class, cut to sad smile. Full mouth, sheer coating of muted lipstick, maybe even just Chap Stick . . . ? Honey tone to voice. Bring up volume, wail it, voice, no background, her whisper . . . shoot in full color, then go to black-and-white. Swivel of hips, her head cocked to the side. Capture. Attitude. Storyboard it. Bass notes. Rhythm section as she walks . . . God, capture walk, rear shot, reverse, hand on curve of hip. Hair, bouncing curls—percussion interlude. Natural, curly yet silky, a wisp near her delicate earlobes and at the nape of her neck. Close up. Hands . . . delicate structure, tapered, wondrously smooth looking, probably velvet touch . . . uses them to talk. Follow them, on tracks; stay with the hands. . . .

Unaware that he was dreaming, he could hear her laugh, and could trace her mouth with the tip of his finger, which was *soooo* soft to the touch, which made her grow serious, and made her stop laughing, and caused her magical eyes to drink him in, which brought his face toward hers, and he removed his finger from her lips, and replaced it with his own, and his tongue found hers, and her taste was sweet like her smell, and her teeth were smooth, just like her touch as her hand slid down his chest, and her collarbone begged for equal attention, which he lavished with a row of tiny kisses upon her velvety skin, and those kisses made her gasp . . . and her gasp quaked his skeleton, and forced his tongue to her skin, until neither of them had on clothes, and they were in his sleigh bed, and she had transformed his pillow into herself, and she moved against him in steady cresting waves, and she felt deep and warm and wet like the sea at home . . . and dear Lord it had been so long . . . and she suddenly became the ocean, and he grabbed her to keep her from flowing through his fingers, and she laughed deep down in her throat as he began to drown from pleasure, and her waves lapped against him hard, and her legs spread to yield a lush valley, and he scooped up her fertile black earth as his arm slid under the small of her back, and he couldn't pull himself into her hard or fast enough, and she closed around him, becoming molten lava, then cried out until he woke up with a start upon the last sudden convulsion while calling her name.

Opening his eyes, he blinked twice, then sat up abruptly as he heard footsteps. Disoriented, he gathered the covers around him, shivering, then looked down at his pillow with disgust.

"Dad," a small, sleepy voice said, "I heard you talking, and you said you were going to tuck me in."

Panic tore through him, as he tried to adjust his eyes to the darkness, using the light from the moon and streetlamp that was pouring into his window to help him make out the small frame of a child at his bedroom door.

"I'll be there in a moment, need to find my slippers," he lied, frantically hoping that the child would not budge from where he stood.

"I'm scared. I don't sleep here that much, and . . . can I sleep with you?"

The million-dollar question . . . Jesus. "No, uh, look, dude, you and I both sleep diagonal in the bed. Go hop back in yours, give me two minutes to pee. I just woke up. Cool, and . . . and . . . I'll read to you, okay?" His mind stuttered the words in his mouth. "Uh, we'll talk about this in a second, just let me go to the bathroom."

"You don't have to read to me, Dad. Sammy already did, and I know you really don't want to, anyway," the dejected voice replied from the shadows. "It's cool."

"No. No, for real, son," Trevor stammered. "Listen. I just have to go to the bathroom. Give me a minute. I'll be right there."

"But, who's in here? Who were you talking to?"

Nearly too embarrassed to respond rationally, Trevor could feel the child's persistence wearing his patience away as though it were grinding down mill flour. "Nobody. I was just working out a script in my head, and was talking to myself. Can a man go to the loo?"

"You said something about Miss Hamilton . . . you gonna make a movie with her in it?"

"Yeah, yeah, yeah," Trevor said, sighing. "Now go ahead and let me get myself together, dude. I'll be in there in a moment."

He waited until he heard the little footsteps shuffle down the hall, then he let out his breath hard. Of all the stupid, adolescent things that had ever happened to him. Why today? Why now? God forbid if the boy had been in the bed next to him! The chilling thought immediately propelled him out of the bed with the damp sheets wrapped around his middle. He searched in the dark for his old robe, which hung in the closet, and yanked it on. Stumbling and cursing, he left the sheets in a pile on the floor, flung the pillow on top of it, went into the bathroom, and shut the door behind him, then ran the water.

Washing up, he splashed his face. Everything had to change. Everything. He was a dad. Now, he had to do laundry at one o'clock in the morning—well before Scott ever saw him lugging it up the basement steps and definitely before his sister saw him. Pajamas. No more sleeping in the buff. He wasn't on the road, alone in his own hotel room, and he wasn't in one of the flats. He was home. *Purge that woman out of your head.* It was a temporary lapse, but a dangerous one.

Becoming calmer as he looked into the mirror, he suddenly turned away from his own image and slapped off the light. Knowing the hall by rote, and using the dim glimmer from Miquel's night-light to keep him from stubbing his toe, he slipped into his son's bedroom and sat down on the edge of the bed.

"You really gonna stay with us for a while?" the child asked, peering up at him with an expression so open that all Trevor could do was nod.

"I missed you, Dad. And I miss Grandma, too."

"I missed you, and I miss her. Nothing wrong with missin' people you love."

"Did you ever miss Mom?"

The question stunned him and nearly broke him, but he quickly marshaled an internal shield so that he could answer. "I miss who your mother was when I met her, and I miss all of the time that I should have spent with you," he murmured. "But a lot of things change . . . some things change for the better—like me knowing when to give up the road so I don't ever have to miss you again."

"For real? You really gonna stay forever this time?"

Trevor paused, because again, for the third and what he knew to be final time this night, in this moment, whatever he pledged would have to be his word of honor. The child held his gaze in an unfaltering request for his promise. Blood rushed to Trevor's ears until he could hear his own heartbeat while panic seized the air from his lungs. There was no time to think about this, there was no back and forth about it. His son wanted an answer—a commitment. Not a hedge, not a parental "we'll see," not a maybe, only an honest-to-God commitment.

"Yes," he heard himself whisper. "I promise. I'm not going anywhere, unless I take you with me."

"Swear on Grandma's grave," the child challenged, tears filling his eight-year-old eyes. "Swear."

Trevor looked down at his son and wiped away his tears, and as he did so hot moisture filled his own eyes, blurring the image of the face that demanded an answer. "I swear on my mother's grave that I will not abandon you, Miquel. Any of you. Daddy promises."

He swallowed hard as the little boy sat up and wrapped his arms around Trevor's neck, burying his wet face in his shoulder. All he could do was rub the small back that heaved with sobs of relief, and try his best not to follow suit and wail like a child himself. His mind went to all of the times his own father had been there, steadfast, stern, but there on the scene. Like granite, like a mountain, his father had always been there . . . and the shame of his own path of benign neglect was all too clear. A child clung to his huge male frame, seeking refuge, solace, support, and begging him not to leave. Trevor rocked them both, and hushed them both, until the child trusted him enough to allow him to tuck him in and leave him to sleep.

Guilt battered him as he walked down the hall to the bathroom and turned on the light. No child should ever wonder about whether he would be abandoned.

No sister of his should have to live with a pillow as a lover for ten years. No nephew should have to follow the streets to raise him. No niece should have to try to get male attention by showing off her new womanhood as though it were for sale. . . . Trevor's hands found the scissors in the medicine cabinet. His videos should not corrupt children. His gift from God was to make art, not to make mothers worry. His hand found the first lock, and steel separated it from his scalp. His gift was not supposed to drive a woman into the arms of heroin. The next lock fell. He was not supposed to make images that promoted all that he didn't believe in. The next lock fell, and hot tears streamed down his face as his soul bled from the mutilation. His life should have been balanced enough to allow his son to sleep with him. Two locks fell into the sink as disgust made his fingertips tingle and the coldness of the metal in his hand sent a chill through his system.

His self-control, where was it? Another lock fell, as did more of them . . . faster and angrier, they fell and dropped into the porcelain. Years of careful cultivation, of spiritual power-center, male physical prowess, woman magnetizing, politicizing, artist gathering, rhetoric talking, image making, def-defying video creating . . . Jamaica calling, exotic extensions of who he was fell away . . . leaving him naked and fragile, his chest heaving with sudden realization cast in white porcelain.

Seven

Dawn came to him in her normal vibrant, spring colors, pouring through the window with a profusion of sunshine, her sounds the orchestra of birds that still held their own against the city. Traffic mixed with their song and the brilliance of the light forced him to recognize her and fully awaken.

Unfurling his cramped body slowly, Trevor stretched the mangled part of him that had been bent into contortions to fit the overstuffed chair by his bedroom window. An immediate headache echoed through his skull, and he ditched his sketch pad onto the floor. It had been bad enough that he had to wait for the excruciating, slow process of the laundry to get done in the wee hours of the morning. Then during that wait, some type of anal-retentive side of him had taken over his body to force him to clean every surface of his basement sanctuary. But the fact that, once all of the sheets and pillowcases had been restored to his bed, he still couldn't sleep, totally annoyed him. The only solace he had found was to storyboard his mental visions in pencil.

Leaning forward, he stretched his legs, then his back, and stood, avoiding the long walnut-framed mirror as he searched for his clothes. This morning, after he showered, he'd leave a note on Miquel's dresser so his son wouldn't panic at finding the first-floor unit empty, then make breakfast for his sister and all of the kids, and begin his life anew. This was day one.

Smelling eggs and something sweet and oily, Gretchen shuffled down the long hall. Which one of the kids could be up at this hour cooking? she wondered. Only when her mother was alive did her kitchen come to life on its own—especially in the morning. Following the only man-made light in the unit, she moved slowly toward the scents and sounds of someone moving around. Then she stopped in the doorway and covered her mouth.

Hot tears immediately rose to her eyes, and she didn't know whether to scream, or to reach out and wrap her arms around the male figure that had his back turned to her. Immediately seeing the crisis, she was transfixed. And she waited for her brother to turn around and face her.

Hearing someone behind him, Trevor spoke to whoever it was without looking at the intruder.

"Got johnnycakes going, fried fish, and eggs. Juice is on the table," he muttered. "Hope I didn't mess up any plans for using these ingredients for dinner."

When the person hovering in the doorway didn't answer, he kept working at the stove with his back to the individual.

"Might as well sit down and eat. I promise I haven't poisoned it."

Then he heard his name whispered in a thin female voice, which brought him around to see his sister standing in the doorway in her robe with her hand partially covering her mouth.

"What have you done to yourself?" she gasped, her eyes glistening with tears and obvious shock.

"I've made breakfast for me family. You changed shifts last night, am I right? And nobody really ate what you labored over. So I'm trying to take the burden up from you so you can go to the day schedule with something under your belt. Sit down," he added quickly, avoiding her penetrating stare. "Eat. I'll dish a plate for you. Coffee will be up in a minute."

He noticed that she didn't move.

"What have you done?" she repeated, now moving toward him very cautiously until she was before him.

"I have changed."

"No," she whispered in a hoarse tone. "This is like penance." She reached her hand up and allowed her fingers to gingerly touch his butchered mane.

"I'll fix it later this morning. Didn't have clippers to give me a clean, close crop. Won't look so bad after I put Scott's equipment to it. No matter."

"Yes, it does matter," his sister murmured, now embracing him and suddenly holding him back in her arms to keep eye contact. "This is not what I wanted. I never wanted your spirit to be broken."

"My spirit is not broken," he said plainly, pulling away from her hold to tend to the stove. "It's like discipline."

"Discipline?" The horror that shone from her eyes forced him to look away.

"If a man goes into the military, one of the first things they do is cut his identity away from him. His hair. If a man goes to prison, they shave his head. If a man goes into a monastery, he must give up everything, including his hair. It is purely an act of contrition. Atonement." Fixing his sister a plate, he ignored her gaping expression and shoved it in her direction. "Eat your breakfast."

Still standing next to him, half-mute, she accepted the plate but didn't move. "This is not atonement, Trevor, it's sacrilege."

He laughed a hollow chuckle, and shook his head. "Always doin' da wrong thing. I'ree."

"No," she argued gently. "Not the wrong thing for

us, but the wrong thing for yourself." Gretchen moved away from him, placed her plate on the table, and sat down wearily. "I love you so very much, you crazy fool man." She'd made the remark while wiping her eyes and shaking her head. "Look at me," she ordered in a soft tone. "Last night you brought my son home to me in one piece, and for the first time in months, he stopped into my bedroom, sat on the edge of the bed, hugged me, and apologized. I don' know what you said to that boy, but there was an awareness in him . . . almost like he had grown up a little bit."

"We just talked man to man," Trevor said with a shrug, dismissing the compliment that he didn't feel he had the right to accept.

"And you know what?" Gretchen asked in a soft voice that made him stare at her. "He went in the other rooms and got Janelle and Sam, and brought them back into my bedroom, then made them sit down and listen to what he had to say. But he didn't yell, or cause confusion. He told them that they were beautiful, you had said so and now he saw it, and that they should be respected—so they had to respect themselves. And my son is going today to find an afterschool job. His sister and his cousin were so touched that the three of us were crying. I got up, after all of dat, and went to the closet where I had thrown your gifts . . . and I started pulling out things from the bag."

"I know you don' want anythin' I have to offer you, but I jus' wanted—"

"No, Trevor," she interrupted. "I was wrong on that note. I didn't want material things from you, but I never realized what you were giving beyond that. The subtlest gift of steadfast kindness, never forgetting us, always concerned, always trying to make a way."

A sad silence fell between them, and he turned away, filled with emotion, using the task of clicking off the burners and covering the pots as an excuse not to face her.

"We all get tired, Trevor," his sister whispered. "We all get fed up. Yesterday, I was just at my limit, but there's no way I could sleep at night if you gave up yourself, who you are, in the process of being with us. How could I, when I know what that feels like, and when I love you so?"

He couldn't answer the question, and was grateful when he heard another set of footsteps coming down the hall, sleepily shuffling toward the destination of food.

"Hey, Uncle T," a yawning young male voice said. "Smells goo—oh, man! Yo, Unc, what did you do to yourself?"

"Leave your uncle be," Gretchen warned. "Don' ask questions. Just go find your clippers."

Trevor glimpsed the two exchanging looks as his nephew immediately responded to the command from his mother—which sounded like a family call to arms. Next he heard two more sets of feet running down the hall, then screech to a halt with gasps at the door. Wasn't anything private in this family? Couldn't a person undergo a metamorphosis for his or her own personal reasons without a family council having to convene on the merits of one's sanity? When he heard the hallway's second staircase door creak open, and a child's footsteps running, he turned his back to the throng and held on to the edge of the sink for strength. He could feel his shoulders bending under the weight of their stares, while sudden anger ignited at the base of his spine.

"Could everybody just sit down, eat the food that has been prepared, and begin the day without extra commentary? What is the big deal?"

He heard a collective murmur, and the sounds of chairs scratching across linoleum, and finally all of the shuffling ceased. That's when he began dishing plates again and setting them in front of each family member without making eye contact. Then he fixed his sister a cup of coffee, and began dispensing logistics for the day, continuing to ignore the way they stared at him with pity.

"Miquel," he said sternly, "after you eat, wash up and get ready for school. I'll look over your homework. Then we'll walk—"

"Are you going to the barber shop first?" his son asked plainly, while staring at his head.

The honest question nearly broke Trevor's resolve to remain calm.

"No! There's not enough time. I'll wear one of Scott's caps, if he'll let me borrow it."

"Why don't you let me walk Miquel to school this morning, like I always do," Samantha interjected nervously, obviously trying to keep the peace.

"Yeah, Unc," Scott said quietly. "How about if I touch you up and give you a smooth fade before I go out this morning?"

"He's really good at it," Janelle added, her gaze nervously flitting from face to face as she picked at her food. "Right, Mom?"

His sister only nodded and looked away, still seeming stricken.

"Yeah, Dad, let Sammy walk me, and you can come and pick me up after school like we were gonna do? Cool?"

"Nobody wanted me here the way I was, and now with a change, nobody wants me in their space either! Yeah, that's cool." Embarrassed by his own outburst, and feeling trapped between worlds, all he could do was storm out of the room.

Scott immediately stood and put his hand on Miquel's shoulder. "Look, little brother, your pop is just going through a lot of changes right now. He didn't mean it, and he'll be cool after I give him a real shape-up. The lion has been wounded, and he's gonna snap and growl at everybody till he gets right."

When Miquel relaxed, he ruffled his young cousin's

hair and boxed his shoulder. "Eat up, dude," Scott said, chuckling. "Your Dad ain't mad at you. He's just mad at himself."

Receiving a tentative high five from Miquel, and a nod of approval from the women around the table, Scott pushed back his plate and went to the stove to begin fixing a plate for Trevor.

"He's not going to eat, you know," Scott's mother said in a weary tone. "You two are just alike in dat regard. Now he's probably on some type of religious fast. . . . Oh, my brother . . . what are we going to do with him?"

"He'll eat later. After the demon wears off."

"The demon?" Gretchen remarked.

"He's not on drugs, is he, Scott?" Janelle whispered. "Not my dad . . ."

Scott turned around with a smile that seemed to visibly relax the group and help Samantha remove her hand from her covered mouth.

"No, y'all. It ain't like dat," Scott said with newfound confidence surging through his veins. "It's just a man thing, and y'all wouldn't understand."

Knowing exactly where his uncle had gone to lick his wounds, Scott carefully descended the basement staircase with a plate in one hand and a pair of barber's clippers in the other. He knew that this was a delicate entry—going into a wounded male lion's den, you had to throw him a bone before attempting to pull the thorn out of his paw.

Setting the foil-wrapped breakfast down on the coffee table, Scott sat in the butterfly chair adjacent to the sofa. Considering his uncle's prone and angry position, he hung his head to keep the wide smile on his face from being seen. He knew how it felt to be so amped and so trapped that any slight gesture could be construed as additional injury to the ego.

"Brought you somethin' to eat," Scott said in a forced casual tone.

"I ain't hungry," Trevor spat back, then flung his arm over his forehead.

"A man's gotta get his grub on, particularly when he has a lot to do and think about."

"I said, I ain't hungry," Trevor boomed, shutting his eyes against the intrusion.

"Okay, man," Scott said amiably. "But we gotta buzz your head. I have a reputation to keep, and I can't have my uncle running around the streets looking like a piper."

The comment shot adrenaline through Trevor, and he sat bolt upright and turned on Scott. "I'm not goin' anywhere, and you can put your shears away!"

"Aw'ight," Scott said, with a laugh. "That's cool. You gonna live in the basement forever, never leave the house till your dreds grow back . . . maybe take ten to fifteen years to get 'em back. By then, Miquel should be outta da house; me, I'll be long gone; and Janelle and Sam, if they here, can bring you food down in the dungeon. Mom's gotta work, so you might starve to death if the girls don't feed you. I'll let 'em know."

Trevor leaned forward with his elbows on his knees and stared at the floor. Even to him, his outburst sounded foolish, if not vain and trite. But his dignity was in total shreds.

"What were you workin' on last night?" Scott asked, totally changing the subject.

Trevor knew the tactic well, and had even employed it himself to get to the youth that now used it on him.

"I was storyboarding somethin' I been meaning to work on—but never got around to it."

"Can I see it?"

"No. It's not finished."

"Will you teach me how to use this equipment down here, then, since you ain't usin' it?"

The question made Trevor go still. This was his sanctuary. This was his haven. . . .

"You know how many brothers my age would kill to have somebody in their family teach them how to use all of this electronic stuff?"

Again, Trevor couldn't answer.

"You sitting here feeling sorry for yourself, right?"

That kid was getting on his nerves.

"You can teach me and my crew how to use this stuff, and show us how to set up a video, and make movies about stuff we care about. You know, you know. It's somethin' you could also teach Miquel—since you care so much. Cuttin' off your hair didn't do jack but put you in a tailspin. What was this Samson and Delilah thing all about? Drama."

"Samson and Delilah?" Trevor looked up briefly and scowled, then returned his gaze to the floor.

"Grandma did make us all go to church. I know some stuff. So why'd you do it, man, cut off your strength? What, she don't like dreds?"

Trevor let his breath out hard. He needed space.

"You barkin' up the wrong tree. Ain't got nuttin' to do wit nobody but what I was dealing with meself!"

"Okay, okay, man," Scott said, grinning. "Don't go ballistic. Chill. I'm just tryin' to get to the root cause. But you startin' to slur your words back to home. You know you and Mom do that when you get uptight."

"I'm not uptight," Trevor growled, checking his diction.

"Look at all this stuff, man," Scott said in awe, changing the subject again while standing and walking around the basement. "You got soundtrack equipment, cameras, I don't even know what this is," he said, swishing his hand past Trevor's digital editing system. "If you tryin' to make a complete overhaul change, and since you being dramatic, then each one teach one."

"I ain't no teacher," Trevor grumbled. He refused to be baited this morning.

"Why, 'cause you can't get phat paid from teachin'?"

The question deeply disturbed his sense of self-righteous indignation and began chipping away at it.

"What was you workin' on, Unc? For real, for real. Man to man."

"A documentary," Trevor mumbled, peeking at the plate of cooling food.

"On what?" Scott shot back, moving closer to sit beside him on the sofa.

"On kids . . . showing the people who help inspire them, and what they have to deal with around the world—but some of them don't lose hope, because somebody cared."

"Can't talk the talk, brother, unless you gonna walk the walk," Scott said casually.

Again, Trevor couldn't answer, but the statement had begun to seep in.

"Instead of you being in control of the images, why don't you let kids from every age group make the jaunt—from our point of view. Let us tell our own story, man. Let us explain who influences us, and why . . . and tell what we're scared of. Nobody hears us—they always tellin' us from their perspective, what dey think is wrong wit us."

This time, Trevor sat back and studied his nephew's face. The pure simplicity and brilliance of it all held him in artistic thrall—and, above all else, it got his attention.

"I wanna go up to the school, and see if Miss Hamilton would allow me to film her and her students. Maybe even if she would entertain making this a class project."

"She's all that, ain't she?" Scott said with a wink.

"She's an old-fashioned, care-about-her-students teacher—who hasn't lost her passion for the job . . . and she has kept close tabs on Miquel, filled in the gaps, you know? Film what you know, ground level."

"Yeah, I'm feelin' you," Scott said. "And, like I said, she's *all that.*"

Trevor ignored the comment. Corey Hamilton being all that, as Scott said, had nothing to do with his work in progress, or the direction of his career.

"You might have a point," Trevor murmured, " 'bout lettin' the children storyboard their own experiences, then script out the narration, find and make their own soundtrack . . . then the older brothers could layer on their perspective and do the same—so it would be a mentoring and collaboration between an elementary school and a high school—showing the gaps, the transition into adulthood, and all of the traps that can derail innocence. You dig? This could be large, and pivotal . . . and important work. In the long run, it might help educators, parents, and the children themselves to see what's really happening on the street, at ground zero."

"Yeah, I'm really feelin' you, Unc," Scott said with a glimmer of admiration reflecting in his eyes. "You know, if we had something positive to work on like this, with a brother like you who has been there, this could be phat—and maybe get the brothers focused on something positive."

"Dat's what I was thinkin'. But we cannot forget the girls."

"True dat, Unc. True dat. The females is part of the problem," Scott said with a sly smile.

"Yeah. True dat," Trevor admitted, taking the foil off his plate as his appetite began to suddenly return.

"Then if you're going up to the school to negotiate this project, you oughta be lookin' your best," the teenager remarked casually, standing to retrieve the clippers. Returning to his seat next to Trevor, he held out the small black instrument and considered it as though it were a scalpel. "Gotta do some heavy surgery to repair the damage," he remarked coolly. "Image is everything. And a good shave wouldn't hurt you none, unless you doing five-o'clock-shadow-urban-grunge as a new look."

The statement made Trevor's hand go to his jaw and rub the stubble beneath his palm as he exhaled.

"She's got you all jacked up, man, admit it." Scott chuckled and gave Trevor a sideways glance. "Don't forget, I've seen her—been up to school with Miquel who don't talk about nothin' else but the nice Miss Hamilton. She's *fine*, man."

"I told you dat—"

"Man to man, and for real, for real," Scott argued, ribbing Trevor mercilessly as he punched his uncle's shoulder.

"It's about the doc. That's it. Got a lot on my mind. Changing careers, locations, responsibilities, and—"

"And she got you jonesin' so bad that you was up doing laundry at one o'clock in the mornin', dude. Like you told me last night—been there, seen it, done it. But your secret is safe with me."

Eight

It had been silly of her to think that she'd get a call at the school from Miquel's father after her unseemly outburst. She'd probably driven the man underground for good, and had also probably destroyed that child's last hope of ever having his father fully participate in his education, or his life. Morose feelings crowded in on Corey as she dismissed her class for the day and watched from her window as the children spilled out into the schoolyard.

Slowly collecting her pencils and markers, she did her normal sweep through the room to tidy it up, only to begin the routine all over again the next day. When her door opened, she didn't even look up immediately, and she expected to hear a young voice asking her to repeat the homework assignment she'd just erased from the board.

"Miss Hamilton," a deep, exotic male voice intoned. "May we begin again?"

The sound of the voice immediately snapped her head up and riveted her attention to the tall, clean-shaven, and elegantly dressed person who stood in her doorway, hesitating in a manner that seemed to ask her nonverbal permission to enter. It took her a moment to process the new image that accosted her. Nothing in all of her formal training, or her home training on basic politeness, could stop her from staring at the stark contrast . . . where were those gorgeous locks? What had the man done? It was like witnessing an individual's private religious experience. Without thought, her hand briefly went to her mouth, then she quickly lowered it.

"Mr. Winston?"

"Yes," the man said softly. "Trevor."

"Please come in. Do come in. I'm sorry," she stammered, glancing at him nervously. "You just look so . . . I mean, different from yesterday . . . and I hadn't expected you to . . . what I'm saying is, I owe you a sincere apology for my outburst yesterday, and for judging you so unfairly."

"No," he replied in a gentle tone. "It is I who owe you an apology. I came into your class unannounced, created confusion, and did not respect what you had been trying to communicate. I also had not responded to your numerous attempts to get in touch with me on the extremely important matter regarding my son."

He loved the way she smiled and allowed her gaze to slide away from his briefly. Without words, the simple action told him that all was most likely forgiven, and she'd accepted his overture to begin again.

"I'm so glad that my attitude didn't permanently drive you away," she admitted, seeming to relax. "I get so wrapped up in the children sometimes, and I forget that there are mitigating circumstances. It's just that Miquel has so much potential, and he's such a wonderful kid. But I forgot to give credit where credit is due. He couldn't be so special unless his parents and family had laid the foundation. My apologies for being so presumptuous."

"No offense taken," he replied with a smile, then looked down. Her warm compliment and apology almost made him forget why he was standing there.

God, he was handsome . . . and seemed to be so much more complex than she had given him credit for earlier. His gracious acceptance of her awkward statement made her relax even more. Perhaps his involvement with his son's life was salvageable.

"Your coming here has made a difference," she said quietly. "I know Miquel appreciates it. All he could talk about today was that his father was coming to see his science project, and had promised to stay for a while. I didn't realize that the child meant you were coming again so soon . . ."

"Yes." Trevor grinned self-consciously. "I told him that I needed to talk to you, and then we'd retrieve it together and go home. I'm planning on staying in Philadelphia for a long time."

"Really?" she remarked before she could catch herself.

"Yeah," he answered, casting his gaze out the window. "Time to stop globe-trotting and put down some roots. I thought, what better place to begin than with significant involvement in my son's education?"

"We could always use a spare pair of adult hands around here," she replied, letting her breath out in a rush of excitement and growing more comfortable as the exchange wandered down a perfect path.

"Well," he began slowly, trying to find the right words and hoping that she'd be interested in his offer, "I know that some of the artistic projects I've been involved in have not necessarily been community-building in nature. Did a lot of soul-searching about that." He stopped to look her squarely in the eyes, and when her gaze slid away again, he knew that she was going to be kind enough to defer comment. "But," he added, continuing with conviction, "I've had this documentary about children, and the influences on them, knocking around in my brain since forever."

He watched the fire ignite in her eyes when her gaze held his, as a broad smile suddenly overtook her lush mouth. Witnessing it sent an inexplicable sensation of pride through him. It was an indescribable rush, and something that instantly made him aware of just how much he cared about her opinion of him.

"Oh," she murmured, flattening her palm against her heart. "That would be wondrous!"

The way her words flowed out, and her eyes went to slits of ecstasy, and her delicate hand covered her petite bosom . . . dear Lord, where did this angel come from?

Recovering himself quickly, he let his words tumble out in an adolescent rush. "I was thinking of it as a teaching moment . . . you know, I could come in and show the young people how to sketch out their ideas on storyboards—which helps build analytical skills; then coach them on how to write the narrative script from their perspective—which helps their literacy skills; then begin introducing different forms of digital equipment, cameras, and lighting techniques—which require math and other cognitive skills . . . and then they could shoot footage, which they can edit in my studio over on Springfield Avenue . . . if you think that would be okay, and it would help them get along, team-building wise, because film is such a collaborative process . . . maybe even annex the high school, so that some of the older kids who they are trying to emulate could get involved in the process, from a positive mentoring capacity . . . again, only if you think the idea has merit."

He waited for her approval, nervously twisting the silver bangle on his arm . . . waiting for this teacher to grant him absolution . . . waiting for her to say, "Job well done."

"If I wouldn't mind . . ." She gasped. "If I wouldn't mind?" Corey Hamilton sat down slowly on the edge of her desk, covering her mouth as though her legs had gone out from under her.

The sight of her sheer delight had begun to take a toll on his reason, but he could not stop himself from staring at the gorgeous creature—who had just gone weak in the knees from his offer.

"Jesus . . . Mr. Winston . . ."

"Trevor."

"Corey," she said, shaking her head slowly. "I don't know what to say. . . ."

"*Yes* is a good place to start." His heart was pounding so hard that his ears had begun to ring.

"Most of the parents that come in here to assist simply put out cookies and crayons, or help with the bake sale, or the spring festival . . . they don't rewrite our entire curriculum. . . ."

Immediately, his hopes were dashed, and, crestfallen, he quickly interjected an apology. "This was all too presumptuous, and, well, I just don't know anything but filmmaking. I could come in and help with the fair or repair broken—"

"Oh, no, forgive me," she cut in fast. "Oh, no, I'm not at all pushing back on this wonderful, magnificent offer. Please, Mr. Winston—I mean, Trevor. I'm just flabbergasted. It's like someone handed our students a lottery ticket to knowledge and exposure, and I just don't know what to say."

Nervous relief swept through him so hard that he laughed to release the internal pressure.

"Good, then," he said quickly, before she could change her mind. "It's sealed. We have a film project together, then?"

He extended his hand to shake hers as she broke out into an ecstatic giggle that rippled through him, and was immediately accosted by the smooth warmth that filled his palm. It took everything in him not to bend down and kiss the back of that gentle structure. God, her hands . . . just as he'd imagined them to be. Velvet electricity. No wonder his son was so smitten. Just standing there with her hand in his had literally blown him away.

"How do we begin this lesson?" he asked, his voice dropping an octave of its own accord, while he still held her hand.

"Why don't you come to our class, if your schedule

permits, tomorrow? Or as soon as it is convenient for you. Then you can begin by telling the students about your idea, and then I'll list the elements and steps of putting together a film on the board to familiarize them with the process."

He could only stare at her. How could she do that, when she didn't know the industry?

Her smile became so rich and brilliant that he ached for his camera to capture it. But it was her eyes that actually sparkled with an inner light. . . .

"That was my major in school," she whispered, her gaze becoming self-conscious and shy. "I have wanted to do a documentary on the children for *soooo* long, you have no idea how much of a dream come true this is for me, too."

Her hand slid out of his, and she walked away from him and looked out the window. He studied her proud carriage, and the way her voice became so gentle that it almost cooed to him. It was becoming difficult to breathe as he realized that he was talking to a fellow artist. Never in his life had he been so completely devastated by a woman. She knew the craft. She knew the imagery. She knew what he did and loved it. She was professional, and kind, and beautiful from the inside out. And she'd be working with him. He was seduced and taken. . . .

"I never knew," he found himself whispering. "I just assumed . . ."

"No," she murmured, her gaze lovingly cast in the direction of the schoolyard. "I wasn't always a teacher, but I found how rewarding it can be. My mother became ill and died, there were bills to pay, and I couldn't just up and leave and gallivant around the country. Plus, the process of getting funding was so rigorous that, at the time, I just didn't have it in me," she added in a sad voice that made him want to move toward her and wrap his arms around her.

"I am so sorry to hear about your loss," he said quietly, now also realizing why she'd confronted him so fiercely. Just like his sister, the women always seemed to stay and defer their dreams, while he, like most men, got to continue with theirs no matter what.

"Corey," he said in a quiet voice, approaching her side. "I know what it feels like to lose the most important person in your life. I ran from that. I'm not excusing my absence from Miquel's life, but that was part of it . . . and I couldn't imagine what I would do if I couldn't make films."

She nodded and looked up at him, her wide, brown irises reflecting gentle respect. "I wanted to run, too, but I didn't have anywhere to go," she said with a self-conscious smile that faded with her next words. "Guess there were a lot of wrong assumptions that got us off on the wrong foot."

"Truce?" he asked, but didn't trust himself to extend his hand to her again.

"Truce," she said with a grin that eclipsed the sadness that had momentarily overtaken her face.

"This will be the best project I have ever committed myself to," he murmured, holding her gaze. "It's too important, and there's too much riding on it. I give you my word, I will use every contact, call in every marker, and exhaust every resource I have at my disposal to make this something that gets national attention, Madame Producer."

"Producer?"

"Producer," he confirmed, "with the children all getting screen credits for each aspect of their work. These kids should not only walk away with knowledge and experience and growth, but also résumé, portfolio, and options for their future. Each one teach one," he added, shoving his hands in his pockets to keep his fingers from reaching out to trace the delicate line of her jaw.

"I'll have to get releases from the parents so that the children can work on this unfettered." She didn't know what else to say, and this man who loomed over her like a fairy godfather was stealing her breath, her reason, and all of her professional decorum at the moment.

"Tomorrow . . . what time would you like me to be here? I'm all yours."

She couldn't immediately answer him, as the last part of what he'd said made her face warm. "How about nine?" she replied after the brief pause she required to pull herself together. "Does that work for you?"

"Nine it is," he remarked with a wide smile, then promptly went to the back of the room to her science table. "I cannot forget this again." He laughed, picking up the large clay volcano that was mounted on a wooden board.

"Never," she said, laughing back. "Miquel was so proud of that thing when it spouted lava that he concocted from food coloring and baking soda and vinegar. Please, put it somewhere very visible in your house—it's a shrine."

"Might have to go into Claymation at some point." Trevor chuckled, lugging the monstrous project past Corey Hamilton. "Animation takes the patience of a child."

All she could do was shake her head as Trevor Winston slipped out of her classroom and walked down the hall.

"Stop, gurl!" Justine screamed into the telephone receiver. *"You are lying!"*

"No, for real," Corey said in rapid-fire response. "Oh, my God. Oh, my God. . . . Girlfriend, you should have heard him, should have seen him, never in my life would I have expected . . . Lord, have mercy! What am I going to do? How can I process this? He's coming back tomorrow. I have to notify parents, my principal, redirect the curriculum for this opportunity of a lifetime for the kids—"

"For the kids?" Justine cut in with a mischievous giggle. "Not just for them, doll."

"Oh, no, Justine. Don't even go there," Corey argued, feeling her face get hot again. "No. That would ruin everything, and it's way, way out of line. This man has just done an about-face, has no interest in me beyond my capacity as a teacher, and it is totally inappropriate to even begin to allow my mind to—"

"Begin? Oh, pullleeze," Justine said in a huff. "That man invaded your nervous system the moment you saw him and—"

"Not true, and totally off the mark. Besides, we'll be working shoulder-to-shoulder with all the kids, and none of the kids, especially little Miquel, can perceive that there's anything other than professional respect and conduct between the adults that are working with them. I can't have an entire class, and possibly a contingent of high school students, not to mention parents, or my principal—thinking there's any thing inappropriate going on, and besides—"

"Y'all can be discreet until the project is over—"

"What?" Corey found herself hollering into the phone. "Never. I don't roll like that. And there has been no evidence of anything from Mr. Winston other than sheer resp—"

"The man cut his hair for you, gurl."

"He did not!" Corey jumped up from the sofa and started pacing. "Oh, you are so exasperating sometimes, Justine."

"He went total monk on you."

"What are you talking about?" Corey shouted, pacing into the kitchen to boil water for some tea.

"The brother had some type of overnight epiphany, did some soul searching, and is putting down roots in—"

"If anything," Corey fussed back, searching for her teaball as she filled the kettle with water, "perhaps my words sunk in, and made him evaluate his relationship with his son, but I had nothing to do with a haircut, or his new project idea. He said it had been on his mind to do it for a long time."

"All right, if you insist," her girlfriend replied in a blasé tone, "but something significant was his catalyst. I think that something was you—because in the last twenty-four hours, first he was yelling at you, and now you're yelling at me, and I say—"

"I'd say, you're crazy, and I don't want to talk about it."

"Okay. But one last question," Justine said with a snicker. "What are you going to wear tomorrow?"

"Get off the phone!"

"I love you, too. Bye."

"Yo, Uncle T," Scott boomed as he came into the duplex's kitchen. "You look good, you look good. How'd it go?"

"Miquel's downstairs with Sam, both doing homework—check out his science project when you see him—Janelle's in her room on the telephone—as usual—and your mom should be in from work soon—dinner will be ready in about—"

"Aw'ight, aw'ight, but, that ain't what I'm asking you. How did it go?"

"Cool," Trevor said, trying to keep the excitement out of his voice. "How'd you make out with landing an after-school job?"

Scott eyed him suspiciously, but his expression contained mirth. "Got a good lead on a gig at Rite Aid," he said casually. "Did she go for it?"

"That's good," Trevor replied. "I hope that comes through for you."

"So, what, now you got selective hearin', Unc? I asked you, did she go for it?"

"I wasn't trying to get Miss Hamilton to go for anything—not like I'm scammin' her. But, yeah, she liked the project idea."

"So, could that be why you're buzzing around the kitchen all in a big jangle, wit too much energy like you on speed, or somethin'?"

"I'm not in a janglement. I just promised your mom—"

"Yeah, and look at you. All efficient, can't stop smiling—"

"Get out of my business," Trevor warned, but his voice just couldn't seem to muster the timbre of authority he needed at the moment.

"Oh, so now she's your business, huh?"

"I didn't say dat, an' you know—"

"You slurring your words again, boss, and goin' Island on me."

Trevor bent his head and laughed from deep down in his chest. "Son, you're trying my patience and gettin' on me nerves, is all it is."

"I'd say, from the way you all lit up, you ain't got no nerves left for me to git on."

"She wants me to come to the class tomorrow morning, and is very happy about the idea—and was thrilled about the high school students mentoring the younger ones. You should have seen her face. . . ." he mused in a lapse, then quickly corrected himself, taking on a businesslike tone. "I'm going to ask her if you can help direct, while she produces, and the younger ones create. Okay? Everybody should be happy. Now, can you leave me to my pots so that I don' burn da meal?"

"So, now you done gone from storyboarding into casting, huh?"

"Yeah," Trevor said in a huff.

Scott leaned against the kitchen door frame and rubbed his chin, smiling all the while and nodding in satisfaction. "You done good, boss. Kill't two birds with one stone. You go, boy!"

"I didn't kill no birds! And, this project ain't about no woman. It's about redirectin' my focus and my art."

"Then why you gettin' so touchy? Look at'cha. All amped, and whatnot."

" 'Cause you in my way and gettin' on my nerves! This ain't about nuttin' but de project!"

"Yeah, I know," Scott said coolly. "For real, I know you worried about Miquel, and what's going on in the neighborhood—that's serious. But I also know that it doesn't hurt that this *fine* honey is happy about the new direction your energies are takin' in her classroom. Like I said, you done kill't two birds, brother. So I'd say, from where I stand, the lion is back."

"I'd say, from where I stand, that you have an overactive imagination," Trevor argued, tending to his pots on the stove and refusing to look at the youth, who mocked him.

"Naw, naw, for real . . . you got injured, used to go big game huntin', was the baddest mother in the jungle, you got shot, had to nurse your wounds, been lookin' at prime rib and salivatin' for a long time, and now you got it cornered. All of a sudden, the two birds dat you just kill't ain't enough to fill you up . . . and that fine antelope is makin' you slobber on yourself. It's been a *long time* since you felt the hunt. And now, you just scared 'cause you don't exactly remember how to bring down big game anymore."

"What, boy? You been watchin' *Lion King* videos or somethin'? I'm not tryin' to go there wit dis woman—she deserves the utmost of respect! Don' ev'r let me hear 'bout you talkin' of her outta turn like dat! She ain't no game I'm runnin'. I'm—"

"See what I mean?" Scott chuckled, obviously unperturbed. "Just the thought of it is giving you the gotta-hunt shivers, like an adrenaline rush, the heebie-jeebies, making your fangs come out and what's left of your mane stand up—prob'ly everything else, too." The teenager laughed harder as he slipped out of the room, yelling a parting-shot comment over his shoulder as he sauntered away. "You gonna be hard to live wit until you handle your bizness!"

Nine

He had changed his clothes no less than five times this morning, something that he never paid attention to before. Settling on a pair of khakis, combat boots, and a simple beige polo shirt, he looped his digital light meter over his head and let it fall. Why was he so out of sorts, and so nervous about going to school with his son to speak to a class full of fifth graders? He'd taught graduate level courses at the university, had been in heated negotiations about contracts. Now, a group of fifth graders had cowed him?

Trevor studied his reflection in the mirror. Maybe Scott was wrong; the old lion was definitely not back. Or maybe it was because he didn't want to be perceived as a carnivore by the lovely Miss Hamilton. Either way, his nerves were piano-wire taut.

After three trips up and down the steps while his family watched him without a word, he had all of the gear he wanted to take to the class. Stopping to catch his breath, he wiped his brow and leaned on the kitchen door frame.

"You about ready, sport?" he quipped to Miquel, who instantly shot up from the table, almost toppling over his cereal.

"You bet, Dad!"

"Cool, dude. Let's roll. We'll see y'all tonight," Trevor said in a forced casual tone, avoiding Scott's fish-eyed glimpse.

"Not so fast," the teenager said, chuckling. "Let me check you out. Make sure you representin' proper. Kids are a tough audience. Don' wanna get booed like you at the Apollo."

Even though Trevor tried to play off the comment and act like it didn't matter, he waited for Scott to get up and inspect him.

"Yeah, yeah," Scott murmured, walking around Trevor like he was a drill sergeant. "You check out," he added, reaching up to dust imaginary lint off Trevor's shoulder. "You smooth."

"Thank you," Trevor replied with relief in his voice. "What'chu doin' this morning?"

"Going to school," Scott said. "Why, you need backup?"

"Thought that since you and Janelle, and even Samantha, are supposed to do community service work to graduate, I might be able to draft you all to oversee different crew positions?"

"Ooooh! For real?" Janelle exclaimed, almost knocking over her chair.

"Oh, that would be fantastic!" Samantha squealed.

"What's all the fuss?" Gretchen muttered, entering the room in her robe and slippers with her hands on her hips. "I have to work tonight, and you all are in here raising pure Cain, thumping and bump—"

"Mom!" Janelle exclaimed, cutting off her mother's words. "Uncle Trevor is going to make us crew captains, or somethin' like that—and take us to Miquel's school this morning to—"

"What? Have you all lost your fool minds? Can't just be up and goin' places without telling your teachers about—"

"No, Auntie," Samantha protested. "All of us have to do community service to graduate, and this is perfect!"

"Oh, I see," Gretchen muttered, swallowing a smile and trying to remain peeved. "So, Uncle Trevor strikes again, out of the blue, and has made the one family member who does have any sense, Sam, lose her mind, too, eh?"

Trevor noticed the wide grin on Scott's face, and how his nephew tried desperately to act like he wasn't fazed.

"We'd need a note, and everythang—can't be just bookin' up without an excuse, ya mean. Moms would flip, like she just did, and I don't need no more unexcused absences on my record, since I'm about a positive vibe now. . . ."

"Oh, yeah," Trevor sighed. "I forgot all about that. Gotta do this by the book."

"You are correct, Mr. Trevor," his sister warned, wagging her finger in his face. "Now, instead of sleeping, I have to call two schools, speak to counselors, because somebody woke up with a bright idea this mornin'."

"Oh, *pleeaaaase,* Mom," Janelle begged. "Just this one time, then we'd have a set schedule and wouldn't have to miss any school."

"It's for a good cause," Miquel lamented, his shoulders dropping at the merest hint that the idea would get squashed.

"Nahhh," Scott sighed. "Maybe we shouldn't go and try to participate with this kiddie thing." Yet he beamed with mischief as his sister and cousin protested with a series of teeth-sucking and eye-rolling grunts.

Not ready to give up so easily, Janelle pressed on, her voice escalating and sounding tighter as she spoke. "Look, Unc, if you call the school counselor this morning, give them the rap about this project, then you can bust us out of L-seven. Later, if Miss Hamilton sends a note from her school, everything will be smooth."

"That could work," Trevor said quickly.

"Oh, pullleeze. Your uncle don't have time to be callin' no schools, let alone know what to say once he got ahold of a counselor. I'll make da call, on the one condition that you all stick with this project," Gretchen said firmly, folding her arms and thrusting up her chin before she laughed.

"You mean we can go?" Samantha shrieked, while jumping up from the table before another doubt could derail the plan.

"My whole posse's going to school with me?" Miquel asked, laughing and becoming so excited that he did a little jig in the middle of the kitchen floor, which made everyone laugh.

"Oh, my goodness," Samantha swooned. "Wait till my friends at the university hear about this!"

"All right," Trevor said, regaining his confidence and authority. "Let's move out. We're about to run a full-scale production company. No slackers, no bein' late for crew call. Got it?" Turning to wink at Gretchen, he blew her a kiss. "Thanks, sis."

Teenage banter, whoops, and loud music that blared from his four-by-four's radio punctuated the entire ride over to the school. What had he gotten himself into? Moreover, what had possessed him to bring a teenage contingent along to the most frightening new project he'd ever embarked upon? Indeed, he must have been mad. But one thing was for sure: Soon he was going to have to trade in the four-by-four for a van in order to carry all of the equipment and cart around all the kids.

Having restored some semblance of order, he was finally able to marshal the excited teenagers and his son, who was bursting with pride, down the hall to Miss Hamilton's class with a little in-school-so-be-quiet decorum.

When they arrived, toting heavy metal cases, Corey's face lit up, and the children went dead silent. Trevor surveyed the room and noticed that the school's principal was also in attendance. He glanced at Corey Hamilton nervously and drew in a silent breath. It was show time.

"Please, come in, come in, Mr. Winston," Corey said beaming, almost pulling him by the arm as he set down a case. "And who else do you have with you today?"

"Well," Trevor said, pacing himself, "I brought some crew captains with me from the local high school and college who can help us with this project. Meet my director, Scott; script analyst, Samantha—a college intern; and Janelle, an aficionado of hip-hop music and wardrobe. Miquel I'm thinking could be the art and animation director."

"Oh, absolutely," Corey said with a wide smile, her voice filled with merriment. "That's quite a crew."

He almost laughed as the teens stood a little taller and their faces grew extremely serious, and he and Corey exchanged a pleased glance. But he loved the effect it all had on his son, who nearly saluted when his title was announced.

"Mr. Winston, it is indeed an honor and a privilege for us to have such talent among us, and a talent so willing to spend this type of valuable time with our students. We will be on our best listening and following-directions behavior, isn't that right, class?" The principal had stood and walked toward them, sweeping her arms in front of them like a proverbial mistress of ceremonies, then directing the class into a unison response of "Yes, Mrs. Williams." Then, stepping off the imaginary stage, she turned and smiled at Trevor and his motley crew. "Do proceed, Mr. Winston. Do proceed."

Nodding to his crew to take a seat, Trevor began writing on the blackboard next to Miss Hamilton's neat script. Somehow, as he began talking about his craft, and answering the children's questions while opening cases and showing them the equipment, years seemed to melt right before him. Energy surged through his veins as their eager minds snapped up the information faster and with more acceptance than any college level class he'd ever encountered. He found himself laughing with them as they asked simple questions that were deeply profound, and he knew. Yes, he was home.

She'd watched the man captivate her students for two hours, walking among them with the ease and grace that only consummate teachers were known to possess. He not only held their attention, but opened the world of possibilities before them, and had pulled thought-provoking questions from their minds.

She was mesmerized by his comfort level with the children and the way one could actually see them grasping the subject matter as he skillfully introduced each new concept. Her own heart was racing with the excitement of a schoolgirl as she drank in his teaching style and the way he simply made the information that was old to her new again. For once she was so glad that she had followed her hunch, staying up the night before to rewrite her curriculum, then proposing those changes to her principal that morning.

Corey's mind reeled as she thought about ways to incorporate their English lessons, math lessons, and science projects all around this central project. It was an integrated approach, whereby they could write scripts, learn about light and units of measure, and art . . . oh, it didn't get any better than this!

Finally, having to be the bad guy and force the children to go to lunch and recess, she gave Mr. Winston the two-minute warning to end his first day in class amid a series of moans and groans from the children.

"All right, all right," she said merrily, clapping her hands. "We are going to give all of our guests a big round of applause for their time, and they'll be back during the rest of the term to work with us, so we must let them go on with their days."

She couldn't contain herself as the boys argued and fought for position around Trevor and Miquel's cousin, and she had to turn away and laugh secretly as Miquel puffed up and showed off his teenage cousin as though he'd brought a pit bull to class. She wasn't sure whether she was more tickled over Miquel's stance, or the fact that the teenager seemed to absolutely bask in the adoration. Then, of course, it was the girls who flocked around the two teen-women, all giggles and admiration over their clothes, hair, and makeup. Trevor Winston had brought her a teacher's dream!

Although it took longer than usual to get her class to file out to the lunchroom, to the point where Trevor's teens had even offered to hang with the younger kids and to escort them down the hall, she finally got her classroom back.

"Wow!" Mrs. Williams exclaimed. "Just *wow* is all I can say. If you were the Pied Piper, Mr. Winston, our kids would be out on the Ben Franklin Bridge right about now. I see why Ms. Hamilton made such a fuss about your magnetic charisma—oh, and what you have done by getting teenagers involved . . . there are simply no words!"

Corey felt her face burn. It had not been her intention to be so effusive about this project in front of Mrs. Williams, and it was definitely not something that she wanted Trevor to know—at least not the comment she'd made about him being magnetic and charismatic. Oddly, that part of what her principal had said embarrassed her now. However, it was indeed the truth.

But she smiled when she glanced at Trevor Winston. He looked so self-conscious from Mrs. Williams's comment that she was sure he'd say, "Aw, shucks, ma'am, it wasn't nuthin'." Why that delighted her so, she wasn't sure. What she did know was that this man had a gift.

"I just hope I didn't overstay my welcome," he said in a self-deprecating way that rang true. "I wanted the children to become excited about what has been my passion since longer than I can remember. If they're excited about it, then they'll grasp the concepts and learn."

He'd cast a nervous glance at both women, and Corey noted that his expression held a hopeful expectation in it, in much the same way adult students who'd approached her mother on the streets used to. . . . Then it dawned on her—he was truly nervous. It mattered to him that he did well here today. Oh, my God. . . .

"Of course, of course, Mr. Winston," her principal immediately interjected. "Oh, you were fabulous, just fabulous, an absolute delight. I, myself, learned so much, well, as I said before, we are truly in your debt."

"No, the thanks is mine alone. This was the most fun I've had in years, Mrs. Williams. Thank you, and Miss Hamilton, for allowing me to participate."

Seeming to blush at the compliment, the rarely flustered Mrs. Williams gathered her folders and nodded. "Well, on that note, I think I'd better get back to my administrative duties. It was a pleasure, Mr. Winston. Do come again."

So many emotions and thoughts were going through Corey's mind all at once that she didn't know what to do, so she opted to lean against her desk until Mrs. Williams had closed the door behind her.

"You blew 'em away, Mr. Winston." She chuckled, shaking her head. "You totaled my class. Don't know how I'm going to keep the lid on them until June, and then next year." She laughed again, throwing her head back. "What will I do for an encore? They're ruined."

It was with no small measure of satisfaction that he soaked in her praise. It had been so important to him to do well. Until she'd completed her comment, he hadn't realized it. Up until now, he'd tricked himself into believing that it was purely his worries about not messing up in front of his son's class, only for Miquel's sake. Then, he'd lied to himself and said that he'd dragged the teenagers along to give them exposure—but, when it came down to it, he'd been terrified to walk into her classroom alone and in front of fifteen pairs of little eyes.

But something had happened to him as he was working with the kids . . . something indefinable that ignited within him. Passion had filled him, and images and plans had besieged his brain, and for the first time in years, he was no longer doing something by rote. He'd begun to create again, to realign form and pattern, to see the unseen and cosmic connections, and was left fulfilled and spent. And when he looked up at Corey Hamilton, she, too, seemed to have taken the ride with him, leaving her exhilarated, yet spent.

Feeling guilty that his motives weren't as clear as he'd hoped, Trevor began packing away his light kits and cameras.

"I was hoping I would do all right today," he admitted, never looking in her direction.

"You did more than all right," she said in a warm tone that made him glance up at her briefly, then look away. "You're a natural."

He smiled and caught her gaze, this time not running from the compliment. "I love this work," he confessed, "and when I talk about it, and create on the run like we did in class today, it's like the sensation of weightlessness—it's like flying."

"I know. . . ." she whispered, her wide smile beaming with pure satisfaction. "Oh, God, I remember, and I know."

The way she'd said what she had said tugged at a side of his brain that he was trying to ignore. Her voice had that effect on him, and her choice of words, or maybe it was her intonation that always messed with him . . . either way, it always sent images to him that he didn't dare acknowledge.

"I was thinking," he said casually, trying to sound as nonchalant as possible. "Maybe I can get some T-shirts and caps made up for the kids—you know, crew gear with their names on the back of it. I know the older kids love that stuff, and I figure the younger ones will, too."

Corey laughed so warmly as she doubled over, slapping her leg, that he had to begin packing equipment again.

"Oh, yeah! But the school doesn't have the budget—"

"My treat," he interjected, cutting her off. "Look, the fair is next weekend, and I can have a buddy of mine print them up so they can film and strut their stuff at the event. By then, we'll have the kids in teams, some working on the storyboards, some working on the script, some working on the equipment—with each squad getting a turn to teach their peers about the aspect of this that they are working on. I'll get Scott and Janelle to recruit some of their high school friends to help the small fries with the more dangerous things like the lights when we use them. The big kids can crew sound—with the boom microphones—and the younger kids can learn the lavalieres. But we need crew uniforms, just like a Little League team. It builds unity and identity."

"Mr. Winston," she said, letting her breath out in a pleased rush that washed through him. "You have already done so much . . . the film alone, and your time . . ."

"What, I can't donate a few T-shirts and baseball caps to some schoolkids? And, by the way, I'm going to start calling you Corey, so I hope you drop the formality and will adopt Trevor as my tag line." He chuckled when she blushed, feeling her positive spirit coax his courage out of hiding.

"We can never repay you for all of this," she whispered. "This is so wonderful."

"There's no debt attached to this," he said quietly. "I am the one who is gaining so much from this experience. Have you any idea what being in this class did for me today?"

He watched her studying his face, and the mirth and acceptance in her eyes told him that she did.

"What are you doing after school today?" He tried again to make his voice sound casual.

"The usual," she replied slowly, but she was still smiling. "I'll probably go home, mark a few papers, maybe grab a bite to eat. Why?"

"Want to see the studio where the kids can edit? It's not far from here—and I could take you by when I come back to get Miquel this afternoon, if you aren't busy," he said quickly, then wished he could have ripped out his own tongue. The offer sounded so pat, and he also wasn't sure whether or not he was trying to lure her into his lair, or to show off. Either choice was wrong, and he admonished himself for being so weak as to tempt her beyond the walls of the school using the children as bait. That was lame!

"Really?" she squealed, hopping off the side of the desk. "Oh, that would be so much fun! What do you have down there?"

Trevor let out his breath as slowly as he could to steady himself, and to retract any hint of fangs that might be showing. Scott was right; he was nearly slobbering on himself.

"Uh . . . an Avid . . . couple of Beta decks . . . some sound stuff," he said with a shrug. "Nothing special."

"Are you mad? You mean that you have your own Avid sitting over there on Springfield Avenue? Do you know how we used to fight in graduate school to book lab time on one of those? Jesus, man . . . these kids don't know . . . Oh, I'd *love* to see it. Oh, yeah!"

He almost closed his eyes to keep her voice from threatening his composure any further. Taking his breath in on a deep inhale that he disguised with the exertion of picking up a heavy camera case, he nodded. "Cool. Pick you up around quarter after three. You like Jamaican food?"

"What are you trying to do, Trevor," she said, laughing. "Make me crazy?"

Somehow he couldn't keep his fangs back as he hoisted another heavy metal case off a student's desk. She'd been good to his boy, passed the family litmus test, used his name in that sultry voice of hers, made him feel like a million dollars in her class, knew what an Avid was—and he was sure she could make it sing, and now, she admitted to liking the food of his culture. Plus, she was leaning against her desk and flashing that brilliant smile . . . her long, shapely legs crossed at the ankle, while she traced her collarbone with her finger—just like he wanted to . . . oh, yeah, he had to get out of there and get some fresh air. Immediately. He was already insane from the hunger she stoked in him. The question was how did one approach her?

"I'll come back for the rest of this when I pick you up," he said, moving quickly. "You like red fish and rice and peas . . . spicy cabbage and johnnycakes . . . with a little ginger beer on the side?"

"Get out of here, Trevor Winston," she said, her laughter ringing out, "before I follow you home for lunch. I haven't eaten all day, and now you're making me drool."

Although he only chuckled as he paced out of her classroom and down the hall to collect his teens away from their fans, his mind was a million miles away. . . . If she only knew how much the thought of her following him home for a nonchaperoned lunch right now was making *him* drool. . . .

Ten

For the balance of the day she was a bundle of nerves. How in the world was she supposed to calmly conduct her class and act like nothing out of the ordinary had happened? Trevor Winston, in three days, had turned her sense of order upside down.

First it had been his incorrigible nonchalance and then his outburst when she was in the right—or, at that moment, seemed to be in the right. Then he had done a complete one-hundred-and-eighty-degree about-face, even down to the way he looked. Now he had swept into her class as the parent of the year! Worst of all, he was potentially more than a parent was; he was a possible suitor. Maybe it was her mind playing tricks on her, but there was something in the way that he looked at her, and the way he smiled at her, and definitely in the way that his presence made her feel things that she wasn't supposed to feel.

Brushing off the uncomfortable thoughts, Corey busied herself in tidying up her classroom and trying to keep her routine. She carefully put away all the pencils, crayons, and markers just as she normally would do. She erased the board, and began to pack her briefcase with the children's homework to be marked. Today was like any other day, she told herself in a bold-faced lie. She was just going by a studio to see another learning venue for her students, much like she would site-inspect a future class field trip—since that's all there was to it.

Yet, for some odd reason, the more she held on to the concept that Trevor Winston's only interest was to show her a teaching venue, and his offer of dinner was just a hospitable gesture between teaching colleagues, the more morose she became. And the more morose she became, the harder it was for her to continue to fool herself into thinking that she wasn't interested in the man beyond his role as a partner in teaching a group of children. That mental peeling away of her internal shield was frightening to her as she cleaned up her classroom, because it led her down the path of demons she'd already had to slay.

Like the infamous Hydra, the no-good-man-demon had multiple heads and too many faces to count. Each one had its own sharp claws and fangs that could dig into a woman's tender soul. "Been there, seen it, done it," Corey said, sighing. A man like Trevor Winston, even if he were interested in her, probably had women stashed in every conceivable port in the world. Tall, fine, handsome, eligible, with a level of notoriety, oh yes, this dragon had teeth. This was the kind of guy who stopped, dropped, and rolled 'em. This was not a family man, despite the sudden transformation. This was indeed Dracula 2001 A.D. Urban legend.

This man had the potential to possess her spirit at the most vulnerable point of entry, something more precious to her than her art—her students. This guy could seep into her brain, make her believe in fairy tales of happily ever after, set her up in a mirage, make her believe his oasis would be lasting, then seduce her through her art, and finally into his bedroom—where she could only imagine that he'd be skilled to the point of making her lose her mind . . . especially after her drought and toil through the desert of almost two years of celibacy. Why, she'd probably become a zombie for him after he turned her out.

Plus she had read that she was supposedly in the midst of her sexual peak as a woman, between thirty and thirty-five. . . . Oh, hell no! *Get thee back, Satan,* she told herself firmly as she flung a stack of her students' papers into a manila envelope. She would not allow her interaction with Trevor Winston to even remotely go there. If he wanted to play, then there were plenty of women with whom he could toy. She hadn't gone through the agony of almost two years without a date to break her fast on the ultimate evil. She had to keep that in front of her as she entered the devil's lair, Corey reminded herself.

No matter how good he smelled, or how good he looked, or how wondrously smooth his voice was . . . or how nice he was to her students. None of that mattered. She wasn't going to fall for the oldest photographer's line in the book . . . *"Hey, baby, let me show you my studio."* Hmmph! After all, she wasn't stupid. No. She had a Xena sword and shield. She had strength of character. So if she had to walk through the Valley of the Shadow of Death to get her kids what could change their lives, this was a mission, like going to seek the Holy Grail for them.

Sure, there'd be demons and dangers along the way, she told herself. There would be tests of faith, tests of fortitude, tests of discipline. There would be boundless temptations, and ultimately, He-Who-Would-Remain-Nameless would show up when she was at her limit, at her lowest point of fatigue, and he would offer her a cool sip of water and a quiet place to lay down her head. But she would be strong, for the cause!

"All right," Corey whispered. "You can do this."

But as the clock ticked to ten after three, she still couldn't understand why instead of demon battle jitters, her stomach felt like it had butterflies in it. Instead of being indignant, why was she unable to shake off the feeling of anticipation? And if she was going into a spiritual street fight to give the devil an old-fashioned beat-down, then why was she putting on lipstick and studying herself in her compact mirror?

Corey checked her neck quickly for the signs of vampire fang marks and laughed to herself as she closed the tiny case. "Oh, hell," she lamented on a whisper, "I've probably already been bitten!"

Letting her breath out slowly, she surveyed her classroom to see if anything else needed to be put in its place. She strained and listened for heavy footsteps down the hall, which she soon heard. *This guy is definitely the baddest mother in the valley,* she remarked to herself. *He can even come out in daylight.*

He stopped at the door for a moment to pull his head together. This was it. He was going to pick up the balance of his equipment and escort Corey Hamilton through the schoolyard, pick up Miquel, and the three of them would get into his car. Two hours' worth of dashing about three levels of the duplex, from the basement, to his unit on the first floor, to the second floor to make sure everything was in its place . . . then running to the local Caribbean market to handpick the best fish and vegetables . . . then checking if his sister had left enough rice and peas, had been a godsend. He had been too busy to get nervous since the tasks at hand required action, not thought.

But now, two inches from Corey Hamilton's classroom door, all of his sublimated worries caved in on him. What if she had a change of heart? By what right did he assume that he could kindle any interest within her beyond the joint project? By what right could he suppose that a beautiful woman like her wouldn't already have plenty of men flocking around her, vying desperately for her attention? And he was the walking wounded. . . . How was he going to stack up to that potential competition?

After all, he had a track record with women that, if he were a felon, would incarcerate him for the rest of his born days. He had a son to watch and a dependent family . . . and she didn't have any children, and was a free agent. He couldn't just pick up on a whim, or take her to paradise for the weekend, much less take her out on the town without undue scrutiny. He didn't have a private bachelor's pad to bring her home to so he could open champagne for her and lavish all of his pent-up desire on her.

Anyway, even if she did grace him with the opportunity to get next to her, where could that possibly happen? At her place? A hotel room? Perish the thought. . . . that was not how he had been raised. A man had to come to the table for a bride with a bride price, something more than just his sex to offer her. How in the world was he supposed to woo the woman of his dreams with nothing to offer? Those other guys after her were in full metal jacket. He was standing out in her hallway trying to joust for her honor with no horse and a bunch of camera equipment. Stupid!

Trevor stood very, very still. Did the word *bride* jump into his brain? Oh, no . . . Two years of abstinence was definitely making him take leave of his senses. He didn't even have a career left . . . A bride? Not this brother. Forget it. He would go in there, pick up his equipment, and cancel. He had been letting the little head think for the big one, allowing a pretty face and a gentle spirit to coax him into purgatory. She was the worst sort of demon—the marrying kind. The kind that transformed a man's entire universe after he was hopelessly entangled in her web. A seductress. A soft, cooing siren that called free men to dash their dreams upon the rocks . . . while they were loving every moment of their own drowning. Hell, no.

He had to get himself together, get his life organized; his sister had been right. He'd been in Philly for three days, and here he was picking out potential . . .

he couldn't even repeat the word in his mind. After the Jennifer fiasco? No, he wasn't going out like that!

Gathering his courage to face the seductress, Trevor turned the doorknob and entered the room. Then she smiled. Why did she have to do that?

"I was so excited about seeing your studio that I was like a big kid for the rest of the day," she said merrily. *Why did I say that?* Corey thought, groaning inwardly. She was already in midtransformation and on her way to zombie status!

Why did she have to say that? Trevor let his breath out slowly. "I couldn't wait for you to see it, either," he confessed, feeling the siren pulling the truth out of him, despite his resolve to shoo her away. "You ready?" he heard his voice ask.

"Yeah, let's go," she heard her words reply.

The next thing he knew, he was opening the door for her and following her down the hall. He could see the rocks coming. It was a potential iceberg, in fact, and he was the R.M.S. Titanic. But, oh, how beautiful the northern lights that beamed in front of him were. At least he'd make history, and go down with a full crew . . . dancing in the ballroom.

Dracula was escorting her to the nest. She could turn back now and drive a stake through his heart. But her feet kept going, and her heart kept pounding, and her head was beginning to tilt on its own accord to expose her neck. . . . Maybe living forever as an immortal with this guy wouldn't be all that bad. . . .

"Ready, dude?" Trevor quipped as he approached Miquel and interrupted a crude game of soccer.

"Yeah, Dad!" the child exclaimed with a laugh, running to him and abandoning his friends. "Miss Hamilton's going, too?"

"Yup. Gonna show her where we can make the film," Trevor said in a casual tone, not looking at his son or Corey as they walked.

"Whoah . . . Miss Hamilton," Miquel said in a serious voice. "Nobody gets to go down into Dad's studio. Not even Scott."

The boy's comment made him cringe, but Trevor shook it off and let the comment slide. How did one do this with a chaperone—an eyewitness who would turn state's evidence on his father on a dime?

Corey only smiled. He didn't take other women there . . . so Dracula had picked her . . . this was not a good sign. She was going to get bitten for sure. . . . He was definitely taking her to the inner sanctum! And just like all horror movie heroines, she wasn't picking up on the cues, as the audience screamed and shouted at the screen. He even had an innocent day-walker, one who could run errands when the big vampire was asleep—his son. Oh, Lord help her. . . . He was actually coming to her side to help her up into his four-by-four, which in another era would have doubled for a black vampire coach—and she was getting in!

Trevor was glad that he didn't have to make small talk on the drive over to the house. Miquel took care of that. His son was so excited that he talked in a constant stream of non sequiturs, telling every conceivable bit of family information in the process. Occasionally, Trevor glanced over at Corey, who seemed to hang on every word that Miquel spoke. . . . He knew what that felt like, and certainly couldn't blame the boy for wanting to impress her. Hadn't he experienced the same exhilaration from having her undivided attention bestowed on him today? There was something about the way her eyes bore into the speaker and seemed to absorb every facet of what was being said. The woman listened not only to the words, but to the person's soul, and that had been what had totally seduced him.

"All right, all right, champ." Trevor chuckled as they pulled into a parking space. "Give Miss Hamilton's brain a rest and help me get some of this stuff into the house."

She watched as Miquel popped out of the vehicle

to assist his father, and she was mildly taken aback when Trevor Winston rushed around to her side of the car to open the door. Oh, yeah, Dracula was smooth. Men didn't do that any more. Old-school, perhaps old-world . . . all he needed was a cape.

Corey cast her eyes up at the magnificent Tudor structure that was three stories high, complete with gabled windows, stained glass, leaded beveled glass doors, and arches. Only the gargoyles to complement her mental picture were missing.

"This is beautiful," she found herself saying, and she watched a shy smile form on Trevor's face . . . one not wide enough for her to see fangs yet.

"I'm glad you like it," he said in an octave so deep and sexy that he might as well have said, "Good evening, welcome to my castle."

The thought made Corey's smile deepen. Yup. She was losing her mind. But it felt so good. So she followed them. Curiosity had gotten the better of her as Miquel squirmed about on the porch while his father turned the locks.

"This is our half of the house. Aunt Gretchen lives upstairs with my cousins, and then there's the attic. Dad's studio is in the basement—but it's all fixed up, you'll see," Miquel immediately said, dragging her over the threshold by her sleeve. "Check it out. Dad put my science project right there," the child said, pointing with pride toward the large clay object on the coffee table.

All she could do was laugh as her gaze scanned the upscale Swedish modern decor that was contemporary and of minimalist design. But there was a lush contrast of gorgeous art on the walls that gave added texture and depth to the room. She noted his taste, which was so similar to hers. Strangely, being here made her miss her old apartment, the one which she gave up to move into her mother's old-fashioned furnished home.

Corey looked around and gave a nod of appreciation to Trevor Winston. The living room was sparsely furnished with a black leather sofa, architecture-style lamps, and black wrought-iron chairs covered by sumptuous pillows—all of which faced the HDTV and music epicenter. Then there was the clay volcano.

"I see that your dad found a very special place for your wonderful project," she replied with a giggle, then glanced at Trevor with approval. The man had a heart.

"Let me show you my room," Miquel said proudly, again dragging her by the sleeve before she could speak.

"Let her catch her breath, Miquel," Trevor warned to no avail as his guest was whisked away, leaving him only one option—to follow them.

Corey broke out into a full laugh as she clapped her hands and turned around in a circle. "This is simply a wonderful, fun place," she said, looking at Miquel's upturned face, then glancing at his father. "Look at all of this cool stuff you've got in here. Man, I'm jealous!"

He loved the effect she had on Miquel. Trevor stood at a strategic vantage point by the doorway and watched his son practically swoon from the teacher's approval. God, what a difference the right woman made in this space. And the effect she was having on Miquel was quietly spilling over to him.

"The bathroom is down the hall, between me and Dad's room," Miquel added, again starting to whisk her away.

Trevor noted that she had put on the brakes.

"Those are private spaces in people's homes, Miquel," she protested cheerfully. "Your dad doesn't need to have some teacher going—"

"He doesn't mind, do you, Dad?" Miquel cut in, his face filled with a hint of worry as his eyes begged for permission. "His room is even cooler than mine, and besides, I wanna show you how he put a shaving mirror down low just for me."

"It's okay," Trevor said, feeling suddenly exposed, but not knowing how to diplomatically wrest himself out of the predicament. His son's crestfallen expression immediately changed.

"Really, Miquel," Corey protested again, "I don't think—"

"Oh, c'mon," the child said, laughing. "Nothin' to be scared of, even though it's dark. Dad, put on the hall light."

This time both adults laughed as Corey was pulled along by her outstretched hand down a narrow hallway. Peeping into the bathroom to satisfy Miquel, her female radar clicked on without her permission. No sign of any other female life. . . . Then she banished the thought as she praised the boy-sized mirror that was adjacent to the man-sized one, and she took note of how clean the room was, despite there being no obvious female inhabitant. Then she couldn't help herself, and she went in and openly gaped at the deep claw-footed tub.

"Oh, man . . . will you look at this thing. . . ." she whispered. "They don't make these anymore."

"You like that old tub?" Miquel asked with disdain and a shrug. "Girls . . ."

Trevor laughed and nodded proudly. "It came with the house."

"How old is the house?" Corey asked with surprise.

"Circa eighteen-nineties," Trevor answered, feeling pleased that she would even ask or care. "I put a lot of work in here to restore it."

"I can tell," she murmured, looking around like a Realtor. "Wow."

Trevor let his breath out slowly. She liked the bathroom. That was a good thing. Any man knew that.

"C'mon, guys," Miquel urged in a bored voice. "We've still gotta lot left to see."

Both adults laughed as Miquel barged into Trevor's bedroom and spun around like a magician.

"Check it out," the child said, giggling. "He doesn't let me come in here much 'cause I mess it up with my toys, but his bed is the coolest." He whooped, flinging himself on the king-size sleigh bed. "It's like a Santa Claus sled, but only with a mattress."

Trevor felt his face go hot as Corey raised her hand to her mouth and giggled behind it. If only she liked this room as much as the bathroom . . . But then again, it really didn't matter, did it? There was no time and space for him to really give her a proper ride on that sled. He had to get hold of himself.

"This is pretty cool," she said casually, glancing around the room. "I love the windows," she remarked, "I bet you get a lot of great light in here with the southern exposure."

"Yeah," Trevor said in a blasé tone. He was too embarrassed to say much more.

"C'mon, you guys," Miquel fussed. "I can't figure it out. You like the tub and the windows, Miss Hamilton . . . the strangest stuff."

This time she was happy when her student pulled her to the next room. Her stomach had done flip-flops the moment she'd stepped over the threshold of Trevor Winston's den of inequity . . . which, no less than she'd expected, was phenomenal. Massive mahogany structures of hand-carved Caribbean woods had drawn her in and threatened to swallow her up . . . armoire, dresser, heavy end tables, exquisite mirror facing *the sled,* lush, forest greens and burgundies, velvet, overstuffed chair, pillows enough to shame a sultan . . . and the smell . . . male, distinctly masculine . . . She'd had to put her hands behind her back to keep from touching anything in there, including Trevor Winston.

"We don't usually cook down here," Miquel explained as they entered the kitchen in the back. "We always eat upstairs with my cousins and my aunt, but sometimes when Dad is tired, he makes something quick down here."

Again, Trevor held his breath. This room, possibly more than the bedroom and the bathroom, had to pass inspection. This time, he cut his son a glance to be still, and somewhere in the remote regions of the child's brain, Miquel must have sensed that something in the environment had changed, because he let Corey walk around without chattering to her and sidled up to his father.

In that moment, Trevor was not sure if he wasn't indeed teaching the boy to hunt as Scott had so crassly put it. Rational thought had left him when she'd entered his bedroom under mild protest. He couldn't tell if he'd finally been driven to the fertile, National Park–forbidden lands by an urge to bring down prey. All he did know was that his young cub had to be quiet for a moment and be still in the tall grasses to watch Daddy hunt.

Something very primal took over the human side of his brain as Corey slowly entered the kitchen, looked around to see if it was safe, and lowered her head again to inspect some other aspect of the environment. But she was skittish. He could tell that, as memories of his years of big game hunting recoiled and then snapped to the forefront of his awareness. God, he was hungry . . . and she looked so good . . . and she was oh so close. . . .

But experience told him to wait, because if he didn't he'd flush her, then have to chase her, and could possibly lose the only opportunity to get next to this one. Adrenaline coursed through him as he summoned patience.

"You like it?" He found himself nearly growling.

"Like it? Are you kidding?" she asked, laughing easily, going around and touching the stainless-steel refrigerator, the stove he'd surrounded with wood in the middle of the floor.

She was at the watering hole . . . then she moved, so again, he had to wait. Corey momentarily turned her attention toward the large bay window, and he breathed in slowly, standing downwind from her. Suddenly, she turned around to greet him, her face all smiles as her hand swept across the butcher-block table housed in the nook of the window seating area. . . . It was as if one minute, she knew that he was there—just waiting to pounce—and she was taunting him, then the next, she seemed unsure. This was a very smart antelope . . . no . . . a lithe, dazzling gazelle . . . fast, fluid, magnificent . . . one that would give him a run for his money. . . .

Then she turned her back on him again, and he felt the muscles twitch in his arms and legs. Her hands went up to touch the wine rack and copper pots, and he was sure that she'd forgotten about the lion. . . .

Occasionally she'd make a comment, which he would respond to with a low rumble in his throat. Then she'd look up nervously as he stayed motionless by the doorway with his son by his side—who excitedly glanced between his father and the doe that had come within striking distance. Oh, yeah, without a doubt, he was drooling, and his cub needed the kind of nourishment she could provide.

"But this isn't what I wanted to show you," Trevor said, laughing, regaining his composure, and wresting the torrid images from his brain.

Then he waited to break her off from the herd.

"Oh, yeah," she replied, seeming startled. "Let's go see that studio."

Again, Trevor gave his son a glance, but this time Miquel smiled in a way that slightly disturbed him. It was as though the child had picked up his primal thoughts by telepathy, and was only too happy to see his father bring this one in.

"This is the best place of all, Miss Hamilton," Miquel quipped, taking the lead, then stepping back. "This is Dad's place," his son added with a grin. "*He* should show you this room."

A combination of pride and sudden exposure momentarily flustered Trevor as his son hung back to let him turn on the lights and lead Corey Hamilton down the stairs. His son was going to give him running room to bring this prize in. The boy had instinct.

Miquel hesitated at the bottom of the staircase as Trevor walked behind Corey's timid start-stop motions. She was cornered, stunned, and he was only two inches behind her . . . easy does it . . . don't mangle it. . . .

Standing in the middle of the floor, Corey covered her mouth, turned around. looked at him wide-eyed, and squealed.

"Oh, my God! Trevor, this is magnificent! Look at this place!"

Kill effective. All he had to do was drag her back upstairs, later, to the feeding den.

"I told you that you would like it." Miquel laughed, jumping off the bottom step to join the feeding as his father stood back and let the littlest lion eat off her adoration first. "You know how to use this stuff, too, Miss Hamilton?"

Uh-oh . . . change of plans. Not a gazelle. Lioness. A sexy, perfect female match . . . possibly in heat, too . . . now stalking him.

"Do I know how to use this?" Corey laughed. "Honey, I can make one of these stand on its head." She giggled as she went over to his Avid, appreciating it with her palm. "May I?" she asked, her eyes almost narrowing to slits before she retracted her claws.

The Avid wasn't the only thing she could make stand on its head, he noted from a remote part of his brain . . . *Oh, yeah, you can touch it.*

"I'd be delighted if you fired up my system," he breathed.

Then she paused . . . and then she smiled a different kind of knowing feminine smile . . . one that made him sure that she had fangs, too. Double entendre noted, but it didn't even make her flinch. *Go ahead and kill me, baby,* his mind whispered inside his skull.

A different kind of hunger seemed to pass between both of them, and it hung on a thick, brief silence, only interrupted by his son's comment.

"There's more," Miquel urged.

"I'd like to see everything your dad has down here," she said in a low tone, thrown in Trevor's direction.

So she was hunting big game, as well. . . . He loved it. Now it was a test of endurance.

"While the system is booting up, let me show you where the kids can develop their still shots. We have to let them take photos of the process, the making of their documentary, all of which can be used in the trailer for the film and to help promote it."

Trevor stood back, trying not to show the exertion after round one, and trying not to breathe hard from his mental tussle with his female match.

"You have a darkroom?" she purred. "Oh, show me what you've got in there."

Again, he gave his son a glance to be still. She was good . . . real good.

"Enter," he commanded, sauntering over to the door and switching on the red light. Sentence structure was becoming difficult. She was messing with him and winning this match. He had no endurance . . . she was kicking his butt.

He waited for her to lope toward him, and noticed that Miquel was on her heels.

"This is nothing short of phenom," she said in a husky voice, "and your stills are fabulous," she added, appraising his hung work with the eyes of a professional. "These black-and-whites are awesome."

He could not breathe, much less immediately comment. His son was about to witness his father being brought down and slaughtered on the spot by a female of the species.

"It's just some dabblin'," Trevor said in a rush that

made his son cock his head to the side and give him a funny look.

"What are you talkin' about, Dad? This is some of your best work, you said so yourself."

The little one was overanxious and spoiling the hunt.

"It was just—"

"Your father is too modest, Miquel," Corey corrected, holding up a photo of an elderly man. "He has true vision and genius."

And she was a fair sport . . . a true queen, because she'd allowed him to escape unchallenged in a near miss. She'd made him back up and respect her capability to tangle toe-to-toe. She wasn't going down without a fight, and she definitely wasn't going down in front of a kid. He had to give her that. He also knew enough from this tussle that all she had done was swat him and growl back. She hadn't used full force, and what she did show him was enough to put him in check. She would decide if and when this would happen, that much was also made clear. It had been a long time since he'd done this, and it had been even longer since he cared so much about the outcome.

Although maybe she was also enjoying the practice hunt, too, and was just toying with him . . . to let him know she was interested, but just not now . . . But at least she didn't punk him down in front of the boy. That was class—in any jungle.

"Let's go see if that Avid is ready for a spin," she remarked casually, now taking the lead in his domain.

When she sat down in his pilot's chair, all he could do was watch her. She owned him, and was eating him alive.

Eleven

For once, the sound of teenagers slamming doors and running overhead had been a true blessing. It had given him a viable excuse to wrest Corey away from the digital system so that he could stop the mesmerizing effect she was having upon him as she edited some of the clips he'd loaded. The way she sat there oohing and aahing over the sample shots he'd taken in her class, and the way she burst out laughing at the children's comments, just tortured him. One day, if his libido could tolerate the agony, he'd have to record her voice.

He hated to admit that possibly the most frustrating part of watching her was that his son had gotten the prime position—right in the center of her lap.

As his son's teacher delighted herself with the raw footage of her students, her favorite child had sensed the opportunity. Miquel seemed to have enough courage to just walk up to her, hug her around the neck, and hop into the chair with her so that he could allow her to show him the computer keystrokes and how to trim a clip to perfection using the mouse.

All Trevor could do was pace a bit, morosely watch, and hanker for a little of her cast-off affection, the crumbs that Miquel would allow, as the child soaked up her petting and admiration. The boy was good—obviously better than his father. Miquel was a quick study, too, for in no time he had made the woman gasp by deftly manipulating the small bits of footage and combining them in a way that landed him a full-blown kiss on the cheek.

But the teenage crew upstairs gave Trevor an earnest reason to call her away—food had to be prepared for the incoming hungry brood of adolescent hunters in his pride. So, with a low disgruntled growl, he summoned Miquel and Corey upstairs, leaving them behind as he took the stairs with heavy blows to the hard surface of the wood.

"Yo," he said low in his throat when he entered the second-floor kitchen and spied Scott rummaging. "Chill. Got special company. Don't you see the table set?"

Scott glanced around the room quickly, then peeked his head out of the doorway past Trevor. "Yo, dude!" he said in a harsh whisper. "You got her in here . . . that fast, and boxed her in? You good, boss. I take back what I—"

"Shhh!" Trevor rumbled. His line of vision nervously shot to the back staircase, knowing that Miquel and Corey could appear at any minute. "I'll kill you if you even hint at—"

"Chill," Scott whispered. "I got'chure back. I know this is da one. I won't blow it. You ain't never brought nobody here. *Ever* . . . This is deep," the adolescent lion cub murmured in awe. "Good thing Mom won't be here tonight."

"I know," Trevor admitted. "Gretchen would have a heart attack if she thought I brought some lady up here without warning, and before she could clean the house good. But it happened sorta fast. Dig?"

"You *baaaad,* brother. I gotta watch you work." Scott bobbed his head and loped into the kitchen to take a spectator's position as they heard Corey and Miquel coming up the steps. The expression of pure male-to-male awe on Scott's face made Trevor self-conscious. Jesus, what was happening? What kind of message was he sending to this kid? And he didn't want Scott to get the wrong impression that anything did, or even could, transpire. He'd have to clean up the carnage later, and talk to the boy on the steps. Corey didn't deserve to have her reputation put in question, all because he'd made an unplanned move to bring her by the house.

But at the moment, he'd have to get through dinner, with all eyes watching. Heavy social immersion. This was a really stupid idea. Why didn't he just ask her out to dinner away from all of this? Or had Scott been correct all along . . . had he brought her there to box her in, get a sign-off with the family having his back? What, he was going to teach two young lions how to hunt and drop fresh gazelle at their feet? Was he tripping?

No. That wasn't it at all, he reminded himself. Then he admitted the truth. He just didn't want to end the sensation of being in her company, and he would have withstood any humiliation to keep her near. It was just that when she entered his bedroom, he couldn't get that image of her standing in the doorway out of his mind. That had turned him mentally primal, and his entire thought processes went into call-of-the-wild mode.

Glad that Corey had offered to show Miquel how to properly shut down the system, which put them several paces behind him, Trevor let out his breath and went to the refrigerator while Scott sat on a high stool focused on the door like a cat watching a mouse's hideaway.

"Hi, Scott!" Miquel hollered out. "Guess what? I was editing on Dad's system, and Miss Hamilton knows how to edit as good as Dad!"

"Hello, Scott," Corey said, laughing. "I wouldn't say all of that, but I am familiar with the equipment."

"Hey, Miss Hamilton," Scott replied with a smile,

closely studying his uncle's demeanor from the corner of his eye.

"Familiar . . ." Miquel echoed in disgust. "She's *all that.*"

"Yes, she is," Trevor concurred, ignoring the sly look and smile Scott gave him.

"Miss Hamilton's here?" Janelle yelled as she ran down the hall.

"You are so late," Scott grumbled as his sister bounded into the room.

"Oh, shut up!" Janelle snapped, starting a teenage feud of play slaps and pulled punches. "Hi, Miss Hamilton. He's so ignorant. Samantha will be in real soon—she'll be glad to see you, too. She's at her college class right now. My mom will be sorry she missed you—she works nights at the VA."

"Who are you, Eyewitness News? Got a bead on everybody's location?" Scott huffed.

"Look, would y'all cut it out?" Trevor boomed, his nerves beyond frayed. "I need to get the fish on, and heat up the rice and peas and cabbage."

Scott immediately jumped down from his stool and gave his sister a look that momentarily stilled her. "Why don't you go help Miquel with his homework?" he ordered in Janelle's direction. "I need to get on mine."

"Why don't you go help Miquel with his homework, and anyway, Sam will be in here in a—"

"I don't need no help doin' my homework, and y'all don't help me no other time," Miquel argued, obviously taking offense at being separated from Corey.

"How about if Miquel and I go over his homework, and you guys help your father out in the kitchen?" Corey suggested with a barely suppressed smile.

"You are such a chicken-brain," Scott fumed, plucking his sister in her forehead, which only made her scream and start trying to hit him back. Holding Janelle away from him in a basketball defensive move,

Scott glanced at Trevor with an I-got-chure-back anxiety expression, then tried an unproven recovery tactic. "Yo, Miquel, why don't you walk me to the store to go check on my boyze, then us fellas will get away from these females. You can do your homework after dinner with Sam, like always—you see Miss Hamilton everyday, all day. Dam—I mean dag, Janelle. You so stupid!"

Mortified, all Trevor could do was stand there and witness the last of his chances evaporate with an unseasoned teenage ambush. One of them, Janelle, had made too much noise and been oblivious to the stalk. The other didn't wait for range, and the littlest one was in the way. The adolescent male thought he was helping, but in his eagerness to assist, had flushed her, and she'd be gone.

Leaving Corey's side instantly, Miquel took the tempting bait to hang out in the streets with his older cousin—something even the lovely Miss Hamilton couldn't hold sway over. Trevor sighed. It didn't matter now. It was too late. Despondent, he just turned toward the stove.

Then, as if a very slow lightbulb had just gone off in her brain, Janelle issued a last slap at her brother before conceding. "As you can probably tell," the young girl said in her best approximation of diction while pecking her neck, "We don't get a lot of outside company around here, and my brother is still ignorant—'cause he didn't even offer you *a chair.* Sorry 'bout that. But I do have some homework to do, Miss Hamilton. . . . Since the table is already set, I'll do the dishes, Uncle Trevor. See, some of us have manners." Then, like a hurricane of hormones, Janelle flounced out of the room and shut her bedroom door.

"C'mon, dude," Scott called after Miquel, which sent the youngster scrambling behind him. Picking up on the strong male mental telepathy his uncle was sending him, Scott's shoulders sagged with defeat.

"Sorry, man," he whispered as he passed Trevor. "Next time."

"Be back in no more than an hour," Trevor mumbled, then shook his head and leaned against the sink to study Corey Hamilton—the one who got away.

It was truly a sad day in lion country.

She had never been so filled with laughter and warmth in her life. Nor had she ever been so flattered in all of her days. The entire kitchen scene was comedy at its finest, as the teenagers made assumptions, and tried so hard to unobtrusively clear out to give their uncle what they assumed would be operating room. All she could do was shake her head when her eyes met Trevor's, and his warm chuckle clinched it for her. She liked this man. Really, really liked him.

"And you do this each and every day with fifteen of them?" he said, laughing, any and all of his sense of bachelor smooth having been decimated. "Let me get on my knees to the saints who teach." He bowed low and swept a wooden spoon before her. "My apologies, Saint Corey. Won't you please sit down and have a moment of peace before they all come back?"

"They were just trying to be helpful, and were mixing messages, sending wrong signals, making wrong assumptions, and trying to be on their best behavior for girl company. God bless 'em," Corey said, grinning. "You have a really, really nice family, Trevor."

Her gracious acceptance of his melee and the way she just came out and said it made him grow more serious than he'd intended. He really, really liked this woman.

"They may have been inept . . . but maybe they hadn't totally made the wrong assumption," he said quietly. "Kids can detect fraud a mile away. They like you. So do I." Then he turned back to the stove and began stirring the pot of cabbage.

She couldn't move, much less take a seat at the table. What had he just said? All she could do was stare at the man.

Bad move, he thought, tending the cabbage for longer than necessary. *Just as bad as Scott. Lost your touch. First he flushed her, now you're in a flat-out sprint across the plains trying to catch a gazelle who can outrun you—all 'cause you're so hungry for her that you can't even think straight.*

He could feel her eyes boring into his back, and knew that at some point he'd have to turn around and face her. But when he did, instead of finding an angry scowl, or a sarcastic, yeah-in-your-dreams smirk, he turned back to see her wide-eyed and stunned . . . standing where he'd left her. The sight of her still in range made his pulse tear through him until his ears rang. A new rush of adrenaline shot though his system, and he could feel the muscle in his jaw throb. Then he let out his breath.

"I didn't mean to offend you. . . . I mean, what guy in his right mind wouldn't find you totally captivating? . . . And I know a lot of men are always in your face, so I'm not trying to do that to you, and I respect the obvious limitations of . . . I mean, I know you're a teacher—an excellent one. The project was—is—sacrosanct. It's the right thing to do, I didn't just dream it up as a . . . but, at the same time, when I saw you down there with Miquel, and I've watched the good spirit you have inside—not that I'm saying the outside isn't gorgeous, too, but, the whole package is just. . . . I just never saw. . . . I mean, you're different. Never mind. I'm just confusing you. I know. Probably offending you. That wasn't my objective at all. Look. I like you. Your style, the way you are with kids. I like you. There, I said it."

If the linoleum would only cooperate and part like the Red Sea, then swallow him up . . . It was the most botched, awkward, stupid, nonsensical bunch of rambling rhetoric he'd ever espoused in his life. Dear God . . .

"That is the sweetest, most flattering thing anyone has said to me in a long time, if ever, Trevor Winston," she murmured and sat down cautiously. "I like you, too."

He could feel a smile developing on one side of his face as she looked down shyly and began toying with the flatware.

"Guess you aren't Dracula, huh?" she said, chuckling, then peeped up at him.

"Dracula?" He gave the image a moment to sink in and then laughed.

"Came on kinda strong with the visit-my-lair thing, you think?"

"A little bit." She laughed again easily, then gave him a sly wink. "But Miquel took me around and showed me that I was on hallowed ground. So even if you did have less than honorable intentions, I wouldn't get bitten tonight."

She was so smart, and all he could do was laugh as he flung the marinated fish into the pan.

"No, you're safe—tonight."

"I can't breathe," Corey said, laughing as she pushed her plate away and declined a piece of coconut pound cake. "For, real, for real, you've outdone yourself, but I have to get ready for school tomorrow."

"Aw, Miss Hamilton, can't you stay for a little longer?" Miquel whined.

"You gonna see the lady tomorrow," Scott fussed. "Give her a break, dude."

"Well, at least my ignorant brother could have offered to wrap up a piece of cake for you to take home, before *he* hogs it all. Won't be none left by tomorrow,

Miss Hamilton." Janelle jumped up and went to fetch some aluminum foil.

"I've had the best evening of my life," Corey said, smiling amid the chaos. "We even got some spectacular work done here. I love the production company name, Miquel—Reel Community Film and Video. And Scott, my goodness, your logo design is awesome."

"It's aw'ight," Scott said, beaming.

Trevor laughed as he watched Scott practically roll over on the floor to let Corey Hamilton pet his belly. Some pit bull, he thought. But he could dig it.

"And Janelle, you are so good at matching the right sounds to the beginnings of the storyboard—you and Sam are going to be monstrous working together."

Again he watched as Corey seemed to be able to quell any chaos in her midst. Janelle and Samantha had fallen silent and demure, accepting her compliment as though she'd bestowed the title of princess on them.

When Janelle brought back a piece of cake, Corey pinched off a little bit, popped it in her mouth, and closed her eyes. "Oh, Trevor, this is *so good* . . . Did you make it?"

The teenagers immediately scanned him with unseen radar, as though the low timbre of Corey's voice had reverberated through them before it locked in on him as a target. They also seemed to know he was a goner when he only swallowed hard and couldn't immediately respond to her question.

"It's nine o'clock, and you need to get your bath," Samantha ordered in Miquel's direction. "March."

"Do I have to, Dad?" Miquel protested, looking at his father, who was only looking at Corey Hamilton.

"Yes, you do, bubble-head," Janelle said quickly, pulling Miquel's chair out to make him stand.

"You coming right back to tuck me—"

"Don't be a baby, I'll check on you. He's gotta take her home, man," Scott chimed in, his voice having dropped to a military octave of male reinforcement. "Do what Janelle said."

Then, as though a time bomb had been set at the three-minute mark, all of them got up, said good night quickly, and cleared out. He'd never seen anything like it in his life.

The kids knew, she mused. They had to know something was up—even though she was pretty sure from their earlier bumbling and bumping into one another that this was not rehearsed, and this was not a drill. It was like being in the rainforest when a storm was approaching, and all the bird and lemur chatter went still. What in God's name was headed her way?

She tried to get a read on Trevor Winston's weather station. He had not spoken a word since she'd complimented him on the cake. What gave?

"You don't have to go to the trouble of taking me, I'm only a few blocks away, and—"

"It's no trouble," he said, almost too quickly. "C'mon, it's getting late. Hope dinner was all right?"

"Dinner, and all the company, was wonderful. Thank you."

This was not a good sign, she thought, as he showed her down the steps and out the door. She noted that he'd dropped the keys once in trying to lock it, and that Samantha had told him she'd get it, so he'd left it to his cousin. Then Corey found that she almost had to walk two steps to Trevor's one, his long strides outpacing hers. Then he'd dropped the car keys. Twice. Plus, he hadn't even given the kids an idea of when he was coming back. And unless her eyes were failing her, she could have sworn that his hands trembled slightly as he'd opened the car door and helped her in. Oh, no, that was not good.

"Don't you want to know my address?" she asked as he pulled away from the curb. When he came to a sudden stop, and turned to look at her, that's when she knew he indeed had fangs. And it was dark outside, and she was no longer on hallowed ground.

"Yeah," he murmured without a smile. "My bad."

Her bad, actually, she thought, quickly rattling off her address, and noticing that he'd touched the radio button to put on smooth jazz.

"Kid music . . . wears you down after a long day," he said low in his throat.

Oh, definitely, this was not a good sign. He'd added soundtrack.

"I know what you mean," she said as brightly as she could—then couldn't think of anything else to say that made sense.

The one-on-one proximity was becoming like a thick, static-charged tornado that was gathering in the tight confines of the vehicle. As they pulled up to her home on Larchwood Avenue and sat under the shadowy canopy of wide oak trees, she was sure that she could actually see flashes of lightning from her position within the eye of the brewing storm.

"Thanks so much for sharing your studio, your home, your dinner, and your family with me tonight. This was awesome," she murmured, not knowing whether to invite him in or what. It was way too soon, but Lord the man had swept her off her feet. No, she decided. Not yet.

"Thank you for allowing me to show you my most cherished possession, my family. And I thank you for appreciating them and my art, and where I lay my head. All I wanted to show you, Corey Hamilton, was who I am. Most people don't know who that is."

His gaze held hers in what now felt like a hypnotic trance, while his voice lulled her into a near state of semiconsciousness. His family was his most cherished possession . . . oh, man, her resolve was crumbling. He was pushing all the right buttons.

"Then they've apparently missed a lot," she whispered, being more open with her comments and abandoning long-ago-rehearsed lines. This man had taken her to meet his family . . . had showed her his home . . . it was so old-fashioned, and very, very dear.

"Can I be honest with you?" he asked in an octave so deep that it made her squeeze her thighs together. "I want to get to know you better, but I have enough respect for who you are not to try to learn that all in one night."

The passion with which he said it, so close to her face, evacuated the air from her lungs slowly as something way down in her belly ignited.

"I appreciate that," she whispered, not trusting her voice to say more. There was an element of him that she couldn't define. It was something so palpable, so visceral, and it fused with the primal side of her brain in a way that made her trust him. And his statement was again turning all of her assumptions upside-down. She wanted to know him more, too. Who was this complex being who'd simply jetted into her life?

Almost as though he'd read the unspoken question in her gaze, his eyes took on more intensity. It was as though his personal lens had opened to full capacity, letting her glimpse through it to capture him in still, one excruciating frame at a time. Unwittingly she braced herself for another layer of his texture to develop in the shadows like a strip of darkroom film. Mutual anticipation seemed to be the fluid between them.

"I made a vow on my mother's grave," he murmured, staring into her eyes as he spoke. "Two years ago I promised that I would change, and not just run the streets all over the world any longer. I had to be there for my family, especially Miquel. No games. Time was too precious, she and my father passing as they did, taught me that. If ever I had a woman in my life again, it had to be someone I could see beyond one night. That was two years ago, and I haven't broken my fast yet. Then I met you. And that's why I'm sitting here two inches in front of you, tremblin', girl. But I am a very patient man. You can't rush the process, or you will ruin what's delicately evolving in the frame."

"Seems we both have a lot at stake," she began carefully, trying to remain rational. "Until you brought me by your house, I hadn't a concept," she admitted, allowing that reality to wash over her. "What made you step out on faith so fast?"

"My son . . . and knowing human nature enough to know that some things can't be manufactured . . . like the tears of sudden anger and frustration that you held back when you fussed at me. You care. And when I spent a day in your class and watched the way you were with the children, you held every one of them enthralled—like you did me. . . . And maybe it was the way that you captured my family, and wrapped that rowdy bunch around your little finger . . . and then it was the way you popped a bit of sweet cake into your mouth, closed your eyes, and murmured how good it was . . . and, in that moment, I wanted to be that piece of coconut pound cake so badly that I couldn't answer you, woman."

His words threaded through her veins, connected with the base of her spine and forced her motor senses to nearly close her eyes as her vocal cords responded without her help. "I made the same vow at my mother's funeral, nearly two years ago . . . and never in my life have I wanted a man to be as impatient as much as I do right now."

His breathing was coming in short bursts now. This woman had just told him that no man had held her in two years . . . and she'd chosen him to break her fast, to reconnect her with one of the sweetest aspects of life itself. . . . This angel who had bestowed self-esteem on countless children, and had taken his son under her wing, and had protected the boy until his father found his way home, and had walked through his home casting her light and her blessings, and had resurrected his art so that his soul could live again . . . this woman, who had as much said that she would not only lie with him now if he just asked, but wanted him to in the most urgent way . . .

"If I move in less than an inch and do what I've been aching to do all night, it won't stop with a kiss. . . ."

"I know," she whispered back, her voice full and husky.

"And if I walk you to your door, most likely I won't stop at the threshold. I'll carry you over it."

"I know."

"Two years is a long time . . . and two minutes can feel like two hundred years . . . and two days can feel like two seconds, when somebody makes you feel like this," he breathed, daring to reach out and trace the delicate line of her jaw. When she closed her eyes, his fingers caught on fire, and he felt the silken edges of the fine hair just behind her ear.

"Two years can feel like forever, and two days can feel like a lifetime . . . making patience so hard to come by, but I know that this is worth taking slow," she murmured, touching his bottom lip till it quivered.

She had breathed the words out on cake-sweetened breath, and he inhaled the scent of coconut and butter, wishing he could run his tongue over her flawless white teeth, and allow his tongue to explore all of the places where some of it might still be hidden. When she exhaled again it burned him so thoroughly that his stomach tightened as his groin muscles constricted, and he had to remove his hand from her cheek.

"And, if that happens, where we lose all of our patience, then children will be home alone tonight, and tomorrow the class will have no teacher, because I cannot promise you when I'd be able to stop taking it slow," he whispered, feeling a sensation of immediate cold on his mouth where her fingertip had withdrawn.

When he'd admitted that, a tremor opened a dam

in her forest, sending a rivulet of warmth to flood the thickened valley of it, and she sipped air to keep from nearly passing out.

"I know," she whispered sadly, bringing her mouth dangerously near his, the smell of him edging her toward delirium.

"Then let me watch you walk into the house before we both forget 'bout what we know. . . ."

"Then you have to back away and break the magnet between us, because right now I can't," she murmured in earnest.

And she watched him ease deeper into his seat and away from her with pain glimmering in his eyes, then lean back until the base of his neck touched the headrest. And she watched him repeatedly take in a deep gulp of air and slowly exhale it through his nose. And each time he did, she threatened her hand not to touch him, and ordered it to obey and open the car door, which it eventually did. Then, with all her might, she willed her legs to resist the jelly-spell that he'd cast upon them, and she begged them to walk. And she admonished her breasts for feeling heavy, and chided her lower self for giving in so immediately to being wet. And she fumbled for her keys without looking back, turned the locks, and made it inside.

He sat there for a long time watching her door, watching the pattern of lights glowing on until he saw a bedroom light go on through her window. Checking the rearview mirror once, he just wanted to be sure that he still had a reflection.

"Hey, Unc," Scott said in an unusually quiet tone. "I figured I'd stay down here till you came back—just to keep an eye on Miquel."

"Thanks," was all Trevor could muster.

"Sam said she'd help Janelle clean up the kitchen

right, so Mom don't have a bird when she comes in this morning. Figured you'd rather run into me than one of the girls, anyhow. Even got Miquel straight on it bein' all right to say Miss Hamilton came by the studio about the class project, but not to give up the tapes about her coming upstairs, on account of he know how his Aunt Gretchen is about people visitin' before she cleans."

Trevor prayed for mercy from the constant teenage banter. He knew Scott was feeling some sort of male-bonding moment, but right now, he just couldn't deal.

"Is Miquel in bed?"

"He's cool, snug as a bug . . . but you look—"

"Please, man," Trevor said, sitting down heavily and leaning forward over his knees with his head bent and eyes closed. "I'm not in the mood."

"Frankly, I was hangin' out down here 'cause I didn't think you was comin' back so soon."

Trevor let the adolescent question hang in the air. Caught between being a father figure and a big brother to the boy, he knew that Scott just wanted some much-needed skills-building bond-time, but right now he didn't have it to offer. More than anything, he needed a cold shower and a Guinness Stout.

"Neither did I," Trevor finally answered, then let his head drop another two inches.

"What, she don't like you?"

"Yeah, she likes me."

"What, you crazy, man . . . you don't like her?"

"Are you insane?" Trevor grumbled.

"Then . . . what?" the youth asked with a dramatic shrug.

"Can't always rush it if you want it to be right," Trevor mumbled, no longer believing his own rhetoric.

Silence prevailed as Scott sat back and looked out the window for a moment, then returned his attention toward Trevor.

"She's the one, ain't she, Uncle T?"

"Yeah . . ." Trevor murmured again, not even caring that he'd been so honest and had so completely exposed himself to someone so young. Losing blood flow to his brain had probably been the culprit. God, his body hurt for that woman.

"You coulda, but chose not to, till it was right . . . you tellin' me that?"

"Yeah, Scott. I'm tellin' you that I respect the woman and like her, too. She's more than just a conquest—or I wouldn't have brought her by here. She ain't like dat."

"Deep. She's got you slurring your words again, dude."

"She's got me goin' blind, to be honest," Trevor grunted.

"Den if she's feelin' your vibe, and you feelin' hers, why you lookin' like you just lost the championship?"

Seizing the teaching moment, Trevor gathered his last ounce of strength and pushed himself up from the chair, holding the kid's gaze in a lethal one of his own. His stare was designed to bring closure to the conversation.

"Because, the state of *almost* is kickin' my butt . . . and knowing that it's also kicking hers is wearing me out."

Twelve

Corey took in a deep breath of fragrant spring air and hummed as she worked, packing the children's sketches and getting all of their items ready for the fair. Today was their maiden voyage to carry the cameras into the street. And what a day for it. Clark Park would be loaded with people beneath the gorgeous sunshine and topaz blue sky. Vendors would line the sidewalks and grassy plots with international foods, crafts, and games.

Marking each milk crate with a Sharpie pen as she stacked them in her foyer, Corey tried to think only about the day ahead of her. But, as always, her brain snapped back to collect retrospective footage.

The week had gone by in much the same way their project was unfolding, in an odd combination of streaming reels of activity stopped down into agonizing still frames that were interspersed with playful animation. True to his word, Trevor Winston had visited her class daily, introducing new facets of the basics, with his teenage crew enthusiastically helping out in the new after-school film club.

Those were the streaming moments, filled with laughter and the frenetic energy of youth. But the still moments came when she'd finally leave for the day and her fingers ached to dial the telephone to call the man who'd opened his inner lens to her.

However, he was obviously keeping his distance,

seeming to understand that the situation was much too volatile to ignite with a late-night call. She respected that. His conversation had been subtly personal, but kept to the focus of what they were working on. Only his eyes belied any further interest in her, and even that was sparingly shared in quick glances that made her stomach quiver to even think about them. The man was a professional, and had kept it that way in front of her students.

She only wished she'd had the presence of mind not to give up the tapes to Justine, who now harassed her daily about the progress of her situation. Justine nagged her like an agent impatient for a script to be finished in order to make a sale. And each day Corey's response had been the same: "We're taking it slow to let things develop naturally."

Yet Justine would hang on the telephone for hours, going over and over the same ground trying to wrest a kernel of new information from her. That was getting tired, because Trevor had become more to her than an interchangeable male commodity to be discussed and traded on the open floor. His worth to her was priceless, in her mind, and he was a treasure whose personal unveiling was to be guarded.

He couldn't wait to go pick her up. Trevor paced about in his new T-shirt and cap that had Scott's logo emblazoned on it. Unabashed pride had swept through him as he'd looked at all the kids in the household who whooped and shouted in excitement when he gave them their crew gear. When they'd all stood together, he'd snapped half a roll of film before he was satisfied enough to drop them off at the park to begin the shoot setup. Now all he had to do was go collect Corey.

Almost pulling up on the sidewalk, he brought the four-by-four to a fast stop and paced toward her steps, taking them two at a time. Ringing her doorbell incessantly, he couldn't wait for her to open it, and as he'd hoped, she hopped up and down, screamed, laughed, and pulled him over the threshold.

"You think they'll like 'em?" He laughed, spinning around in a circle to give her a full view.

"Oh, *maaan!* They are going to flip!" she cried, making him turn around again and giggling in the process. "Let's get out of here and get over to the park!"

It had been her only way to keep herself on point. She had to get that fine man out of her living room and out of her house. The way that black T-shirt clung to his torso, showing off his strong upper arms and every block in his washboard abs . . . When he turned, bent, and picked up three crates at one time, the sight of how the fabric strained against pure sinew, and traveled down into a deep valley that gave rise to a backside so tight she could have bounced a quarter off it—yeah, they had to get out of there.

It was easier to summon her cool once they got out of the car. Immediately, kids from all over the neighborhood and the school flocked to watch what was going on. A group of teens joined in and got their shirts to stand next to Scott, Janelle, and Samantha, who helped sort them out for the littlest children. But the sense of pride inspired in her fifth graders kept Corey on cloud nine all day. The man was a genius. Parents and passersby all stopped to watch the kids, to offer words of encouragement, and to everyone's surprise, a news team showed up and shot a bit for the local news after a parent phoned in.

By six o'clock, the end of the festival, all the parents present had to literally drag their children away. The only way to stop the loud youth complaints was for Corey to reassure them that on Monday they could see what they'd shot, while reminding them that patience was a virtue. The sheer irony of having to tell them that made her laugh.

"Whew," Scott said, hauling a load of equipment to Trevor's car. "What a rush! You editing tonight, Unc?"

Trevor laughed. "Naw, man. Tomorrow is another day. Gotta let the images develop in your head first, before you can edit—no matter what's on the storyboard."

Corey covered her mouth and stifled a smile. This man was totally in his element.

Scott, who seemed to be hanging on every word, as was his posse of what had once seemed to be a rough bunch of his friends, all nodded in unison as if Trevor had spoken from the Tablets.

"Cool, man," one of the teenagers said.

"Yeah, dude. It's about the artistic process," Scott reaffirmed.

"Right, right, we do sound after the cut," another said.

"That's my yard. Sound," Janelle exclaimed, strutting about.

"After I work with them to lay down serious script," Samantha said to the shock of the group, which made everyone laugh.

"Yo, y'all," Miquel said, puffing himself up so that he could be heard. "Art director, remember. I'm gettin' with my squad to be sure that we are thematically on point."

For a moment, everyone stopped and looked at one another, then the whole group burst out in laughter.

"Sho', you right, little man," Scott hollered, giving Miquel a high-five of encouragement. "Set the record straight."

"Look," Trevor said with a chuckle. "Why don't we all get this stuff packed up and away, and go get us some pizza across the street from the park? Gotta feed the crew."

"It's sacrilege not to," Corey said, laughing as she hauled a crate to the side of the car.

By nine o'clock, Miquel was yawning, and the pizza shop owner looked like he'd had enough, too. Even though the teenage crew had definitely boosted the store's profitability index with a dozen cheese-steak orders, four pizzas, too many bags of chips and cheese curls to keep track of, and countless sodas, it was becoming obvious that the loud production team had overstayed their welcome.

"Y'all, I'm done," Trevor finally announced. "Can't hang like I used to."

"The night is young, Unc." Scott laughed, giving his buddies a round of high-fives.

"We got out there at nine o'clock in the morning, and by my watch that means we've been hanging for twelve hours."

"You know you used to this, dog," one of the young men said, laughing with affection.

"Yeah, I remember," Trevor said, chuckling. "But twelve hours is twelve hours."

"I have to confess I'm wiped out, Uncle Trevor," Samantha admitted with a yawn.

"What's the matter, can't hang?" Janelle giggled, nudging her sleepy older cousin.

"What'chu talkin' 'bout," Scott yelled over the din. "Your butt needs to go home, too."

Trevor glanced at Corey, who seemed to be fading fast. Gathering all the paper place mat–drawn storyboard edits, which had been the center of artistic bickering all night, he handed them to Corey. "That's a wrap for the day. I'm taking these ladies and Miquel home, then I'm going to drop off Miss Hamilton and all the equipment. You gentlemen can continue on until the sun comes up, if you like. Peace. We out."

"Aw, can't I stay with Scott and the fellas?" a sleepy little voice asked.

"Next time, dude. You the art director, and gotta get your snooze on so them images be crisp in the morning," Scott teased in good nature, trying to assuage Miquel's wounded ego.

"Aw'ight, Scott," Miquel conceded. "For the project, man."

"Yeah," the teenage males said in one voice, saluting Miquel with power fists. "For the project."

"What a day." Corey sighed as they brought the last of the milk crates into her living room. "But the kids were so good, I mean fired-up good, Trevor."

"Yeah," he said as he set down a heavy crate with a thud. "There's nothing like that feeling in the whole world. The teenagers, though, wow . . . they have some incredible insight, too. No wonder they're leading the pack with the music scene, cutting it raw down to the bone. The ones that aren't just trying to get paid have some profound concepts and messages worth listening to."

Corey flopped down on the sofa and yawned. "I hear you. I love to watch you work with them. This is so much fun, Trevor. I can see how it would be hard to stop doing it once you start." She covered her mouth again and yawned. "You want some coffee or some tea?"

"Yeah . . ." he said slowly, for the first time that day realizing he was actually inside her house, inside her living room, and all alone with her. Now, *that* was profound. They had gotten so swept up in the shoot for the day, then the after-gathering of crew, that it hadn't even dawned upon him.

He allowed his gaze to take in her environment, which was well-appointed, turn-of-the-century Victorian. Seemed totally unlike her . . . but then again, maybe not. She was complex—both a conservative and a risk taker. Old school and new millennium. The living room seemed to be where she sprawled and relaxed, he noted, but as they walked toward the kitchen, he stopped as he passed the dining room. "May I see the photos in the silver frames?"

"Oh, yeah," she said immediately, as though caught off guard, but open. "Sure," she added with a laugh, flipping on the light. "Those old things . . . me, and Mom, and some of her girlfriends. Happiest time in my life."

"Stunning," he whispered, appraising the black-and-whites and deeply appreciating being given a glimpse of Corey then and now.

"I guess Mom or one of her girlfriends took the ones of me. Later, when I got my first camera, I started taking pictures of everything, but especially of Mom. She was my heart—my best friend."

"Yeah," he said quietly, selecting another black-and-white photo of Mrs. Hamilton, studying it with reverence. "You can tell how much she meant to you, and you to her. Look at how beautifully you captured her, and look at how she's looking back at you with adoration. And you captured that joy in an instant . . . in a timeless moment when she just so happened to look up at you from her garden. Natural. Not posed. Just captured."

One day, he told himself, he would capture Corey Hamilton with that same reverence . . . her beauty already indelibly etched in the images of his mind.

He handed her the shot to look at it more closely for herself, and he watched her smile become gentle and sad as her fingers traced the lines in her mother's face.

"I miss her," she whispered, setting the picture back down on the buffet. "Well," she said, sighing, "Time changes everything."

"It does," he murmured back, putting a stray wisp of her hair behind her ear. "But aren't you blessed to have a mental lens . . . one that you carry inside your head, so that even fire could not destroy that photo, because you've cataloged the most important ones within your heart. You carry images in your soul, Corey Hamilton. She's in there."

His fingers traced her cheek, and despite the ember that had begun to glow within him, he didn't want to take her here, like this, in her sanctuary. This room was reserved for her images. It was where she and her mother had probably laughed at the dinner table together, and had shared hurts, and had worked out problems. This was her darkroom. So he let his hand fall to catch hers within it.

"How about that tea or coffee?" he whispered. "Thank you for opening this vault for me."

Trevor's tenderness and the way he knew to revere this room amazed her. Another texture of him had been revealed, and she led him to the kitchen, to the laughing place in her house. This was where any memories from the past were allowed to be superimposed on the present. This was where there was no barrier between yesterday and today.

The shift in her mood was so subtle, yet so palpable. Trevor sat down at the table on one of the padded wood chairs, becoming filled with awe as he considered what that meant. She was an environmentalist, one so sensitive to the vibrations of her surroundings that she could almost blend in like a chameleon or be irreparably damaged by it if it became toxic.

"How do images come to your mind?" he asked out of the clear blue, following a concept that now nagged at his brain.

"Uh, I really never thought about it, actually," she replied, pulling out the teakettle without looking at it and beginning to fill it with water. "Why?"

"I don't know," he said honestly. "Just a thought, is all."

"How do you conceive of your images, then?"

He sat back for a moment and closed his eyes. "Move around the kitchen," he commanded. "Humor me."

"Okay." She laughed, intrigue filling her voice.

He loved it. "Talk to me," he whispered, listening to the water hit the metal and her feet move across the floor, while she giggled at his request, and the metal of the pot slam against the burners when she set it down.

"Sound," he murmured, then opened his eyes slowly. "Maybe that's why music videos came so easy. I don't know . . . but I love the sounds within my environment. Percussion, water, and your voice like a ripple in a pond when you laughed. . . . You are water, moving earth. That's what I see in my head. Blues, and rich browns, and translucent overlays to all of that as you shift shapes and flow."

"Wow," she whispered, now studying his face hard, neglecting to turn on the burner under the kettle.

It was the sexiest thing she'd witnessed . . . the way he oozed creative essence from the most simple process of listening.

"Try," he urged. "How do you find yours?"

She allowed her gaze to sweep the room. "Spaces. Some spaces laugh, others cry, some are still, some frighten, some seduce . . ."

He swallowed hard. "Okay. Close your eyes and think about the spaces you've had these emotions in. What images come to mind? Don't think too hard. Tell me colors."

"Deep forest greens, and burgundies, and rich velvets. Deep browns . . ." she whispered, breathing in through her nose. Then she opened her eyes.

He could only stare at her for a moment. She'd described his bedroom. One day, he'd have to take her there to see what she'd create in that space as he listened to the sounds that he'd help her make.

"The emotion that went with it?" he asked, trying to remain in control of his own thoughts.

"Extreme desire." She looked at him plainly, and then turned her back to fetch the kettle off the stove, then returned it, realizing she hadn't turned on the flame under it. "What color goes with that for you?"

"Aqua," he murmured in a way that made her turn around and forget about the tea. "Water . . . I always hear different timbres of water in your voice. Soothing, a rush, a trickle, and bubbling, then stillness, then a sweeping, passionate hard rain. Water."

She stared at him and leaned back on the sink. Silence enveloped them, and he closed his eyes again, not sure if he could withstand the sight of her languidly poised there, comfortable, legs crossed at the ankles, hands on either side of her hips, head slightly tilted . . . just as she'd stood against the desk in her classroom.

"Right now, as you stand there," he whispered, "you are a waterfall, breaking over the edge of the sink, which is now a cliff, and you are long, flowing, but rushing through my system. And I am considering whether or not it is wise to walk over and quench myself in that fast-rushing current . . . for I might be swept away."

"Is it hot outside?" she asked in a sultry whisper. Then she closed her eyes and leaned her head back.

As much as he wanted to move toward her, the sight of her creating the image in her head had him transfixed. . . . She was siphoning his vibe, then filtering it in her mental processes, to give back to him.

"It's sweltering outside," her voice intoned in an octave so low it made his groin throb. "You are heat waves across sandstone. . . . You could be desert now, but then you have your own life force. Desert is not dead; it is patience personified. It is life in stasis, waiting for water to renew it."

"Renew me, Corey Hamilton," he whispered, low in his throat and praying for her rain.

"You are massive. . . ." she murmured, seeming unashamed to so openly want him. "And you have isolated canyons in your soul where mighty rivers once ran. There's now a close-up—of the pores of your skin . . . that are now grains of sand, which ache to drink in water, and drop by drop large splotches of summer rain come down slowly at first, then quicken, and overtake your surface until you are covered and quenched. . . ."

He was looking at her through half slits as she spoke, and her voice poured out over lush, silken lips like the tender petals of an orchid. The effect of it was devastating, and he found himself going to the waterfall to quench his barren earth, and he felt it flow against the most neglected terrain of him—his mouth.

First he sipped her in slowly, like a cool drink of morning dew, reveling in the delicate texture of the surface of her mouth before he entered it with his tongue. He took his time to move across the smooth, hard surfaces of her coral reef, tasting the pungent hint of garlic and cheeses before he plunged into the depths of wet softness to intertwine his tongue with hers. Moving closer, his hand found a warm jet stream of desire as it trailed her back and covered her bottom. Her hands became liquid motion and drenched his shoulders with the warmth of healing fluid touch, while his other hand explored the soft moss at the nape of her neck until his fingers slid up the base of her skull to become tangled in the sea grass of her hair.

Unable to resist, he found his body lunging into the spray of her full current, undulating with her waves as he allowed his chest to move against the tiny pebbles under her shirt surface. Bending and kissing them through it as she moaned made him need full-body coverage from her. Moving with her hard until he couldn't stand it, he heard her voice echo in his brain. Soon each wave of her crashed against his shore harder and his belt buckle began to swipe past hers, creating the clacking sound of friction as though two rocks were being struck together.

Broken, he tore his mouth away from her lips to drink more of her in, and found solace in the soft surface of her neck. But the sudden avalanche into a new part of her pool drew a gasp from her that rushed past stalagmites in his mind. And a part of him quaked and issued up earth core–heated rock from the lowest regions of his terrain, causing her to become a molten spring, that wrapped a leg around his and pulled him into a deep eddy, where he knew he would surely drown.

It was her voice that finally fractured him into sand as he dissolved. Her sharp gasps collided with short pants as he moved his hand to pull up her shirt, and she yanked his shirt up, till she covered him like a fast torrential rain. Skin to skin at their tops, bellies pressing, hardness meeting softness, he drank from her, making the underground stream in her flow with a deep moan.

It was as though each knew the other blindly. . . . Her hands slid down the valley of his spine, and he tugged her pants to her knees. Swept by her hard current, he worked at the dam of fabric between himself and the river it held him back from now . . . dipping his fingers in her well as she urged them in deeper, until he shivered so hard with want that the continental plates in his brain collided. Her whimpers were creating evolution and forming new landmasses that made him block her delta with mountain. . . . And suddenly she stopped flowing, and put her palm in the middle of his chest to hold back certain disaster.

"We have to use something," she breathed heavily, sending more molten current into his ear.

"I know," he gulped, trying to get his bearings. "I know. I didn't think to . . . I didn't know it was gonna happen tonight. . . ."

He rolled away from her and held on to the side of the sink beside her, sputtering and taking huge amounts of air into his lungs. Perspiration ran down the center of his back, and he kept his eyes shut tightly as he listened in agony to her pulling up her pants. "I'll go get somethin'," he whispered. "I have to get something, before I lose my mind."

"Come upstairs," she murmured, her smooth hand tracing his cheek. "I already brought something. . . . The day after we had a near miss in the car, after the first night I went to your house. I didn't know when it would be, but I knew."

Her words nearly buckled his knees, and he found himself pulling her to him, this time drinking her in hard, absorbing her scent, his hands and mouth reveling in the texture of her hair and her skin, and soaking her up like a desert that so desperately needed rain. He clung to her and tried to pull her inside of him, as each time he attempted to let her go, the ache that briefly separating created was unbearable.

"We won't make it if you keep this up," she gasped when he broke away from her mouth to indulge her collarbone.

"Then take me up there now." He breathed in short bursts, as he searched her face with his eyes, trying to explain what words could not. How could he get her to understand that his body hurt so badly for her that each step was going to send that ache through him. Each footstep forward was almost destined to make him cry out.

"C'mon," she whispered with mercy in her voice as she led him out of the kitchen, through the dining room, toward the living room, and up the stairs.

He tried to gather his breath as he allowed her to set the pace, but as he ascended behind her and watched her bottom sway in half-undone pants, he had to hold on to the banister to keep from falling.

When they got to her room, he stopped, sensing her mood shift again as her environment changed. This was her private space, her comfort zone, and he looked around at the high-set four-poster bed that was covered in beige and off-white tones . . . This is where she started with a blank canvas and added color, he thought . . . watching her slowly disrobe before him without losing eye contact.

Steadier now, having a brief respite from her touch, he kept her in his gaze as he peeled away the remaining clothing barriers until he stood before her nude. When he took off his pants, her eyes went half-mast and her nostrils gave only a hint of flare as her chest rose to take in the silent breath she drew. However, watching her so aroused did something to the rational side of his brain, and he couldn't move for a moment as his eyes again drank her in.

The sight of her flawless caramel skin that rose into even petite mounds, only interrupted by two tiny brown pebbles, made him draw an audible breath . . . and he watched that sound draw another inhalation from her. His gaze traveled down the length of her to the region he desired to claim, and he moved toward her slowly across the center of the bed as though it were his only bridge to get to her on the other side.

Near enough to touch her, he watched intently as she moved to her nightstand in what seemed like slow motion, and took out a small box and tossed it to him. He caught it in one hand. Without looking at the package closely, he sat back on his heels, opened it, and found a passport that would allow him entry to her oasis.

Her hands were trembling as she pushed the drawer closed, and she watched him work at the protective layer that would be the only thing between them. He sat on his heels in the center of her bed like dark earth in contrast to the eggshell tones that surrounded him, and she could feel a slick, hot river beginning to crest and threaten to spill down the tops of her thighs. . . . Sound . . . he loved sound . . . and tonight they'd have a soundtrack to replay for the rest of their lives. The image he was creating now as he stared so deeply into her eyes burned into her spirit in a way that could never be captured in stills.

Moving to the bed, she joined him, tentatively at first. This was happening . . . and even though she'd hoped it would for what felt like too long, now that it was imminent, anticipation crushed the air from her lungs. Then he reached for her, and truncated years of not being sure into seconds of immediate imperative. And she allowed her voice to spill out into his ear in a deep moan as he pulled her beneath him.

The sound she'd just made when he'd entered her sent shock waves through his spine, and he clenched the sheets in his fists to keep from bruising her arms with his hold. Then she moved against him hard, and he sank deeper into paradise. His own voice blended with hers, creating a primal symphony that came from their depths. Instantly, as he felt himself shudder, he grabbed her under the small of her back.

His words were now staccato as he held her firm. "Wait . . . baby . . . I'm too close to the edge."

"Go over it, then," she whispered sharply and bit the lobe of his ear.

Blinded with desire, he shut his eyes tight with her words. The sound of her voice eclipsed time, and her touch eclipsed sound, until the only thing in his awareness was how her legs wrapped around his hips, and the way her hands pulled at his shoulders as she arched against his hold. His personal restraint fractured under the battering of her relentless waves, and he sank hard and fast. Unison motion drove her up toward the headboard until he had to shield her head with his hands. His mouth found her shoulder, then breast, and he could feel her begin to spasm, which caught him in a tidal wave of convulsions at the very moment she called his name.

Sucking in air, he tried to raise his weight off her, but his arms trembled so badly that he simply gathered her up and rolled over.

"It's been so long," she murmured, "and it was never like this."

"No, never," he gasped back, not finding enough air to fill his lungs.

"Can you reach the box?" he asked on a winded chuckle.

"Yeah." She giggled. "Why?"

" 'Cause, I'm not done with you, girl. I'm still taking in water. Just need something to stop a hull breach. I warned you . . . and I need you again."

"That you did," she whispered, kissing his eyelids so tenderly that it made his chest heavy.

"I'm not going anywhere," he whispered back. "You are my port in the storm. I'm crazy 'bout you."

Thirteen

Weak, satiated, exhausted. Every muscle in his body reminded him how much he was all of those things when he tried to climb the front steps to his house at three-thirty in the morning. Every part of him ached with a wonderful satisfaction, except his heart. The ache from having to leave Corey after a night like that still made it hard for him to breathe.

He chuckled as the recent memory poured over him, thinking about how they both kept saying this was the last time, then kept extending the time beyond reason as he'd torn open each foil wrapper, until the six-pack was empty. The only reason he'd gotten out of there was because their supply had gone dry—and he had to leave to keep from going back for more of her. All he could hope for was that his son hadn't awakened in the middle of the night looking for him.

Entering the house as quietly as possible, he glanced around the living room half expecting to see Scott sprawled out on the sofa. Not seeing him there mildly concerned him, and he made his way down the hall with more haste to check on Miquel. Not seeing his son in his bed, Trevor instantly panicked. What if something tragic had happened during the night? What if this time he'd not been there, and would get the news through the sobs of his weary sister?

Adrenaline instantly sobered him from his love binge. With added haste, he quickly climbed the back stairs to his sister's unit to begin a bed check. The first room he hit was Scott's, and he breathed out a sigh of relief seeing the youth spread-eagled across the mattress in the normal sweat gear that Scott always wore around the house. But where was Miquel?

Rushing down the hall to Janelle and Samantha's room, he drew in his breath and let it out slowly as he saw his son nestled against Sam in her lower bunk and heard Janelle snoring away in the top one. God bless Cousin Samantha.

The sight of her maternal covering of his little boy pulled at Trevor's insides. He hovered in the doorway just watching the three of them slumber. Would there ever be a day when he and Corey and Miquel could curl up in his sleigh bed as a family, sleeping peacefully, awaiting dawn to wash over them? The image stayed with him as he slowly pulled himself away, turned, and had to process the vision of his sister.

"So, look what the cat brought in," she said in a low, threatening tone. "We need to talk. Now."

With no ability to marshal resistance, he followed her into the kitchen, using the small oven light emanating from the room as a beacon, and sat down heavily in a chair. He didn't need this right now. Sudden exhaustion made it hard for him to hold his head up to even look at her, much less tune his mental faculties to a logic channel for an argument.

"So," she said in a mercifully low whisper, fixing coffee as she spoke. "You are to be my backup, my door guard, 'eh?"

The smell of coffee assailed him enough to make him realize that, if she was making brew at this hour of the morning, she meant to interrogate him until he confessed. Sleep depravation was a torture tactic that had been well tried and proven since the Inquisition.

"I'm tired," he murmured in self-defense. "Can we talk about this tomorrow?"

"It is *already* tomorrow," she snapped, pouring coffee for herself and taking a seat in front of him.

"Then can I at least have a cup of coffee, too?" he begged her in a whisper, trying not to totally blow his positive vibration.

"It's in the pot if you want it. Suit yourself. But I know you don' expect me to be your handmaiden after having worked a whole shift?"

"My bad," he whispered, but could not gather the strength to move.

When she switched on the overhead fluorescent lights, he lowered his head to the table and closed his eyes.

"Gretchen, please." He breathed out hard. "The children were with me for twelve hours. I fed them, got them home safe, and Samantha was here to baby-sit while I made a run. I just came up to check on everyone—then go downstairs and slip into a coma. I don' have the stamina left for an argument." He could only hope that his plea for mercy would be accepted, and his mind drifted lazily as his head continued to rest on his folded arms in front of him.

"At least you could look up and speak to me with respect," his sister grumbled, "rather than falling asleep here at my table after you have so disrespected my house."

Jesus, Lord in Heaven . . .

Trevor pulled himself up and leaned his head back against the wall, peering at his sister through heavy lids. She had pulled out a blunt instrument on him, her tongue. Then, he was sure, after bludgeoning him, she would pull out the guilt razor and start carving out the tender sections of his abdomen. Weariness was giving way to anger.

"All right," he said in a low rumble and folded his arms. "State your case."

"How, for the love of God, could you bring some woman up to my home—without my permission, without my knowing? Hmmm? Start there, if you please, Mr. Trevor Winston."

He could only hope that she hadn't pressed the children into a grand jury panel. Knowing this day would eventually come, he just wondered why it had taken this long for her to find out. His sister's detective skills must be slipping.

"Who told you?" he asked, not really caring. He just wanted to know which child he had to give medical attention to after they'd endured Gretchen's kitchen torture chamber.

"It does not matter 'bout who tol' me what," she fussed, her accent growing thick with imploded rage. "The only thing dat matters is dat you didn't tell me 'bout any of dis!"

"You're right," he said evenly, glad that her voice had only come out in a harsh whisper. "It doesn't matter. So, to the best of my ability, here is an explanation."

He watched her sit back in her chair and fold her arms over her chest before he began.

"After Miss Hamilton was so gracious to accommodate this film project for the kids, I invited Miquel's teacher to come by and see the studio where the students will work to complete that project. As a teacher, she just can't allow her kids to be running by some strange man's house, now can she—without knowing it is safe. Things are not as simple as they used to be."

His explanation seemed to give her pause as she mulled it over, then took a sip of her coffee.

"All right," she muttered. "Then if she was site-inspectin' only, what cause did you have to bring her up here and all through da house, answer me dat, Mr. I-got-an-answer-to-eve'ythin'."

Patience was edging away from him, and it opened a door to a question that he'd had locked behind it for a long time.

"I thought she needed to know that, although no

one answered more than five notes from the school while I was overseas taking care of this family, we did indeed have a family structure that tended to the children. So I walked her through the entire house, except the attic—as though she were a Department of Human Services case worker."

His sister seemed stunned from his verbal punch, and she sat back and sipped her coffee. Good. He wasn't taking a bunch of crap at nearly four in the morning for doing what was basic in a house that he'd paid for. Forget that!

"Well," his sister replied, and let it drop.

"Well, what?" Trevor spat back, finding his strength returning as gall ignited his system.

"Well, then it appears you had cause."

"Is that all you have to say to me?" His voice had returned to full capacity, and the authority in it seemed to be the impetus that made her stand to fetch more coffee.

"Why, Gretchen, would you open, then bundle up and mail, five letters from the school, *five,* knowing I had no way to really get to this school? You never offered them a reply, never went over there, and never checked to see—"

"Because," she said defensively as she spun on him, her voice escalating and her hand sloshing her coffee as she did so, "I did it for the same reason you have slinked in here like an alley cat tonight! I needed a break, and some respite from these children, and the only way to get your attention was to *force* you to be responsible for the only one in the bunch dat I did not give birth to. You made Mom and Dad watch him, then me . . . well, I've raised mine, and dey don't need walkin' home from school, homework checkin', lunch makin', clothes washin', tucks into bed at night, or nuttin' else!"

Oh, yeah, she had gone for the big blade, unsheathed it in the middle of the kitchen floor and run him through to the bone. He sat there breathing the heavy gasps of the mortally wounded, the pain so great that he was temporarily unable to respond . . . because hers was the blade of truth.

His shoulders slumped as he felt his spirit dying. Looking up at her, all he wanted was for her to perform last rites. Even a man going before a firing squad was supposed to get a cigarette. But she had gored him on the spot without pomp and circumstance.

"Okay. You're right, and it did draw me here. And I promised I'd stay. What else do you want from me?"

"Yes," she sneered, not seeming at all fazed that he'd validated any and all of her complaints. "And you promised to watch out for the children so I could have a break, and that you didn't need to go out so much, and that I could depend on your time with them . . . and in one week, you are back to your old tricks."

Anger became morphine, and it stanched the pain in his gizzard enough for him to verbally fight back.

"I was not out and up to my old tricks, as you call them, tonight," he seethed from a very low place in his throat. "Do not *ever* go there about this situation."

Gretchen blinked, set her coffee down slowly, and stared at him, then smirked. The reaction confused him, but his rage was already full tilt, and he was not about to back down from the struggle she'd begun.

"Well, I'll just be damned. . . ." his sister murmured. "Miss Cleo was right. . . ."

"Miss Cleo? Miss Cleo?" Trevor was up on his feet and pacing as he waved his hands toward the neighbor's window. "What has she got to do wit where I been? I'm a grown man, and you ain' talkin' ta Scott. How dare you drill me like I'm a chile, and drag me bizness t'rough da neighborhood! I won't have you ruin dat woman's reputation all 'cause you're pissed off about Robert's Rules of house visitin' order, when nuttin' happened to any chile under dis roof while I was gone for a few hours!"

His chest was heaving so hard and fast that he felt light-headed, and the fact that his sister only chuckled made him want to punch out the wall.

"Keep your voice down and have a seat," Gretchen said.

"I don' wan' to sit down, I want peace, and space, an' a good night's sleep!"

"Sit down, and I'll tell you what Miss Cleo predicted at her own kitchen table."

"What do I care what some nosy old woman who—"

"She saw her in the tarot, Trevor."

"This is insanity," Trevor huffed, but found himself flopping in the chair anyway.

"None of the children tol' me anythin,' " his sister said in a demure tone that belied the mirth concealed in it. "So relax."

Oddly, her statement did make him relax. But he was not about to let her know that, at least not right off.

"Now, let's get one thin' straight before I tell you 'bout what Miss Cleo saw," she warned, her voice becoming serious, even though it remained calm. "I didn't have so much of a problem with the fact dat you went out. My problem was in that, as a parent, the kids should always have an emergency number posted somewhere visible—like my work number is posted on the refrigerator. *An'thin'* can happen, in the blink of an eye. Your children should always know how to reach you, and a grown person should know that your kids are alone. *That's* backup. These are basics, Trevor. An' I'm goin' to allow for the fact that you are new to this full-time-parent game, and I'm goin' to allow for the fact that you might not have wanted another livin' soul to know where you had been.

"Notwithstandin' all a dat, this is what makes single parents either snap, bring things in fronta dey children dat children shouldn't see, or become celibate . . . because there's no real space for courtin', the children must always know where you are—which means dat dey will always be in the most private aspects of your biziness, as will some other adult. So, in dat regard, being a parent if you're goin' it alone, you must be prepared to give up the most precious part of yourself—absolute freedom."

He sat back in his chair, stunned, as her words erased all of his anger and let it drain out onto the floor. While somewhere in his intellect he'd calculated these facts, now, for the first time, it truly sank in. His face must have blanched, because his sister laughed and covered one of his hands with her own.

"Dear brother," she said tenderly, but still with mirth. "It's not like when there's a married mom and dad at home, and dey sit up and read da paper and watch television together, and all of the children eventually go to bed . . . and you can hear your mother giggle down the hall as the lock is thrown at the bedroom door, then in the morning, you as a child are oblivious to why Mom is humming in the kitchen, and Dad is in such a favorable mood that he is content to grant you any wish. Remember growin' up in our house?"

"Jesus Christ . . ." he whispered.

"Yes." She laughed, holding his hand tightly. "I have called on the Father many a night, when my nerves were frayed, and my body hurt so badly that if one of those kids crossed me wrong, I might have knocked them over the head wit a pot. And there have been days when my single girlfriends did manage to get me out on the town for an hour or two, and I spied a good-looking, eligible man who smiled at me and who wanted to take me home. . . . But"—she sighed hard—"I had to think about the logistics, which killed any aphrodisiac his smile contained. Then I had to come home horny and wound up to fussin' and fightin' and laundry and bills, and eve'y ordinary thing—wit'out a little pleasure for me. That's why your teacher's letters never got answered. And dat's what's wrong wit dese young kids who have children before dere house is set in order . . . at sixteen, when the sap has just begun to flow, and flow hard, how can your mind and body stand years of such deprivation without goin' off da deep end?"

She looked at him real hard, and although her voice was serious, her eyes contained a gentle brand of acceptance as she tried to teach him love's lessons from her podium at the kitchen table.

"Brother, you and I both divorced, right?"

"Yeah," he whispered.

"Now, don' you remember how bitter the feuds were while trapped in the confinement of an unhappy relationship?"

"How could I forget?"

"Then compound dat wit what I jus' tol' you, 'eh. . . . We took off da burden of raisin' a chile—from *both* of you two while you wrangled. But add children to dat stew, where neither party is havin' dere needs met—but, because of society, dey cannot just go out and do what grown folks must do—if dey have any decency remaining. Then heap on da bills, and an uneven share of da work . . . and add insults and indignity . . . then smatter on lack of affection, and kindness, and appreciation . . . then simmer it wit lack of consideration—and your stew becomes a powder keg. Boom . . ."

Her voice trailed off in a sad whisper, then she looked up at him and offered a weak smile. "All of us wanted what our mother and father had . . . caring and support and mutual respect and passion to the end. There was an old guard who obtained it, and in dis generation, yours and mine, dear brother, we have lost it—and one more generation down has rarely even seen it. . . . And we are searching for it in bars and clubs and now even on the computers—we are so desperate. So don't set up house 'til you build a strong foundation under it. Because when it all comes tumblin' down, dese late nights of passion will all be forgotten—buried under da rubble—and your kids will be crushed from da impact. . . . No one gets out unscathed, at least not witout a scratch. Ask me how I know."

"I never . . ." His voice trailed off, and his gaze locked with hers. Gretchen's statement was so honest, so deeply profound, that he thought about what the children were saying, how they were developing their project around the edges of these issues—from their eyes, which stared up at the adult houses falling down all around them.

"Been building up from the ashes for ten years," his sister admitted quietly. "My babies only got internal bruises, and no broken bones. We were lucky. But I vowed, until I'd raised them up the best that I could, that I'd repave my home foundation wit cement."

She'd paused to allow her words to sink in, and her eyes glowed with a determination that he'd rarely seen in her before. Then she drew a deep breath as though to steady herself.

"I will not put a match to the new wood frame of their existence, Trevor Winston, by bringing in company that I am not sure of. Nor will I leave them to raise themselves in the streets. Nor will I allow even my brother to introduce them to values or see things that I fought for ten years with my own body to keep from my door and out of my house. You may have purchased this house with money, Trevor, but I've built it into a home—there's the crux of the matter. Sacrifice built this home!"

Gretchen's hand had come down on the table with a loud smack as she'd finished making her point—then she sat back and looked at him. She was breathing hard from her sudden burst of truth, and he could only stare at this woman who would not be moved. . . .

"Do you understand that dis is a survival matter, not about a simple argument between grown siblings? If it comes down to your wanderlust and hormones or my children, I will rip your throat out and eat your heart for dinner at my kitchen table. It's my babies or a man, a grown man—regardless that he's my brother."

All he could do was remove his hand from under his sister's, then lean forward and drop his face into his palms. He'd only experienced this dilemma for one week, and had cracked under the pressure. The two years before that really didn't count. He didn't have chicken pox and influenza to disrupt his career schedule. He didn't have to be a constant role model, deal with education, take kids for shots, worry about them day and night, and walk the walk. . . . Now, sending money to fix the problems seemed to be the easiest thing in the world as his sister's truth hammered his brain and cracked open his skull.

Not even his so-called abstinence was really that big of a deal in light of what she'd said, because although he'd taken a vow, he had been free to release his pent-up desire in his bed alone at night, without the possible scrutiny of a child. He didn't have to worry about nightmares and bedwetting, or share his sleigh with anyone but his own body and his own dreams . . . and he most certainly didn't have to hunger for what would always be beyond his reach.

Sensing his quandary, she persisted, relentless in her examination of his soul.

"What if you were working on one of your films, even here in Philadelphia, and one of the kids took sick? Would you walk off the set, abandon the crew, lose the money for the day, and sit home stirring a pot of soup?"

When he didn't answer, she jumped right in.

"Do you know how many women lose their jobs for a simple run of chicken pox—which can last ten days? Do you know how many ear infections, fevers, colds, or other little ailments even normal, healthy children get—and most employers only give you two weeks of vacation, and maybe twelve sick days a year, if you're blessed, in which to handle your family business? And, even then, they are upset if you use that? And do you know how many of these things crop up from birth to kindergarten . . . the entire time dat me and our mother watched Miquel?"

"And," she said quickly before he could speak, drawing a deep breath so she could gather fuel to continue her drilling into his conscience, "do you know what happens when you constantly show up late to work, because a child is not cooperating, or you have to leave early because they have gotten sick at school, or in trouble? Think, man, think!" she urged, using her hands before her. "Me and your mother have paid our debt, we have been there, like thousands of other women around the world, and the most that we receive, if we are lucky, is child support—maybe a Mother's Day card, and an occasional drop-by from the dad who got away. Some don't get that much. But, that's what you did to us, the women you claimed you love!"

Thick mucus filled his throat, and her face blurred as he tried to form words in his mouth. "I owe you and Mom and Dad so much of an apology, dat I don' even know where to begin. . . ."

"Just promise me that you will not disgrace my house by conducting adult bizness before the children, as I have not done. And, if you are courtin', then just leave us a number, so dat we can have a lifeline. That's all. Now, is dat too much of a compromise?"

"No," he whispered in return, wondering how he was going to follow through with such a commitment. Moreover, the debt he owed was beyond repayment. And it also meant that he could not plunge another living soul, not another woman, into this purgatory that was worse than hell. If he followed through with trying to blend normalcy into all of this chaos, it would mean that Corey's business would become family business, which would eventually become school business—

as the children would talk, and all of the parents would know.

Trevor ran his fingers through his hair as his mind struggled to bring the shards of his life together. He'd have to ask Corey's permission about all of this, or try to keep his hands off her . . . which now, after she'd opened a vein, would be almost impossible. So exposing the relationship meant that it had to work out, or the neighborhood could have her smeared as that teacher who had a fling with a student's dad. It was all too crazy and too tangled-up to sort out, and he let his breath out hard, as he tried to kill the memory of the touch that drove him mad.

"It's a lot to take in," his sister murmured as she sipped her coffee. "See the logistics of it, how hard it is to be a do-right parent? Very complex."

"Never in my life . . ."

"Dis is why we scream and yell and beg our children to be careful and not to make children until they can pay the *real* cost to be the boss."

"No lie . . ."

"And will you do me a favor and tell this to my son, who is on the precipice of sowing his wild oats, if he hasn't already?"

"Yeah," Trevor murmured, still too undone to say much more.

"He looks up to you, as all the kids do. You're a good father and a good uncle, and a good brother. But you make me so crazy sometimes, because you see everything in the world, capture it on films and in pictures, but cannot see what is right in front of your very eyes."

"I'll talk to the girls, too," he said slowly, feeling the cycle of entrapment up close and personal for the very first time.

"Okay," she said, chuckling. "But don't overdo yourself, now. These things take gentle handlin', and your reality wound is still tender. One t'ing I know is, children ain't stupid. If you talk the talk, you must walk the walk—or one day they'll throw it back in your face, den' you can't do a thing wit dem. That's why I made the choices I did, because they can never come back to me and say, 'Well, Mom, you did thus and so.' "

He nodded slowly, then caught his sister's gaze and held it, searching her eyes for an answer that he knew even her seasoned wisdom did not contain.

"Actually, it was easier for me in one regard. I didn't fall in love," she said with a warm smile, "so the monkey on my back was imaginary, and its hold could be loosened with a good hot book, a glass of wine, and a long warm soak in da tub. But you got a gorilla chasing you down' da street, and livin' around da corner. King Kong."

They stared at each other for a moment and then both burst out laughing.

"Oh, God." He roared hard and covered his eyes. "It's dat obvious?"

"When da children start coverin' for you, and cleanin' up dishes, and the lady who reads cards is telling me all 'bout a bloomin' romance in my house to the point where I'm goin' ta lock my children in the closet—only ta find out she was talkin' about you—then, yes, I'd say it's that bad."

He shook his head and stood, placed a kiss on her forehead, and stretched. His bed was calling him, and sleep was now an involuntary response beyond his control.

"Timid-lookin' little thing wore your rusty butt out, didn't she?"

He only chuckled and refused comment.

"I'll watch the kids down here this morning to give you recovery space—only because I love you, and as a truce." She smiled warmly, giving him a hug. "And I suggest dat you pull the phone into your bedroom and disconnect the other lines on the first floor of the house when you're talking to dat girl."

"Why?" He yawned, looking at his sister through bleary eyes. His brain was exhausted, his body felt like he'd been in a prizefight, and his soul ached . . . what more?

"Because you can't get out with regularity."

"Gretchen, I'm not follow—"

"I, too, have lived in the world, and I am a veteran at this. Trust me."

"But—"

"Put a lock on your bedroom door, and take the other phones out, if you want to visit her when you can't. This way, one of the children won't pick up an extension and be in your bizness."

"Oh," he said, shaking his head and relaxing his shoulders. "There's not too much I would say on the telephone to her that if Miquel picked up—"

Her wide grin and her slap on his chest made him stop midsentence.

"When dat phone rings at two o'clock in da mornin', and de gorilla has climbed through your window, and it's been weeks since you could break out of child-care prison, and she sweetly says, 'Trevor, I miss you so,' you won't be able to hear the click of an extension being picked up over your own heavy breathin', and none of the kids need to witness that. It ain't pretty, but it's practical . . . and that's why I'm going to watch them this morning.

"Because when you wake up, nose wide open and having just gone back onto love drugs, you gonna be evil, slamming around, bouncing off the walls 'cause you needed a roll-over-and-make-love-again-in-da-mornin' fix, and you can't have it . . . then your hand is gonna reach for da telephone tremblin' like a junkie, and you gonna tell her in baritone, 'Baby, I miss you,' which is goin' ta get her started sighing, and you both gonna be messed up—an' they'll be no livin' with you. Remember, I got teenagers who are mean and surly and havin' crying jags and snit fits and who stay on the phone and rush for it like it was a soccer meet, then wind up locked in their rooms for hours—or tying up the bathroom . . . that's when you know, the end of being mommy is near," she said, sighing. "I'm done, and I'm going to sleep, since that's all I can get around here myself."

He stood in the doorway of the kitchen, mouth agape, marveling at his sister's hard-earned insight and wisdom. He wished he'd known sooner, and could have warned others along the way . . . and he thanked God for having someone who still loved him enough to honestly teach him, so that one day he could tell someone, and have them pass the message on.

Slowly moving down the hall, he descended the stairs and entered the unit, picking up the kitchen and living-room telephones before he went into his bedroom and locked the door.

Fourteen

True to Gretchen's words, as sleep evaporated, an ache for Corey replaced it, and in the sweet space between consciousness and slumber, he reached for her and got a pillow. A deep groan worked its way up from his abdomen as he wondered who was more psychic—his sister or Miss Cleo?

He didn't even open his eyes as he reached for the telephone, punching in the numbers with his thumb as he rolled over onto his back. Although he was aware of sunlight in the room, and could hear light street traffic, televisions, stereos, and children and motion overhead, he wasn't ready to open his eyes.

Reality, and the cold light of day, would be too harsh at the moment. All he wanted to do was pull his respite closer to him and relive the splendor of the night before. Responsibilities would come crashing down on them soon enough. That was a given. But . . . if she would just pick up the telephone, maybe he could salvage a little bit of heaven.

"Baby," he murmured when her sleepy voice said hello. "I already miss you."

"Hmmm . . ." she groaned lazily in a way that let him know she was stretching. "I miss you, too. Last night was wonderful. . . ."

She'd drawn out her words in a sultry, low, morning saxophone tone that made him breathe in deeply and exhale through his mouth.

"I'm sorry that I had to leave you, and couldn't wake up next to you . . . or in you. . . ." he whispered, as the thought gathered, then stiffened in his body.

"Ohhh . . . yeah, me, too, but you had to, honey. I know that," she said tenderly, sending another electric current through him as he imagined what she looked like in the middle of her bed.

"This is killing me," he admitted low in his throat, "and I don't know when I'll be able to get over there again."

"I know," she said on a forlorn sigh. "But we knew this going into it, right?"

"Yeah, I suppose," he concurred with grudging defeat. "But after last night . . ."

"Yeah . . . last night," she whispered, "was transformative. . . ."

He swallowed hard, beginning to see her as water again. "There aren't enough cold showers in the world . . ."

"Or hot baths . . ."

Tension threaded itself through his muscular system as he imagined her fusing with the water in a hot tub, her head back and thighs parted and wishing he were there.

"Oh, God, woman . . . don't talk to me like that."

"Like what?" she teased on a heavy breath. "I thought your medium was sound?"

"It is . . . my Achilles' heel," he groaned, turning on his side and gathering his pillow closer to him with his eyes still closed.

"Ohhh . . . I wasn't sure that sound still affected you so much," she said, giggling softly in a lower octave.

"You know it does." He chuckled, delighting in her game of taunting him. "Be merciful this morning, since I can't do anythin' to fight back."

"Then I have the distinct advantage, huh?" she crooned.

"Absolutely," he whispered, his voice becoming a rasp.

"And what would make me want to give that all up?" she asked, giggling again in a very sexy tone. "Hmmm?"

"Retribution," he murmured. She had reduced him to one-word responses.

"Ah, a threat?" she breathed huskily, then groaned. "I *love* it."

"A promise," he growled.

"Ooooh, I'm so scared."

"I'll be over there in ten minutes," he said, without processing the words.

"But you can't," she teased. "Who's gonna watch the kids?"

Panic wrested back his faculties.

"That's right . . . oh, girl . . . see . . ."

Gentle laughter poured through the telephone, and he sat up and swung his legs over the side of the bed, cradling the receiver as he leaned forward and sighed. Then he began to rock, and think, and try to rationalize his way out of the confinement. It was like being a starving dog in an alley—watching patrons eat with one's nose pressed up against the window.

"You've got me drooling on myself," he said, chuckling in defeat. "Just like the first day you visited here."

Silence met him on the other end of the line.

"Really?" she murmured in a very husky tone that slathered his ear with her desire.

"Yes," he said, both pleased and amused that he'd rediscovered her hot button . . . images . . . Then he fell back on the bed and closed his eyes to conjure up the perfect retribution. Vivid image torture.

"I hesitated at your classroom door before opening it," he admitted, allowing his voice to descend. "Because I knew you'd be standing there, like you did last night at the sink, leaning back on your desk, with your hands on either sides of your hips, your long gorgeous legs crossed, with the rose-orange sun hitting the side of your face, making your hair glisten and your eyes sparkle as it played across your mouth . . . and I, as a man, could not trust myself."

When she only moaned, he chuckled to himself. *Yeah, baby, take that. Who is the master?*

"And when you walked into my bedroom and drew a deep breath, but only smiled, and your gaze tore itself away from my bed, as though it had burned you, I could only imagine you in the center of it, riding my sled. . . ."

Even though she'd let out a little whimper, in truth, his own imagery was also tearing him apart. He needed white space in the graphic in order to collect himself, so he designed it in the form of a question.

"Do you remember any of what I'm talkin' 'bout?" He'd decided to pull out all the stops, and had whispered the question in a lazy, thick accent, just the way he knew she loved to hear his voice.

"Yes . . ." she said in a slow, near hiss that burned his ear like steam.

Silence filled in the gap left by their dangerous play, and he knew that somehow, by roughhousing so recklessly, they'd tumbled into very treacherous terrain. Yet he couldn't stop himself, even now, hovering on the verge of no return.

"Do you have any idea what it did to me to have you so close, down in my studio, being in the most sacred space to me . . . admiring my work, appreciating it for the labor of love that it is, and not being able to put my hands on you?"

Somehow, all of the play had gone out of the game, and he was serious when he asked the question.

"And do you know how it felt to understand that a man, so unsure of how I'd react, would invite me into his home, and hold back from even a hint of impropriety, while standing two inches away from me . . . do you know what that did to me, Trevor Edmond Winston?"

Sound was his curse, not his medium, as he soaked in the way she'd said his full name. "I need you so bad right now," he confessed on a groan, all the mirth gone out of him, as desire became sheer agony. "My hand is about to become you, and you are about to become my hand, if you don't stop."

"I want you so much, too," she said hard and quick, just as her thrusts had been the night before. "My hands have been you all week long. Why should this morning be any different?"

And in that statement, she'd transformed into water. . . .

"You are rushing against me like a current right now . . . and I can't shake it this mornin,' just like I couldn't fight against it last night."

"I lost my patience in the car, when you told me it had been two years, like it had been for me, and all I could think about was bringing you upstairs to my room to quench both of our thirsts. . . ."

"And you crashed against me like I was a cliff in Jamaica—immobile in front of you. . . . And you were aqua, and foaming, and inescapable. . . ."

"You were cliff," she moaned softly, as though her gentle waves were about to crest and break. "And now you are mountain, surrounding a deep, wet, valley pond."

"Oh, girl, I am plundered . . . no longer cliff, or mountain, just gravel at your feet. . . ."

"Then let me wash you deeper out to my sea, and pull you under with this tidal wave that's approaching . . . oh, God, Trevor . . ."

As he went under with her, he could not speak. Her voice had convulsed him, and all that was between them were the sounds of their breathing.

Although he came back to the surface, he had done so too quickly, for the momentary release caused an ache in his soul like the bends. He needed to hold her, to touch her face and stroke her hair. This expanse of technology between them could never replace what he'd found in her arms. He needed more than sexual relief; he needed her.

"I'm comin' over," he said, standing with effort and

walking in a circle like a caged lion at the zoo. "I cannot deal wit dis."

"You can't," she panted. "I will just cause family—"

"I am coming over there, I said, woman. I will fall on my knees, beg my sister's forgiveness, if I have to," he said, grabbing his pants. "I will take her to the hairdresser, wait in line while she goes shopping for herself . . . hire a nanny . . . but this mornin', I am comin' over dere. I have to."

He was pulling his shirt over his head and stooping to find his shoes, and almost dropped the phone twice, then he glanced at the clock and it dawned upon him . . . it was almost eleven o'clock, and it was Sunday. He sat down heavily on the bed, still unable to zipper his pants even after the eruption.

"Church," he groaned. "I didn't wake up in time. She's gone."

"Oh, no," Corey's voice groaned into his ear in a way that made him want to pet it.

"Oh, baby . . . baby . . ." he sighed, collapsing backward on the bed again and shutting his eyes tight. "I promised her," he whispered, hearing the full brood move about in earnest now that his dream state had been altered.

"I knew it wasn't right . . . but I got blinded by . . . oh, God, *Trevor,* we should have never started this mess on the telephone."

Her voice came into his ear in a thick emulsion of defeated want, and the very vibration of it smothered his judgment.

"Yeah . . . now I gotta do laundry," he conceded in a weary chuckle. "The linens didn't make it through the storm."

"Oh, baby," she crooned, low and easy. "I wish I could have taken the brunt of that storm in your bed."

Somehow the mental image she'd just conjured had returned his desire with a vengeance. Feeling her pull even more than before, he grasped at straws. "Why don't you come over here?" he murmured back on a labored bass note. "Just for a little while . . . it will only take a little while."

"What?" she said, chuckling, not as sexily as she had earlier.

"Come ride on my sled. . . ." he pleaded. "Oh, girl, I'm not making any sense, am I? This telephone thing is messin' wit me. . . . That won't work, will it?"

"No," she said, laughing tenderly, but her voice had lost some of its previous deep resonance of passion.

"You're comin' out of your stupor faster than I am. Slap me, woman, please just slap me. . . . I am only a man, and I'm still jonesin' for you hard, girl."

Her rippling laughter only made matters worse, and he kept his eyes shut tight as he spoke to her. "How do you all do it? What instinct is in your makeup that allows you to go from insane to rational in such short order? Is it the ting dat makes women able to hear a baby cry when they're sound asleep? Or is it the ting dat makes her hear a child walkin' down da hall, when her lover is wearing her out in midstroke? Or could it be," he mused, chuckling as he said it, "that mysterious ting dat makes you able to predict the outcome of any situation?"

She laughed with him in an amiable way that made him groggy as the burn she'd caused began to ebb.

"I'll never tell of the secrets held within the chamber of women, silly man," she said, giggling. "That would give you all the upper hand, and you wouldn't know what to do with such power."

"You're so right," he murmured, her voice now warm balm—healing, mineral, and smooth. "My buddies who have small children at home have tol' me about witnessing such mysteries of the universe. . . . Many others went on quests to find the Water Oracle, only to return blind, crippled, and stupid. . . . Some never came back at all."

Now her laugh was bold and deep, and it stirred a

rumbling laughter up from his own core. He loved her voice. . . .

"What is your anecdote, siren, tribe of female, creator of life? Your secret, lady . . . share it with me, please, before I drown? Just between us, since we're now so familiar. Do you know of whom I speak, clear pond? I am on a journey, of sorts, questing for the Water Oracle, and as I stand by your pool, I'm wondering if you might be her?"

"Love," she whispered, her voice having returned to its original husky octave, but now he could hear a new thread of tender flute that replaced the saxophone desire previously in it.

"Tell me this anecdote," he murmured, finding a subtle peace beginning to wash over him.

"It's about caring more for someone than yourself, Trevor . . . knowing that because you exist, someone else can live . . . and it's because you know down in your cellular memory that, if even one generation before you had broken the chain, then creation itself would stop. Life as we know it would cease," she whispered like water evaporating after the summer rain. "That's what's happened in our society. Life as we knew it has ceased."

"How do we get that back?" he asked, stone serious now. "Talk to me, my oracle, and tell me what to do . . . from your woman's point of view."

She let out her breath slowly, and he held his in reverent anticipation.

"From a long-ago concept that has been nearly forgotten, our anecdote of love was simple, oh, wander with questions. A woman would carry that DNA of creation memory between her legs. It would stop her from willingly lying down with anyone who without love could steal a generation from her belly. . . . Men fought wars over love, history was changed because of love, and it was serious magic that women owned. And we gave away our amulets of love wholesale. The gift of prophecy was love, and that used to make us crystal clear about what we wanted for the future generations within us . . ."

"How was that gift of prophecy so employed?" he asked, stunned, as though hearing some of the words his mother used to say, and his grandmother used to clip off in parables, all converging in the modern woman on the telephone now.

"We used to hear what hadn't been said, and know that a child was going to cry before it did. We predicted family disasters before they struck, and we dreamt of fish when someone was pregnant. We were our sisters' keepers, and the keepers of more children than our own. We could shake off momentary passion for a higher cause—because we had the past, present, and future to consider—to love. And we bonded in tribes of female support and comfort, and in love of our sisters, too, we created villages for all the children, and we would excommunicate any male who violated our marriages—and we had one another's backs."

"My sister just told me that this morning, not in so many words. . . ."

Awe stole his voice as the image that she designed in his ear made colors come into focus. Snaps of raw footage rewound and then replayed in his head, and his breath was halted by the significance of what she'd said. Indeed, he'd been given the rare privilege of sipping at the deep ponds of female knowledge . . . twice he'd sipped in one day.

"Oracle," he murmured with reverence, "what do you see when you look at me?"

"I see such great potential that saved itself from being squandered," she murmured, sounding as though she were a myth. "I see a father now developing into a man who my womb could honor with life one day. . . ."

Her voice trailed off and became silent, and he begged her to continue.

"Don' turn away from the vision . . . talk to me, and tell me what it is that you really want."

"What you have all around you . . . family. Children. A place to lay my head and feel secure. Laughter, passion, and trust above all else . . . and respect, hope, and a shoulder to share my sorrows. And a lap to curl up in a fetal position in when I'm defeated and a pair of strong hands to applaud with me in mutual joy. . . . And a home that is a sanctuary against all of the ugliness in the world. I'm too old and too tired to tell you anything other than the truth. You said no games, Trevor, and I believed you. Drink from that fountain of honesty."

"I was afraid, at first that I might be tricked by a fast-moving river, as I had been before. There was so much at stake, and I journeyed with a small child this time, so my route and passage had to be safe. Then I stopped from fatigue, and looked into your pool, Water Oracle," he whispered, "and I was led there by Fate, weary from travel, devastated by loss, and consumed with guilt, yet I had begun a quest. . . . So Fate, as a woman, and in her infinite mercy, was the one who told me through riddle that you had been the primordial ocean, the first and only one for me. . . . Your eyes said you were immortal, and that you had seen the entire world at its birth. Original art—creation."

"How would you know that so soon?" she asked in a forlorn, faraway voice.

"I watched you cradle my son against your breast as you taught him my own craft better than I ever could, and you bestowed calm upon a household of chaos, just as you quell classrooms. Daily, you give young minds a drink of sweet water, and can wage storms out of control when enraged, and then turn to level a man with a wave of passion . . . your water, running so deep, can go so still. And your shores are wide enough for generations of children, and families are sustained by your well of kindness that never runs dry. And you gave this weary traveler safe harbor after he respected the bitter sip of your truth. Then you washed down said good medicine with a hot passion still uncharted. I knew you were the one, Corey. I knew you were not a fraud."

"Oh, Trevor . . ."

The emotion that he heard swell in her voice made his own brittle as it cracked, but he pressed on.

"I knew that I'd toppled into your depths when just intending to bend and take a sip. That first night in the car, leaning over the edge of my own oblivion, I knew your depths were limitless, and that I could not swim out of you once I reached your undertow. So I grabbed on to the edge of your shore, and held myself back that first night . . . and I watched you ebb away from me with a sad smile, shaking your head, knowing how futile my death throes would be once I jumped in.

"And then, like a fool, I came back . . . drawn by something beyond my own will . . . power stripped from me like it is right now, because I had taken one quick sip. . . . I stared into your eyes, and I sipped the cool water of truth. And you reflected back to me what I have always wanted."

"This has to be real. . . ." she said, sniffing. "I can't crash against another false cliff."

Her voice broke him, and it made his arms ache harder to reach out and touch her, his words becoming his hands to reach across the space between them.

"You have seeped into every crevice of who I am . . . you have filled me up and overtaken me. There is no stronger force on the planet than water, and water is inside of every living organism on it. That is why I say you are water. There is no escape from it, and without it you die. Nothing can contain it, nothing can stop it, it can be airborne and evaporate, then seem to disappear, but then suddenly gather itself and rain down upon you. . . . It is collected in clouds, and snow at the highest apex of mountains. It was here at the beginning. . . . Don't you know who you are?"

"No," she whispered sadly. "I'm not sure anymore."

"Corey, woman is water, for she seems to yield and bend to the whims of male hardness, but she erodes it with time and persistence and turns it into fertile soil so that trees can grow, and life on the planet can regenerate itself. It is the cup that runneth over, because it cannot contain such a gift. Precious gift of my life, can't you see any of that?"

He could hear her breathing, but she had not spoken, and his fist clenched as his soul became sand for her.

"Woman, you have eroded the hard edges and ground me into smooth surface. I was once immovable granite, now I'm willing to make way for the new current of you in my life. . . . Do you hear what the earth at your edge is saying to you, baby? You safely carried my son to my shores—back to me. That I can never repay, Water Oracle of my soul. . . . Then you washed me back to myself, returned the little scattered pieces of me at my feet so that I could pick them up, and reintegrate them into the battered coastline of my life. You did that, just now, with your reflected truth and confession about what you wanted . . . and it makes me know that I must again jump in and be overcome by what I was too afraid to say only moments ago . . . I'm in love with you, Corey Hamilton. Jus' like dat, I drowned."

Tears fell from the corners of her tightly closed eyes, and no additional words were exchanged. A river of remembered disappointments and hopes too precious to describe suddenly released itself and streamed down her cheeks. A sob erupted in building waves, crashing against her esophagus, making her vocal cords echo as hurt washed up to her mouth. And he cooed to her and hushed her through the telephone as she curled up into a little ball and wept, knowing that the sound of his voice had become her new medium.

Fifteen

Three weeks had gone by in a veritable blur, to his surprise. As Trevor sat in the quiet confines of his studio facing the Avid, he had to admit the children's project had absolutely riveted him to the work in a way that he'd never imagined it could.

Although day one of physical withdrawal from Corey Hamilton had been the most difficult, when he'd finally accepted the fact that he was indeed captive to the entire family, just as Corey had predicted, oddly a change of focus had made it easier to deal. He was in recovery; though no longer a junkie, he still and always would be an addict.

Studying the rough cut as he let sections of the documentary play back before him, he also had to admit that he was truly impressed with the students' work from a professional standpoint. In a week, they had developed a rough storyboard, and Sam had done wonders with them in coming up with narrative script. Their artwork was exquisite, and he was getting as much pleasure from pulling together the last threads of the making of the project, as he was from doing the actual project itself. *The Way It Is* was going to be a hit. The title was simple, raw, and on target.

He chuckled to himself as he thought about how Janelle and Scott had flooded the basement nightly with hip-hop, self-made original tracks, as well as what seemed like half the neighborhood. It amazed him how the young people took so adeptly to the equipment, and what a difference their involvement in the creative process had made on them in other areas.

His studio had literally become the neighborhood hangout spot, if not the local recreation center for teens, and the sheer noise level, frenetic activity, and endless food-supply runs alone were enough to send him to bed every night too tired to think about anything else. Even his dreams were permeated with their images, instead of the ones of Corey that used to wear him out.

Power 99 and 103.9 FM radio-station music nearly rocked him out of bed seven days a week, and bass notes coming up from the basement practically moved furniture across the floor—and that was more than enough to chase encounters with her out of his brain. But he loved it. They had created a vibe within his space, and the project literally fed off of it as though it had taken on a life form of its own—the music did that.

Many nights, he had to simply surrender to adult fatigue and turn over the basement to the kids, who would not be moved. He knew what it felt like to be on the verge of a creative breakthrough and to want to just finish one more little aspect . . . which then turned into hours that slipped by one unaware, almost like a thief stealing one's sleep.

Per Gretchen's advice, he'd compiled a list of parents' telephone numbers, which were posted on the studio corkboard, as well as his refrigerator. Like a proverbial camp counselor, he kept a stash of extra blankets, pillows and multiple jumbo boxes of cereal and cartons of milk on hand.

Just as Corey told him, he had built it, and they had come . . . flocking like moths to a positive flame, and he was satisfied. Somehow in all of this, he also was surprised to get parent calls—people thanking him for doing something good with their kids, thanking him for giving them, as parents, a stress break. His studio soon became a passport to childhood freedom, because if a child said they were with Mr. Trevor, then it was all right for them not to be home.

And, as Corey also wisely predicted, in their numerous laughter-filled telephone calls at night, that was the best part of it all. It felt so good way down in his bones. Talking about the project, the latest development, what some kid said or did, now added layer and texture to their conversations, which were no longer one-dimensionally focused on the subject that could not be addressed.

It was as though they both sensed that to dwell on it would make them drown in it, so it was better to keep what they had to say to each other light and project-directed.

After a while, somewhere between heavy activity, no personal space to become morose about what he couldn't do, and fatigue, he'd been able to stop allowing his mind to careen into delicious thoughts of being with Corey. It would have been a fruitless mental exercise anyway, given that her after-school visits to the studio were always heavily chaperoned by five small fifth graders and several teenage crew coaches.

It was indeed a wonderful process, watching her work. She had broken her fifteen students down into three groups of five, each team working on either the beginning, middle, or end of the project—with special assignments like art, music, or graphics given out to small specialty crews. Each week, one of the groups got to film its segment, every child taking a turn to shoot raw footage, then edit. It had made for some hilarious moments, as two carloads of kids scrambled about and barked orders so they could get their shots.

The format of the piece was excellent, and Trevor had to take his hat off to Samantha for the genius of it. She had taken Corey's teaching focus of creating stories with beginnings, middles, and ends to another level. The college student had brilliantly translated the concept so that the children could develop their project to begin with statements of how they saw their world, then segue to questions they had about their world, and end the piece with solutions they thought could solve the issues and questions. And he loved the way they blended mediums—crude animation, black-and-white film, stop-frame close-ups of the stills, and both Beta and DV video—in a colliding pattern.

Theirs was a mastery of collage at its finest. And their voices . . . so pure . . . and juxtaposed against the heavy urban music. All he could say was "wow," as he sat back in wonder.

His part of the process was just to supervise and add refinement. But even the rough spots were definitions that he didn't want to cut out. That was the hardest part of it all, because each child's sequence of footage could have been a beautiful project unto itself. Now he understood why parents saved refrigerator art, and despite the expense of keeping every kernel of what they'd shot, he could not bear to tape over it. He'd just keep the kids stocked with film, he thought, scanning a segment, and allowing the children's perspectives to pour over him.

"Look at this . . . just look at this . . ." he murmured to himself, becoming mesmerized by the insights they'd captured. He could only stare agape at some of the sequences. How in the world was he going to cut this down to fit the television one-hour format that really wasn't a full hour, and that required sponsor or commercial bumper interruptions?

Oh, yes . . . this was going on National Public Television. This was going to go down to Washington, D.C. And he was determined to get it up to Martha's Flava Fest during August at the Black Film Festival in Martha's Vineyard. He might even be able to wrangle it into the Sundance Film Festival, especially since the organization had just opened an arm in Philly. Locally, he could get it shown at the Painted Bride and the Prinz Theater. . . . Oh, definitely. This could work.

When he looked at what one of the little girls had shot, he just shook his head, becoming reverent. She'd done a segment on being home alone and feeling afraid. She'd employed a technique that graduate film students would have missed. Subtly, she made the space look like it was closing in on her as the room got dimmer from the loss of natural light, and she spoke about her fears from a tightly framed space in the house. It was spectacular. He was glad that Corey had backed up the child's decision not to use additional lights . . . and the way she'd shot the sun going down, and how darkness closed in on her as she waited for someone to come home. "Breathtaking . . ."

His voice trailed off with an ever increasing level of respect as another child focused on dolls and showed what had happened to her friend. Then another child did a montage of transportation that he had to take, and showed all of the urban decay he walked past just to get to school. But they had also captured funny, happy moments, and he'd convinced them to pepper those glimpses of joy among the more poignant points to give harsher contrasts. He hoped they'd like the cut he was now laying down, and he found himself actually feeling nervous and wanting their approval of how he'd arranged their work. The funny thing was that he was just as nervous about their reaction as he would have been if he had to show it to real industry artists. Yeah, he was into it.

Then he looked at his own son's work and had to stop it down frame by frame. "A natural," he whispered with unabashed pride, as he looked at the shot groupings Miquel had explored with his lens.

With Scott's help, Miquel had obviously taken his camera to the local high school on a rogue shoot away from the group, and had zoomed in on older boys smoking and exchanging money. "Man, kid . . . you went *60 Minutes* on us. . . ." He was proud, but the risk of it all slightly unnerved him.

Trevor made a mental note to use special effects to blur out faces. Not cool. "Must teach him subject-matter etiquette in makin' docs," he whispered out loud to the empty room. Then he sat back. "You go, boy . . . you got lens instinct!"

He laughed as he watched footage of a teen couple necking behind the staircase, and the shot Miquel had taken was low to the floor and scanned up the girl's behind. Okay, he could salvage that by simply trimming the shot before it got to the two engrossed lovers' heads. But he felt his heart slam against his rib cage as a teen opened his jacket and showed off a gun, then zipped it up and dismissed the cameraman with a middle-finger salute.

Trevor sat back and stopped the decks from rolling. Obviously Scott had escorted Miquel past some of this as they gathered additional shots without the aid of the teacher, but he could tell that Scott had left Miquel to creep around and get some of that footage alone. He didn't like it. The dangers of getting beat up for taking shots of the wrong stuff were too great, and even seasoned photojournalists got themselves into jams. Experience echoed in his brain. Sometimes pointing the camera at the wrong person at the wrong time could create issues that a fifth grader definitely wasn't ready to handle. He'd have to speak to Scott about it. But the footage *was* good.

Ever the entrepreneur, Trevor studied the piece, as the business side of his brain reflexively opened a new mental shutter. What if he did enter the project into some of the major film festivals, and even got it over to Canada and Cannes and the kids won something? That could possibly attract foundation funding for the school to set up a student-run, nonprofit production company in earnest. That way they could obtain their own equipment, and maybe some of the more expensive entry-level animation and graphics systems. What he was looking at was too good to be a one-shot deal for the kids. This had potential, and he couldn't wait until their premiere at the International House, when the children would get an opportunity to unveil it for the school, their parents, and the community.

There was a lot of postproduction still to do, he noted, feeling his shoulders begin to ache. He had to pull together a press release, book the venues, get the wrap party for the kids together—as they really deserved a great one after all of their hard work. It was mid-May, which meant he had about four weeks until the end of their school year. He'd talk it over with Corey to make sure that everything synced up, and that he also didn't overburden her, or conflict with her end-of-the-year administrative tasks that had to be accomplished as well.

Trevor stood, walked over to the darkroom, and began selecting still photos. Arranging them, he tried to work on a collection that he could reshoot into posters, and then have reduced into flyers and other promotional materials that could serve multiple purposes. There had to be a way. Maybe he'd call his attorney to see if he could help the school get the paperwork done on the company setup. . . . He then immediately set the thought aside and decided to do that later. He was immersed now, and had taken his cell phone and beeper off-line for anyone but the project team. Calling his lawyer or his agent to help would simply bring him back up on availability radar . . . then the calls would start coming, and he'd have to make a final decision.

Abandoning the photo selection challenge, he walked back to his editing bay much more slowly. What was he going to do, in all reality? Okay, so he'd taken a month-long hiatus, and had talked to people, telling them that he needed some space to work on a personal project. In his heart, he knew that the industry was familiar with artists taking a breather, and his colleagues had been cool about what they believed to be his short break. But he'd neglected to draw a firm line. He hadn't actually told people he was out of the game for good—because he hadn't actually come up with an alternative yet that could feed the beast of bills. That was real.

Switching tapes, he allowed himself the moment he needed to clear his head and brush away the sensation of going stale on the children's work. He'd been looking at it for hours, and he'd kept his focus on it in the rare peace that his sanctuary now offered. Normally it would be jam-packed with teens sprawled out in amusing combinations of sleeping configurations, with some working intently as they polished their piece. Or Corey would be down there directing traffic. But with a Friday-night spring school dance going on, it had become a ghost town.

Gretchen would be coming home soon from her graveyard shift, he noted, and would probably relish the quiet—even though he was sure he would oddly miss the hubbub of activity that had enriched his life and his space. The silence that engulfed him at the moment, however, was a gift that he would not squander with sleep, especially having had so little time and privacy to work on the personal project of his own.

As the tape advanced, the new montage of images made him smile from deep within. He'd call it "Water," and would give it to Corey once they did have some time alone together.

Trevor touched the soundboard without looking at it. Bringing up the levels on the audio, he layered in the ripple of a brook, low in the background, to match the timbre of her giggle. Perfect. All of the video of her directing the children as they worked had given him a wealth of her laughter, her sighs, her praises, and closeups. Frame by frame he watched her and selected the most discreet tilts of her head, captured the way she bit down on her lower lip when thinking, and how her graceful fingers unwittingly trailed back and forth across her collarbone as she was studying something that held her interest.

"Magnificent . . ." he murmured as he layered music and water sound effects under and around her. Selecting his best clips of excess footage he'd collected in his journeys, he located every natural wonder that he'd shot and overlaid them into the piece. Then he found it. The shot that had stayed in his mind for nearly a month; her standing in front of her classroom, leaning back on her desk with a shy smile and her legs crossed at the ankles.

He sat back in his chair and slowed down the tape, making it stream by in a languid visual effect. He remembered the day that he'd captured her in her natural state. She'd been attentively listening to one of the children, and he'd been in the back of the classroom. Then the sun had cooperated as the clouds had shifted, and brilliant light backlit her, giving her a halo. Her soft curls glistened and she began that lazy trace of her fingers, and she tilted her head just so, then the sun overtook her cheek in a golden wash that caught in her eyes.

She was spectacular in that light, and then she looked up at him, and became shy when she realized that he was taping her. That was the look. The demure, semismile that she'd cast his way briefly as her gaze slid away from him. And then a student had said something funny that had shocked and amused her, and she'd closed her eyes, and thrown her head back to laugh.

But the way he'd captured that instant, she could have been laughing or gasping, depending on the edit. He sat there for a long time with the frame frozen, looking at the image, trying to decide the sound of her that he wanted to match to it. The process of thinking about how he would bring her out of that pose made him choose a gasp that he lifted and entered into the background of a waterfall. Then he layered a special effect over that to dissolve her image into a still pond, and brought a closeup of her eyes as a translucent overlay to the pool. His fingers pushed the button, running the sound decks back and forth until he found a part of her speaking voice that said his name.

Connecting the elements, he replayed the short ten minutes of her with all of the sequences loaded, turning up the volume and leaning back in his chair. And when it faded to black on the sound of a wave, he shuddered and stopped the tape.

"Now, baby, *that's* a wrap," he whispered, closing his eyes to the sensations that barreled against his groin. A month of being oblivious, too busy, and project-focused evaporated, leaving him to remember that he'd always be in a state of recovery from his Corey Hamilton addiction.

Winding back the video, he dubbed a copy of it onto a clean tape and took his time to label it—his hands barely able to hold the pen. The footsteps on the outside stairs overhead helped him decide to leave the studio, lest he fall into a reverie that would cause him to backslide. But as he made his way up to the first-floor unit, somehow his legs propelled him up to the second floor.

Gretchen was taking off her light raincoat, and she stopped and smiled at him as he stood before her nearly paralyzed.

"You're working late," she said pleasantly. "Got a whole brood down there and need some more food?"

He couldn't speak, and he just shook his head.

His sister stared at him in the dim hall light, and then cocked her head to one side.

"Trevor," she asked in a voice of concern, "everything all right?"

"Can I talk to you in the kitchen?" he requested hoarsely. "I just need to talk."

She gave him a puzzled look laced with worry and nodded as she withdrew from the hall and he followed her into the kitchen. She then pulled out a chair very slowly, mercifully neglecting to switch on the overhead lights as she sat down.

"Nothin' bad has happened, has it?" she asked in a half plea. "The kids?"

"They're fine," he murmured back, then looked down at the tape in his hands.

"Then Trevor, what is it? What's da matter . . . you look like somebody just died."

His gaze met hers and held it, but her face immediately blurred from the moisture in his eyes that he fought to hold back.

"I'm losing my mind," he whispered. "I need to go out . . . alone, and have some space."

Her worried expression slowly transformed into a tender smile. "I know," she said softly, considering the tape in his hands. "I've seen the way you look at her, and the way she looks at you. And I'm not blind. You filmed her, too, didn't you?"

He closed his eyes, swallowed hard, and nodded, not able to immediately respond.

"There's something more," he finally murmured, unable to look at his sister as he did so, choosing the window as his focal point. "I also want to bring her here—to my domain, my space, my castle," he admitted, then returned his gaze to his sister's face. "I want to take her out to a nice dinner, and give her roses, and wine. I want to let her dress up, and then take her to one of the finest restaurants in town. Then I want to be able to bring her home without scrutiny, and to light candles with her and play soft jazz for her as she sits on the sofa next to me. . . . And where does this paradise exist for a man and a woman who have more than fifteen children at the schools, four live-in children always under foot, and an entire community watching?"

He saw the smile on his sister's face broaden, and he could feel his lungs collapsing as he waited for her reaction.

"Well," she began in a painfully slow drawl. "I'd say

that if a man has made up for lost time by mindin' half of the neighborhood's children . . . and such a man has been a proper gentleman, and wants to take his courtin' to the next level . . . and if he has paid his dues with respect and honor to this lady friend who makes him hurt so bad he has tears in his eyes for her, yet he's man enough to be takin' his time and being consistent and not playin' games . . . then . . . well . . . maybe there's enough mothers indebted from all of his civic service to give him a free night."

"You think so?" he blurted out quickly in a way that made her chuckle.

"Nothin' to it," she quipped. "We mothers spot one another all the time. You just couldn't get no quarter from us before because you hadn't paid into the babysittin' network. Can't make a withdrawal unless you've made a deposit."

His heart was slamming against his breastbone so hard that it made him lean forward with his forearms on his knees. Then he sucked in a deep breath and let it out hard as relief allowed his shoulders to drop a few inches.

"That bad, huh?" his sister said, laughing merrily, teasing him to no end.

Trevor nodded, too relieved to care that she laughed.

"But," he stammered, "what about . . . I mean . . . I don't want them . . . the logistics of it . . ."

"Listen," Gretchen said in a tender tone that was still filled with mirth. When he looked up, she wrapped her hands around his that held the tape. "I don' know what you got in your hands, but it's makin' dem shake."

This time he chuckled and closed his eyes briefly before returning her gaze.

"So it makes me know that we've gotta be real direct with the children, and I'm going to have to leave strict instructions with my girlfriends."

Again she laughed at him as confusion tore through his brain and mortification settled into his bones in a way she'd obviously detected. He could not make this a public display. Never.

"Calm down," she ordered with a smile. "I wouldn't explain the fine points of what will probably happen on that fateful night out," she added with a sly wink. "I'll be firm and tell the children the half-truth, the only part they need to know at their age—that their Uncle Trevor, and father, has a really important date with someone he truly has come to like. And I'll tell them that you've spent a lot of time with them, so it's now time for the adults in question to go out and have some peace and quiet. Since you actually have spent quality time with the kids, they'll begrudgingly acquiesce—or I'll kill 'em."

"God bless you. . . ."

"Then I'll explain that said peace means they should also respect your privacy, and not be up and down the stairs—or be calling you for dumb stuff on your phone, or having their friends stop by unannounced, because you need a little much-deserved quiet time. Then I'll ship them off to their friends' houses for an overnight visit . . . so that your dignity will be intact in the morning. I'll also call in my aces with a few trusted girlfriends, and will explain in the code of mothers that I'm having company—so don't send them kids home until late afternoon. And because all *m'girls* have been in mommy boot camp, we know what that means, and we know how to lock down our troops, and it's a done deal—honor among single moms."

He could only stare at her for a moment.

"You hadn't earned it from us before." She laughed, taking in his expression. "And if you hadn't been nearly starved to death, you wouldn't have appreciated what a gift this is from us. That's why I wouldn't do this for you before. So now, when one of us calls you, you'll respond to the love-starved, nerve-shattered, parental cry for help like you was a marine in the parents' network military—with no questions asked, no excuses, no cancellations, and never leavin' your own. Your butt will hop to it and salute the support system. You've been drafted. Do you read me, soldier?"

Sitting up in his chair tall, a smile broke onto his face, and he issued his sister a mock salute. "Ma'am, yes, ma'am. Reportin' for duty, ma'am. Very humbly requestin' shore leave, ma'am. A-S-A-P, ma'am. Needin' to get out of the house in the worst kinda way, ma'am. *Forever* in service to you, ma'am."

"At ease, soldier." She chuckled warmly, giving him a phony return salute.

"You know it's gonna take me a few phone calls to arrange all dis. May have to give you your walking papers next weekend—"

"—Sis," he cut in quickly, growing frantic, losing his previous cheer. "You can't pull in anything faster than dat? What about Miss Cleo . . . or—"

"Don't panic," she said, giggling. "So this is an emergency outage, and you have to get her back to base camp yesterday."

Embarrassed, he hung his head. "Well, I could . . . yeah, no, I'm cool. Next weekend is cool. I got a lotta edits to do, anyway."

"But . . . you can't think, and you can't work—if you can't see straight, therefore—for the sake of the project you're working on, if I must, I could probably give you a premo Saturday night, like tomorrow . . . but that's a substantial withdrawal from the favor bank—"

"You think you could arrange it?" he asked and stood up so fast that he almost toppled the chair, then began pacing. "I'll replenish the favor checking account with interest," he promised, trying not to babble, "if you'll just extend me a loan. . . . Gretchen, dear heart, I'm beggin' you as your brother. . . ."

"And you're not plannin' to jump on some plane and whisk yourselves out of the city, are you? Remember, I know you . . . as my brother, which don't help your credit ratin' none wit me, so—"

"Zanzibar Blue—it's right in Center City, right downtown on the Avenue of the Arts—you think that's a good place, right? I can probably get reservations—then again, they could be booked. I gotta clean up, get some laundry done. Get to the florist, and stop by the State Store—the wine, and—"

"—if tomorrow's too soon, you know, I could just tell my friends to hold off until you get your arrangements set," she said, smiling as she studied her nails.

"No, no . . . I'll work it out on my end." He stood there looking at her, trying to check his breathing.

"Whoo-boy," Gretchen said, laughing. "This does not wear well on a man."

He ignored the comment and tried his best to be patient and stay as respectful and humble as possible, lest his sister change her mind. She was yanking with him hard, he was powerless, and she made bones about it—she loved it, he could tell. He knew that his only option was to wait for her decree.

"Have you even called her yet to see if she might be available, before I go to all the trouble to look in my phone book for this hefty favor?"

Gretchen dangled the carrot of hope before him and smiled with mischief.

"No," he said quietly, new worry now entering his skull. What if she had plans? Truly, he'd never considered that, and it vexed him no end right now. "I think she'll be able to get away," he finally said in an unsure voice, attempting to recover his dignity.

Again, Gretchen's smile widened, and she shook her head. "I imagine that she will. Okay," she said in a now weary voice. "I'm going to ship the kids as far to the other side of town as I can. Miss Cleo is not an option, because she'd be way deep in your bizness, and the kids would be too close to home, which could represent a possible security breach. But I do have a few rules," she added, giving him a smirk.

"Yeah . . . okay . . . shoot," he issued back quickly, hope allowing him to breathe again.

"Rule number one," she said with a knowing smile. "Although there will be no children in the house, keep the volume down—as to keep your personal bizness to yourselves."

He couldn't even look at her as his face burned with humiliation.

"Rule number two. Bed check is at fifteen hundred hours, three o'clock in the afternoon on Sunday—which means that you have to be back at base, she must be back on civilian territory, and all evidence of your shore leave has to be cleaned up, stashed away, and the place has to be spotless . . . so when the children come home, they're none the wiser."

This time he looked at his sister and nodded with much respect. "Yeah. Okay. You're absolutely right. I can dig it. You've got my word on that. Done."

"Then," Gretchen said, standing and pecking him on the cheek with a kiss as she moved toward the door to go to bed, "request granted."

As she sauntered away from him and slipped into her room, he leaned against the door-frame with an outstretched arm and let his breath out hard in relief. No wonder nobody could hook up and find their soul mate. All of this to simply go out? Subterfuge, espionage, city maps of child travel routes, exit strategies, allied forces, surprise strikes, favor pacts, United Nations summits to lift an embargo and let a shipment come in . . . Man . . . it was like planning a major campaign. . . . No wonder Gretchen wouldn't go through all of this on a chance reconnaissance pass through a club. If a single parent were smart, she'd save up her heavy ground-strike artillery for the real thing, and only deploy it once there was a verified lock on the target.

"Thanks, till the end of time," he hollered down the hall behind her, and continued to shake his head, amazed.

Sixteen

The last several hours had gone by in stagnant, slow increments of the clock's hands inching forward. After hearing Corey's squeal of delight and her acceptance to join him on a real date, all of the dashing around in the world couldn't burn off his nervous energy—especially once he'd returned from the jewelers with gem-replicated water in his hands.

He'd run errands and cleaned like a madman to get things prepared for her visit, and even hollered at the kids not to come down into his lair while he worked. Nonplussed, his son had lost interest in the military inspection-level shine Trevor was trying to put on the house, and had left to find something more fun to do on the second floor. When was their pickup coming?

But with the hour of freedom approaching and everything he could have possibly thought of to do taken care of, Trevor had to pull himself together and figure out how to put his best foot forward in his date's eyes.

There had not been enough push-ups and sit-ups in the world to shake her out of his system. A month of agony, of trying to exercise her out of his system, trying to forget about how she made him feel . . .

Standing in the middle of his bedroom floor freshly showered in his robe, he stared at the options in his closet. Although he'd done this hundreds of times before without hesitation, for some reason selecting an outfit was causing him unnecessary angst. It was a date, for chrissake—not the Emmy Awards! He had to pull it together; this didn't make sense.

Trevor looked toward the doorway and groaned as he heard a set of fast feet coming downstairs. Judging from the weight of the thuds, it had to be Scott.

"Yo, dude," Scott said with a wide grin, barging into the room without asking for permission to come in. "The moment of truth," the teenager said, laughing. He almost flopped on the bed, then stopped himself, catching the warning glare Trevor cast in his direction, glancing at the pristine surface of it, and punching himself in the chest. "My bad, brother. My *serious* bad."

"Knock it off, Scott. What do you want? Can't you see I'm trying to get dressed and get out of here?"

"I see you standin' in the middle of the floor in your robe, dude, lookin' like you in a quand'ry. Let me hook a brother up," Chuckling, Scott sauntered over to Trevor's closet and slid the hangers across the bar.

"I don't need a valet," Trevor snapped, becoming testy, even though Scott's offer to help did begin to take root.

"I know you don't need nobody to drive you over there." Scott grinned, totally missing the point and the meaning of the word. "Been a long time since you had to go the full distance, and pull out all dese stops, ain't it?"

Scott had asked the rhetorical question with his back turned to Trevor as he considered a selection, and Trevor was glad that he didn't have to feel compelled to shrug it off in a verbal response.

"Where you takin' her?" the teenager asked nonchalantly.

"My bizness is my bizness, and you're making me late."

"Okay, I can dig it. Top shelf it is, judgin' from your response. Hmmmm," Scott mused, seeming not the least bit offended—or about to budge. "Oh, here it is," he said, laughing. *"Here it is.* I got you, boss . . . the Armani." He swished the suit out like he was selling it to Trevor. "Oh, dis is *da bomb,* bro. The ultimate, knock-her-off-her-feet threads!"

Going against every gut instinct he had, Trevor found himself taking the suit from the youth's hands and studying it hard. "You think so?"

As soon as he'd asked the question, he knew that he'd never get Scott out of there. It had opened the door for a while-you-get-dressed-overstay-my-welcome visit.

"Think so?" Scott replied in a huff. "You goin' for broke, right—den act like you know!"

"I'm not goin' for—"

"Pleeease." Scott sighed, turning back to the closet. "You don't be cleaning, changin' sheets, running up and down the steps with dozens of roses, and bringin' in bags from the State Store to go on some nice little dinner date, like Mom tried to tell me and Jan—"

"Aw'right, aw'right, look, dude, you workin' my nerves, I got places to go, and, things to—"

"Chill. We peace. I ain't tellin' your bizness to Miquel, or the females upstairs. Besides, you need to get your hookup together, so you be righteous. She good people. I like Miss Corey. She aw'ight wit me."

Before Trevor could respond, Scott had reached into his closet and snatched out another selection.

"Here you go, *boooyie.* . . . The dope combo. Aw'ight, feel me . . . black Armani suit, wit da gun-metal-gray silk shirt, and the monochrome matchin' tie, then play the black Gucci belt, and hook it up wit da black square-toe Gucci lace-ups. . . . Yeeaaah."

Scott had neatly flung the combination across the bed like a Beverly Hills boutique-commissioned personal shopper, then he stood back, folded his arms, and beamed. "You gotta let me borrow some of your rags sometime, Unc. You *got* the threads. You need to play 'em more, boss."

Trevor ignored the request to pillage his closet as he appraised Scott's selection carefully, and he had to admit that the teenager had done in five minutes what had taken him more than half an hour to do—make a decision.

"That could work," Trevor admitted in a low mutter, nodding and walking over to pick up the shirt to put it on.

"The Hugo," Scott nodded toward Trevor's dresser, while leaning on the frame of the closet door. "Total package. Gotta smell right. You did put on deodorant, right?"

With much less resistance, Trevor walked toward the dresser and put on a healthy slap of cologne, and again ignored the secondary ridiculous teenage question about his hygiene.

"Now, don't you feel better?" Scott asked with a chuckle and a wink.

"Aw'right, thanks, man," Trevor conceded on a deep exhale as he continued to get dressed.

"It's gonna be cool, you know," Scott said with an encouraging tone. "She already crazy 'bout chu, all of us know that."

For the first time since Scott had come down to disturb his peace, Trevor stopped what he was doing and considered his young nephew's words. A silent new understanding passed between them as they smiled at each other with respect. Odd how circumstance changed things. . . . Here he was the elder, but the younger of the two men in the room had come down to give him support and encouragement as though he were going to a prom.

Trevor extended his fist for Scott to punch it in solidarity.

"You're all right, man," Trevor said warmly, putting extra emphasis on the word *man*.

The pride-filled smile that Scott returned said it all, and then both of them chuckled and looked away.

"I told you, I got chure back."

"Yeah," Trevor grinned, feeling more relaxed as he finished getting dressed and Scott brushed imaginary lint off his shoulder. "I got yours, too, dude."

Then they both went still at the sounds coming overhead.

"Uh-uh!" Scott hollered, turning sharply as a stampeding herd came down the back steps. "Mom told all of y'all to stay upstairs until Miss Cooper came to get everybody. Right?"

"She late gittin' us 'cause her hairdresser appointment ran over, and I just wanted to see Uncle Trevor before he went out, and see how sharp he looked," Janelle protested as she made her way down the hall with the rest of the contingent behind her to barge into Trevor's room.

Quickly stepping in front of the open bedroom door, Scott spread his arms out wide as if he were on the schoolyard courts, and blocked their entry to the room. "Nope, not in here y'all don't. He's gettin' dressed, he don't need you in his space, and da man got places to go."

Trevor sighed deep in his soul, and one day would have to take Scott to the side to thank him. Yeah, the young buck had his back.

"Oh, Uncle Trevor," Samantha cooed with total appreciation as she stood on tiptoe to see past Scott. "Look at you. . . ."

While her compliment did reassure him, and although he was very pleased by it, the space he'd worked so hard to clean up and keep to himself had now been overrun.

"Ladies, thank you," Trevor replied, feeling nervous tension wind through him again as his lair was exposed to teenage scrutiny. If they would just get out of the bedroom doorway and stop gaping at the candles. . . .

"Why can't I go, too?" Miquel grumbled. "And why all of a sudden you have to clean up and be all dressed up to go pick up Miss Corey, huh, Dad? And what's all da candles for—it ain't no holiday, is it?"

Trevor opened his mouth and closed it as all eyes turned toward him and waited.

"Because, knucklehead," Scott said, jumping in for a rebound, "after all that hard work, and puttin' in all doze extra hours—that the school doesn't pay that nice lady for, and now that the project is almost finished, your dad is cool enough to take her out to dinner. She deserves somethin' nice for puttin' up wit us for a month. Dig?"

Trevor let his breath out in a slow, undetectable stream of air though his nose, and he sent a nervous glance of thanks in his nephew's direction.

While the explanation seemed to temporarily stump Miquel, being bright, he pressed on. "Den why can't we all go like we always do when the crew eats after the shoot?"

"Don't you give your favorite teacher something special at the end of the school year?" Scott interjected again, casting a warning glare at Janelle and Samantha.

"Yeah." Miquel admitted with a shrug.

"Den why can't your father give his favorite teacher a special dinner, and a break from watchin' other people's kids?"

Miquel stood there for a moment and seemed to let the information enter his brain, then go through a battery of logic checks, before it processed a response.

"Yeah . . ." the child finally said, losing the defensiveness in his voice. "But I just wanted to go, too," he added sadly.

"But aren't you and Elliott going to Dave and Busters to play arcade games?" Samantha soothed, trying to take the sting out of the blow of being left behind for her little cousin.

"Yeah, I guess so," Miquel said, sighing. "But Elliott gets on my nerves."

"I'll be home when you get back," Trevor finally mustered, feeling the threat to his freedom night finally about to recede.

"Oooh! Dag!" Janelle screamed from the other room. "Daaaag gooooone, Uncle T! Go head now! This is just like you see it in the movies! Go Hollywood!"

As the gang plowed down the hall away from Scott, defeat claimed Trevor. While they'd focused on Miquel, Janelle had slipped away from the tight gathering outside of his bedroom to inspect further into his den on her own. Scott shrugged an apology and gave Trevor an expression as though he'd passed the basketball to the opposing team.

"See what I have to put up wit around here, dude?" Scott murmured in disgust. Then the youth drew a deep breath through his mouth and bellowed out one word that almost shattered the bedroom mirror with its force. "Mom!"

Too embarrassed by the privacy breach to answer the female inquiries about the roses, and way too stressed out to give his son a logical reason for why his volcano had been moved and replaced by the flowers and a silver ice bucket—or to come up with a plausible excuse for having candles on every nonflammable surface in the living room, Trevor leaned his head back, filled up his lungs, and outroared the junior lion at his side. "Greeeeetchen!"

His roar came from the depths of his male instinct and gained force with his indignity as he elongated his sister's name, and it stilled the cackling girl birds and young monkey swinging off the just-fluffed furniture. It made the hair stand up on the younger lion's neck in respect, and it caused a thundering silence when he was done. It sent the animals scurrying on a stampede out of the unit as the top second-floor step was sounded by the entry of the matriarch of the pride.

He could hear them fleeing in all directions as soon as they saw her, for they knew the rules of the jungle well: The males mostly roared loud, but it was the female lions that brought in the kill, and they had disobeyed her and were now in harm's way. Then her roar was the roar of the slaughter, of body parts being yanked and heads slapped, and wails and screeches prevailed. Then it went silent—as she stalked down the staircase, searching through the tall grasses to assess the damage the male had sustained to his ego.

When she spied Scott standing next to Trevor, his dejected expression turned to one of defensiveness and fear.

"Mom, for real, I didn't bring them down here. Serious," the youth mumbled as his mother backed him up into a corner, threatened to swat him, and showed fangs.

"I ought to box your ears for openin' dat door and bringing them dow' here runnin' throu' your uncle's unit like wild lemmings going over a cliff. After all the hard work your uncle put to cleanin' dis place up—"

"It wasn't his fault," Trevor growled low in his throat, his chest heaving from the sudden burst of rage. "We were just down here chillin'—let it go."

Gretchen backed off the youth, but snarled in her son's direction before she did so, and Scott's shoulders instantly dropped in obvious relief.

"How bad's the damage down here?" she asked quietly.

"I don't know," Trevor murmured, too disgusted to go even look. Then he paced past his sister and Scott in frustration, went into the living room, and stopped, closed his eyes briefly at the sight, and began picking up.

He heard Gretchen's audible gasp over his shoulder, and it cut like a razor.

"Oh man . . ." Scott whispered, and glanced at his mother, who immediately slapped him on the back of his head. "Unc, it ain't dat bad. I'll help you out. You all clean and don't need to get wrinkled up."

"I got it," Trevor said in a very quiet voice. "It's cool."

"Go upstairs, Scott," Gretchen ordered, "and make sure that door gets a deadbolt on it till I knock for you to open it." Then she was mercifully silent as she helped Trevor tidy up.

The destruction wasn't really that bad, truth be told, once he regained his perspective and assessed it. Trevor's eyes followed the path of the kids' wake, and he began to deduce the probable cause from the crime scene in front of him.

Okay, so a couple of pillows had been knocked to the floor when Miquel had obviously lunged on the sofa, and sure, Janelle probably was the one who scattered his CDs across the table as she sifted through them to see what he'd selected from the rack, and Miquel, fighting for position with Sam and Janelle, might have accidentally snapped one of the rose stems when they tried to smell it in unison—leaving a drooping bud looking like it was taking an encore bow—but that was not the issue.

His privacy, and what he'd planned for the evening, had been violated and exposed, respectively. He could not even look at his sister, much less speak to her, and in all honesty, the whole idea of not going anywhere but out to a bar, alone, was becoming more appealing by the minute. The groove blown, what was there to say? In all fairness, he couldn't say anything to Gretchen about the botched arrangements to have the kids gone by the time he'd gotten dressed because, after all, she'd called in every marker to make this happen on a dime. And it wasn't her fault that one of her girlfriends had gotten tied up at the hairdresser . . . but right now, accessing the intellectual side of his brain was no balm to his wounded pride.

"I know how you feel," she whispered, trying to

make amends by smoothing empathy onto his gashed dignity.

He said nothing at first, but could feel a volcano erupting . . . oh, yes, he was stone-cold mountain and, at the moment, he would not be moved.

"All I wanted to do was go out and bring my date home," he whispered through his teeth, "without fanfare, without . . . without . . ."

"Without total, complete exposure," his sister said, sighing as she stood from straightening the coffee table. "Without personal invasion, and now you're on kid radar. I know, sweetie."

Trevor just kept moving, then glanced down at his watch and sighed.

"The room, well, except the one poor rose, didn't get hurt," she said in an empathic tone. "But now, the evenin' and dis space have lost their luster, haven't they?"

"Yeah," he replied sullenly, feeling totally outdone.

"But," she pressed on philosophically, "this was only your first attempt at an undercover escape. The night is young, and your date never knew about dis, and she will probably laugh when you tell her what happened to one poor little rose at the hands of the nosy children in your house."

"I'm beyond through, Gretch. There are no words. This ain't funny."

His sister cast her gaze around the room, and she stifled a smile that he didn't miss before she did so.

"It's beautiful, Trevor," she soothed. "They didn't knock over all the candles, and the lights in here are so pretty down low." Then she turned her head and laughed and covered her mouth. "Oh, honey, I'm sorry. You got cold busted on your first time out tryin' to dodge kids. It happens to all of us. Don't let it ruin your night." Then she came over, straightening his tie, and gave him a military once-over inspection, dusting off his lapels and making him feel better with her unnecessary attentions.

Then she stepped back, saluted him hard, and finally made him smile.

He had been so brief and vague about where they were headed that she wasn't even sure what to wear. All day long her heart kept missing beats with anticipation, and she'd been frantic to be sure that she'd gone to Fresh Fields to stock the refrigerator with specialty gourmet offerings in case he got hungry between devouring her . . . or perhaps even stayed for breakfast. . . . Dear God, help her keep her sanity.

But it had taken her so long to clean the entire house, and then to wash herself pure with a long bath, and to shampoo her hair, and pick out just the right dress . . . and time was becoming her enemy now as it sped along—taking vengeance because she'd cursed it for moving so slow earlier in the day. Now it mocked her for her impatience. Its fickleness gave her just enough time to question her choice of dresses, but not enough time to redo her whole choice and accessorize that change.

So she could only hope that he'd like what she'd chosen. She'd gone for a deep, blue-black sapphire sheath to remind him how much he loved her as water, and she had taken serious time to find her black, thin-strapped high-heeled pumps—housed normally in the back of her closet—which she never wore for another living soul. They still hurt her feet and were a beautiful shopping spree relic usually not on display, but they were the perfect match for the dress she'd selected. But he was worth the pain of such vanity, she'd decided, as she found her small, beaded black clutch that went with them. Then she donned the delicate choker that floated a tiny diamond in the cleft of her collarbone on an invisible nylon thread. Maybe he'd envision it as a beacon star hovering over the deep blue of her sapphire sheath when she again became his sea. Then she checked her total look and worried.

As she glanced at the clock again, she double-checked her makeup and prayed that he would like the matte natural tones she'd selected—what if he was a red lipstick kinda guy? she worried as she blotted her lips again. Naaah . . . He was a naturalist in his core essence, but what if? She primped her upswept hair, then pulled at the tendrils she'd purposely let dangle, wondered if she should have left it all down, and ran for the telephone and heard that it was Justine for the fifth time.

"Noooo. Not yet. I'm getting dressed. Will call you later," she said in a rush. "I gotta go, so he doesn't have to wait. Love you, bye."

She'd lost two minutes, which made her spin around in circles, glancing at every surface in her bedroom. Then she grabbed her clutch and the long, sheer, black oblong scarf that took her more than an hour to find in the stores, put it around her shoulders, and wondered. Everything had to be perfect. Then she looked at herself in the full-length mirror on the other side of her closet door and groaned. Then she told herself she was silly, and she took a deep, cleansing breath, but it only made the butterflies start playing inside of her belly again.

And she nearly had to call an ambulance to jump-start her heart when the doorbell finally rang.

Seventeen

All it had taken was one look. Earlier that evening, when she had opened the door, all of his previous morose thoughts about their night being destroyed, and his foolish consideration of abandoning the concept of taking her out, had receded and been banished. One look at the sapphire blue Water Oracle, and he'd drowned . . . right on her steps, right in the doorway of her temple.

As they neared his duplex, he thought about how wondrous it had been sitting across the table from her, soaking in her beauty and laughter, telling her his plans for the documentary amid her excited squeals of delight. The sound of her voice . . . just being able to talk to her alone, in that lush environment with a sumptuous meal, no interruption of their locked gaze . . . She was his Oasis.

The smooth jazz in the background had perfectly framed his living ocean—who had worn a star around her neck, as though it were a nativity beacon leading him toward his own soul's birth.

A full bottle of the best chardonnay had made them both heady. He liked the effect of it on her, and the way she'd relaxed as the evening progressed and he kept pouring it. Then again, the wine and the vision of her had a decided effect on him, too. Yet somehow it wasn't just the wine alone that seemed to have altered their states.

She glanced at him nervously as he brought the car to a stop, and he gave her a smile, trying to stem her fears about going to his place—fears which were quickly becoming his own.

"Are you absolutely sure this is going to be all right?" she asked softly, glancing at the house, then back at him.

"My sister is aware of how important having some time alone with you has become, and she and I conspired to get all of the kids out of the house for overnight . . . so you and I can just talk."

He felt his smile growing wider despite his intention not to let it. How could he help but inwardly chuckle, when she raised an eyebrow in a mischievous manner upon the word *talk* and smiled shyly at him? No he didn't just want to talk either. He wanted to swim in her ocean. Oh, yes, the Water Oracle knew, and her eyes beckoned him now to jump in.

But she had been enough of a diplomat not to openly counter his small falsehood, and she'd seemed to accept the explanation. Still, her eyes darted nervously between him and the front door as they approached it, as though every step of the way she were asking for reassurance that they wouldn't get ambushed by children.

Now her same silent worry nagged him as he put the key in the door and managed the locks. Everything had been so perfect . . . he just said a quiet prayer that things would stay that way as he ushered her over the threshold. Then he listened—really, really hard—to the sounds of his environment to be sure there was no child intruder as she tentatively entered his space.

"Would you like me to hang that up?" he asked in a murmur, tracing the delicate scarf about her upper arms and shoulders and removing his jacket, casting it on a chair.

"No, that's all right," she replied in a pleasant but unsure tone. "I'll just lay it down with my purse."

Okay . . . she was not comfortable yet. She needed to settle in, listen, feel more at ease, he told himself as he ushered her to the sofa, turned on some more jazz, and summoned patience as his muse. Champagne.

"This is beautiful," she whispered, casting her gaze around the room and appearing to grow shyer as she did so. "You did all of this for me in one afternoon?"

She had taken a seat and set down her purse on the coffee table, slowly pulling the scarf from her pretty shoulders in an agonizingly sexy way, then folding it carefully in a small square to lay it by her clutch.

"Yeah," he murmured, striking a long fireplace match and beginning to light the candles around the room. As the room came aglow, he turned off the dim recessed lights at the wall, paced to the bedroom to light more candles, then went into the kitchen to bring back the champagne. *Patience. Don't blow it,* he reminded himself as he felt his stride sauntering toward her while almost forgetting about the bubbly he was carrying. It took a moment of deep concentration to will his legs to walk to the table to complete the task at hand. *Don't rush her. You have all night. Pour the bubbly, man. Focus.*

He watched her with small glances, checking her approval of his efforts. The mixture of pleasure and demure satisfaction coupled with the way she seemed to be listening for an intrusion sent a tremor through him. She wanted this night, too, he could tell.

More focused, he busied himself with opening the bottle and adjusting it in the decanter to keep it cold, and his eyes spied the broken rose, so he picked it off the stem and brought it to her with the two champagne flutes. Handing her one of the glasses as he sat down next to her, he hesitated, set his glass down on the table, and studied the rose between his fingers.

"These were for you," he chuckled, "but there was a casualty. . . ."

"Awww . . . poor little rose. . . . They're beautiful,"

she murmured, taking the broken bud from his fingers, bringing it to her nose, and setting it down on the table with care. "Just like this whole evening has been, Trevor. Thank you." Then she smiled.

The warmth from her smile and her voice entered his pores and flooded him with emotion that almost took his breath. He took a quick sip of his champagne, set it down, and stared at her, then touched her cheek with his fingers, not ashamed that they trembled ever so slightly when he did. Her skin was as soft as the rose he'd just given her, and he now knew that the rest of the bouquet belonged in the tub with her when he gave her a candlelight bath. Images of that possibility swirled in his mind like a whirlpool, pulling at his groin hard as he envisioned her surrounded with petals and water. After she had taken a languid sip from her glass, he took it from her and set it down next to the rose.

"I've been trying to define how you make me feel," he whispered, "trying to add form and structure to this thing that we have . . . perhaps so that I can frame it and not lose it."

"I'm not going anywhere," she said tenderly, "unless you want me to."

Her statement came out as a blend between a promise and a question, rising on a slight crest as she'd finished saying it.

"I've lost a lot of people I've loved, Corey, because I didn't properly put them into context," he admitted quietly. As he stared into her eyes, he felt truth bubble to his surface, and his shoulders relaxed. She had washed him to an odd place in his soul, and left him stranded between acute physical desire for her and a remote vessel deep within him that wanted to anchor itself to a safe harbor.

Every relationship before this one had been the thrill of the chase with the outcome a hunter's gamble, the disappointment not visceral if he lost what he pursued. It had been a game, but this time he was playing for keeps.

Forming his words carefully, he drew a breath and released it, attempting to find a way to make her understand.

"Since you're a teacher," he said with a gentle smile, "then you know how important it is for a student to understand the meaning of words. Syntax and semantics—which give rise to multiple definitions. So I took the things that I'm about to tell you from one of the oldest books in the world."

He let his hand fall to hers and he captured it, studying the glow from the candles as they shimmered in her wide, dark irises. The delicate structure of the palm he held within his made him brush it with a kiss and briefly shut his eyes before returning to those gorgeous eyes of her quiet storm.

"To love, honor, and cherish," he whispered. "What does that mean, I asked myself, and could I do that if I knew?"

When she didn't speak and her expression immediately went serious, he began again slowly. Although she'd gone very, very still, her eyes scanned his face hard in an intense appraisal, searching, it seemed, for a life raft of her own.

"I have loved many people, Corey," he whispered, "but I had not cherished them or honored them completely." As soon as he'd made the statement, he thought that the admission would be fatal. But, to his surprise, it seemed to relax her as she took in his words.

"My parents . . ." he began, and then trailed off. Emotion temporarily caught in his throat. "I loved them, of course, but I did not cherish them or what they did for me—because I didn't have the maturity to understand the sacrifices they'd made. And, because of that, I did not fully honor who they were. Truthfully, my sister taught me what cherish and honor look like, during our quiet conversations in the kitchen. And I also realized that I hadn't spent the time to go beyond loving my son—to cherish him and to honor him, fully."

She held his gaze and touched his face, tracing his jawline, then nodded as if to tell her student, "well done." With that approval reflecting from her eyes, he drew the courage to continue.

"I cannot take credit for those epiphanies, Corey. I've had excellent teachers. My sister taught me that lesson of familial love, just as you've taught me that lesson about my son. You not only love that boy, but it is evident that you also cherish him . . . you enjoy his company, just being around him, and watching him develop and grow—something I nearly squandered. And you honor who he is in the world, and would fight even me to protect his chances of developing to his full potential. I am sure that he loves you, too—unconditionally. So I studied those definitions for all of these weeks away from you, trying to understand the subtle differences in the meanings of the new vocabulary words I've been given. I'm trying so hard now to use them in an essay . . . to even speak them in a sentence."

Again, he hesitated, watching tears glisten in her beautiful eyes, then burn away, as she waited, too, it seemed, for him to tell her what he'd learned.

"You can love someone," he whispered, "but when you cherish them, you miss their company when they're gone—not just on a physical level—you miss all of their little eccentricities . . . their laugh, their point of view in a discussion, you simply miss doing ordinary things with them. So once I had come to accept that I had initially fallen in love with you, in love, definition Eros—the weeks that have passed between us gave me time to know how much I cherished sharing your space . . . and who you were, and who you've surrounded yourself with to build your world, and I wanted to be a permanent part of what you'd created. Then," he murmured, feeling a gravitational pull to her soul as her gaze slipped away from his, "I knew that I wanted to honor you . . . to have you in my life in a way that gave you my total commitment and respect."

Her stillness frightened him, because there was so much riding on what he was trying so hard to tell her, and he pressed on, not wanting to give her an opportunity to fail him before he'd completed his oral examination for her.

"The way you taught me all of this, Corey Odessa Hamilton, was through watching you spill out unconditional love on others . . . then on me, then witnessing you cherish me—even with my flaws. And you honored me by acceptance . . . acceptance of my family, my work, and who I simply am. That day you wept on the telephone, I thought I'd break from not holding you . . . because in that moment, you trusted me enough to do that—which was an honor, a gift, when you let me know who you really are inside."

When a single tear brimmed and fell, he wiped it away from her cheek, hoping that she would truly absorb all that he was trying to give her through the inadequate reef caused by language. So near to him, her gentle fragrance wafted to his nostrils, fusing with the delicate hint of salmon, wine, ginger vegetables, and the peppermint tea that she'd consumed. The combination of fragrances while staring into her eyes was intoxicating, more than the wine and champagne ever could have been, and he found himself nearly salivating at the thought of taking her mouth to taste all of her in his own.

"Odessa . . ." he crooned softly. "Yes," he admitted, "I looked it up in my study of you. How fitting . . . how cosmically ironic. A seaport on the Black Sea . . . and I have been there before, as I am right now, stranded—waiting on a connection, hoping that I can return home."

"I am the one who is stranded," she whispered hoarsely. "I am hoping that this project will never end, even though I'd never want my students to be disappointed. . . . And tonight, as we talked about all the fantastic plans for the film to be entered into festivals, and the premiere, all the while, I was holding my breath, praying that after the work is done, there'll still be something to keep this magic between us."

He'd looked up her name . . . and called her Odessa . . . just like her mother used to when she was combing her hair as a child. And he'd opened himself up to her as no man ever had, and had given her such fulfillment in her life in a way that she'd never known. His masculine aroma, coupled with the coffee and cognac on his breath, made her want to immediately lean forward and swallow those gentle words he'd just uttered.

"Cherish . . . ," she murmured, as his gaze bore into her, "is to give a person something that is sacred that you have. Trevor, for these last weeks, you gave me your family . . . your passion, your laughter, your son . . . and you have resurrected my art, through this project, and made me believe in myself again. And you comforted me, and trusted me, and hoped with me—making me feel honored by a man, for the first time in my life."

How could she describe to him all the sacred gifts that he'd given to her? There were not enough words in a lexicon. His expression had become so tender that she had to fight to keep from taking his mouth. Before she did that, she needed him to understand.

"Honor . . ." she murmured, her voice growing husky, "has been in your every interaction with me. You have restored my faith that dreams can come true. . . . I just don't want to wake up."

"Neither do I," he whispered, his breathing becoming labored as he spoke. "And I can't. That's why I made you something to let you know how deeply I was pulled into you."

To her chagrin, he stood up and walked over to the television, leaving a coolness to replace the heat in the spot next to her that he'd just vacated. Finally, he came back, sat down beside her and gazed at her before pushing the button to start the tape.

"This is you, Water Oracle. . . ." he murmured in a tone that washed through her. "This is what I've learned."

Curiosity and a gentle smile had overtaken her expression, he noted, then as the montage faded up from black on the sound of a wave, he studied her more closely—watching her face instead of the screen.

At first her finger traced her collarbone and toyed with the tiny diamond hovering at the center of her throat, then her hand slowly reached up to cover her mouth. It was only then that he let out his breath.

She watched in awe at the way he'd transformed her image on the screen, and had blended her into soft dissolves and waves, the way he'd captured the most subtle of her gestures when she hadn't even noticed . . . and how he'd so lovingly compared her to spectacular natural wonders.

"Oh, God, Trevor," she whispered, turning back to him as the video images faded then ended. There were no words, only feelings, and she couldn't sort them out, which brought silent tears.

His arms went around her and pulled her to his hard chest, strong hands stroked her hair, and a gentle mouth grazed her ear. Warmth radiated through her back as a broad palm traveled down it, and she found her face lifting to meet the ruinous sensation of his mouth.

"You like it?" he breathed into her kiss, his eyes remaining only half open as he moved his head slightly to witness her response.

The taste of him resonated after the kiss, and it had worked its way down into her belly, then found her core, which flowed from wanting more of him.

"I love you," she whispered, finding his mouth again and pressing hers to it hard, then sending her tongue to again explore the wondrous regions of his.

But rather than warmth covering her back, a cool gush of air claimed it, as he suddenly changed her position next to him to lift her from the sofa. Her arms encircled his neck and her head found his shoulders, which bulged under the exertion as he paced down the hall carrying her into his bedroom.

He gingerly set her on the edge of his bed, and the room glowed amber around them as he went to his knees before her. She almost allowed herself to fall back, anticipating his intentions, but something in the way he held her gaze told her to let him guide their momentum. His stare reflected a level of fear that she hadn't sensed in him before, and she touched his face to try to communicate without words that everything would be all right and that she was his tonight.

"Corey," he whispered, seeming to hover between blanketing her and speaking. "I am so afraid of this. . . ."

As she stared at him, trying to say something to help him know that she wouldn't hurt him, he lowered his face to her lap, and let out his breath hard. "I've been afraid of this, too," she admitted, cradling his head. She stroked his hair and allowed her fingers to send love to his shoulders, knowing what it felt like to want something so much but to also be terrified of it.

The way he laid his head against her made her body ache for him so deeply that it almost made her cry out. Her fingers raked his scalp, and she said oblations to the universe to heal his vanished mane of locks that he'd sent up as a burnt offering to it. But something in her knew to give him the space to advance or retreat. So she gentled her touch and held back the passion it momentarily contained.

When he reached into his nightstand drawer, her lower belly ignited, and she found her eyes going to mere slits. Her response to his action was nearly Pavlovian as her seam broke with a fresh torrent of wet want. She let one of her hands slip behind her on an outstretched arm to balance herself and to keep from falling backward into oblivion. Her insides screamed for him to touch her as he nuzzled her thighs with his jaw while on his knees just before her.

But respecting his lead as he withdrew his hand from the drawer, she waited and watched him as he held her gaze with his own. And yet, when she stared at him, the hunger in his eyes seemed to give way to something more tender. Taking her hand, he produced the box that she'd mistakenly identified. Blood shot through her veins as her heart beat in erratic answer to the questions contained in his eyes, making her ears ring as he opened his hand.

"I know this may seem sudden," he whispered, holding a small black box in his palm. "I know that I may not have yet earned the right. But never in my life . . ."

His voice trailed off and he looked down. She could not breathe, much less move, and her hand trembled within his as he held it and drew a deep breath.

"I wanted you to have this," he murmured, flipping back the lid on the box and removing his hand to lift the ring from the case.

The brilliant orb sparkled in the amber light, completely surrounded by clusters of sapphires, aquamarines, and what seemed to be blue topaz baguettes. The hand that supported her immediately rushed forward to her mouth, and she sat there mute, as he tenderly took her left hand and slipped the ring onto her finger.

"When I saw you at your door, oh, Water Oracle, I

wondered how you knew . . . the only reason we made it out of your house was because I had to get you here for this. But when I saw you standing there, wearing a diamond at your throat like a star on the sea's horizon . . . and you wore a sapphire sheath as though you were indeed the ocean itself . . . I prayed to God Almighty that you'd accept this, and you'd understand that I had it made to always remind you of who you are to me . . . my burning star in the darkness . . . each color of blue gem representing an attribute of water: deep passion, light laughter, gentle understanding and calm. And Corey, my Odessa, my port, marry me and bring me out of the storm of my own hand's doing . . . please, say yes . . ."

The ring blurred with his face, as tears rose in her eyes, then fell. Her mouth found his as he followed her lead and the encouragement of her hands, which pulled him forward to blanket her. And as he covered her, she wrapped her legs around him, as though he would vanish when she awakened from this dream. Her voice was unable to find its way up from her vocal cords, and she could only nod and say yes with her touch.

She fought with his tie to loosen it as he lifted himself up to kiss her throat. Then he kept his gaze on her as he assisted her in removing it while she unbuttoned his shirt and undid his belt. He took off his large silver bangle and laid it on the nightstand without losing her gaze. His eyes said, *This time I will hold you so hard this piece of metal will hurt you.* In a slow, excruciating ritual, he undressed her, paying homage to her skin as each part of it was revealed, and she honored his as well, with the same tender reverence bestowed in kisses, as they removed the barriers of clothing.

With this encounter, his eyes did not scan her body, nor did hers have to look at his. It was as though they had already captured those images, and this time they were looking at each other's naked souls. And his loving kisses started at her forehead, and gently caressed her eyelids, falling, flowing down the bridge of her nose, until they reached her throat and trailed ecstasy past her collarbone to her breasts where he stopped and had Mass . . . lovingly cupping each mound in his palms before lowering his head to brush the tips of them with his mouth.

Her gasp came up from a depth within her that she'd never realized even existed until now, and as he brought each hardened nipple between his teeth, then suckled the gentle injury, she found her hips responded to the tempo of his lips. Her hands cradled his head as his mouth laved her breasts, and when she arched and cried out, he still would not move away from them, and she felt a wave of release beginning to break.

Hot wetness begged to be answered by the same kisses that he lavished on her breasts, but seemed to refuse to share with her thighs. Fluttering contractions deep within her valley caused the rim of it to burn as it was scorched by the phantom sensations that echoed his touches of her nipples. As though understanding what her body requested, his attentions suddenly shifted, leaving a cool rush of air in the wake of his retreat.

Warm, wonderful, wet kisses mapped her breastbone, then made their way down her belly, and hovered over her navel, before his tongue descended into it. The acute, immediate pleasure almost made her sit up, as it sent a forceful tremor down her spine. In response, her body allowed a new flood of molten desire to escape from her cavern, as she whimpered in reaction to his heated plunge.

Then he nuzzled her so gently, rubbing his cheeks against the inside of her thighs, bringing his tongue behind each swipe of his face, making her delirious with the wait.

"Please . . ." she found herself begging him, as he only rendered light kisses upon the center of her pain. Unable to stand it, she found her eyes closing and the back of her head digging into the mattress as she arched up to meet him.

Without warning, she felt herself being plundered in the way she had pleaded for, and her hands found the sheets as her knuckles turned white, until her voice hit an octave that it had never reached before. Massive hands found her buttocks and held them firm in searing palms, as she chanted prayers out loud, and he drank of her deeply. His mouth pulled at her deepest currents and made her convulse in epileptic pleasure as she begged him to stop what he'd begun.

Her passion-filled cries had submerged his fears, taking his reason along with them. Primal instinct replaced worry and honor as he crouched over her, breathing hard and holding himself up on all fours above her like she were fresh kill.

"In the drawer," he said on a low growl. "I can't move, and I don' trust myself. In the drawer," he repeated, tortured by the wait—this time his command sounding more like a plea to his own ears.

He watched her lean toward the stand and blindly reach for what he needed her to quickly find. And as she retrieved the package, he took it from her and opened the foil with his teeth.

"One day, very soon, you'll be my wife," he said on a harsh whisper as he separated himself from the wetness that his body craved to feel, and summoned the last shred of his intellect—begrudgingly doing what he knew they must. "I don't ever want anything between us. Not even latex."

As he lowered his body into her pool, he shuddered hard, and tightly closed his eyes against the burning, warm eddy that held him in a tight grip, then released him in tiny spasms that made him move like he was mining for ore. Deep lunges against the sensation opened the trapped images he'd held in his mind for weeks . . . for years . . . for an eternity, it seemed, as his shallow pants became one with hers, and their tidal rhythms synchronized upon a harmony of gasps. All he could do was drive hard against her, trying to ride out the storm.

Resistance to her depths was futile. Her body had swallowed him, pulling him into the vacuum of her essence, and he struggled for air against the vertigo that the edge of oblivion caused. He seized twice and bit into her neck. But her legs tangled around him, trapped him, and forced him in deeper and, drowning, his soul could not escape as tiny pinpoints of light formed behind his shut eyes. Then a tremor turned into a quake underneath him, and in his stupor it kept him spiraling, and then everything went still . . . all that could be heard was their united breathing that beat out a stanza of devastated completion.

He wasn't sure how long he'd laid there inside of her warmth, but as she roused, it forced him up onto his elbow, and made him remember to hold on to the top of the thing that separated them while he studied her face and slowly withdrew.

"I take it that's a yes," he murmured, kissing her flushed mouth and finding a substantial peace overcome his spirit.

She gave a lazy giggle and smiled a satisfied smile. "Yes," she murmured into his mouth.

"I was so afraid you'd say it hadn't been long enough," he admitted, hoping that after their lovemaking, she wouldn't suddenly rethink her answer now that clarity had returned for them both.

"How could I say anything else, being hunted by a Leo?"

He cocked his head to the side and felt a smile come out on one side of his face.

"You told me you were born in August, right?"

Her comment, then question, made him chuckle

and roll over on his back. He pulled her beside him, then gently pushed her head into the crook of his shoulder. God, he loved this tempest of a woman, who was always surprising him.

"Yeah . . ." he said slowly, feeling so satisfied that he began drifting off to sleep as he spoke.

"I've been studying you, too," she whispered. "During all of these weeks. So many nights, I was nearly driven out of my mind. A couple of times I thought I might show up on your steps unannounced and beg you for this. Then, I found out you were a Leo, and I even started reading your horoscope in the newspaper, like I was fifteen again . . . and I knew I was totally gone."

He laughed. Touched and very, very pleased by her admission, he nearly purred for her as her hand stroked his belly.

"So, tell me, my water sign . . . tell me about a Leo man," he said low in his throat as his eyes shut without his permission.

She laughed—a tender, sweet, satiated laugh as her hand stroked him from chest to navel. "Ah, you've been reading horoscopes, too, huh?"

"Yeah," he admitted way down in his chest. "It's amazing where your mind will go to scavenge for any shred of connection when you're going insane for someone . . . my July-born, Cancer woman, who has still waters that run deep, and whose sanctuary is a home. Tell me about what you've discovered about us lion men?"

"Gallant . . . flamboyant . . . romantic . . . creative . . . charismatic . . ." she crooned. "Loyal . . . sometimes arrogant . . . but always sensual . . . And you literally hunted me in this house, that first day I came here, didn't you?"

He laughed again, bass notes coming up from his abdomen as he recalled stalking her in the high grass of his kitchen.

"I wanted you so badly that day, but there was no way to break you off from the herd. . . . How did you know?"

"It's always in your eyes, Trevor. They go from laughter to mischief," she murmured in a sleepy voice, "then something ignites, and you go primal. And the shift is exhilarating to watch. . . . I had to get out of here, because it made me get wet."

It was the way she'd said that last part to him that stirred him. He opened his eyes and pulled her up next to him. "I bought a twelve box," he murmured on a dangerously low chuckle. "The six-pack was simply a tease."

She laughed, pushed herself up on one elbow, peered over his shoulder, and shook her head.

"Want another ride on my sled?" he asked in a thick, sexy tone that ran through her skeleton. "Afterward, I'll light the candles in the bathroom and draw you a bath, and I'll crush the roses at your feet. . . ."

Giggling, she fell back and threw her arm over her forehead to shield her eyes. "I'm wiped out at the moment . . . for real, for real."

"It could be a long time before we can do this again," he remarked in an even lower octave. "I don't think I can make it, not being gorged on you. Give me a little something to hold me over, baby. . . ."

"I don't think I can go cold turkey again after tonight, either," she admitted in a hoarse whisper, holding the ring out with admiration as she stared at it, then brushed his mouth with a kiss. "How can I keep my hands off my lion? Trevor, are you sure about this?" Then she shut her eyes.

"Want to hold on and look in the mirror to see if I'm serious?" he said on a hot breath that scorched her ear and made her open her eyes. "You watch my face, and then you tell me whether or not I'm sure."

She swallowed hard, and he nipped her earlobe.

"You're the environmentalist," he whispered, stroking her down the length of her side, and making a tremor reawaken and follow it. "You've already shot, stunned, and tagged this lion with the sound of your voice . . . when we make love, the sounds of your voice . . . Corey, baby," he said with a groan as he captured the tender flesh of her neck between his teeth, then released it slowly, "drives me insane. And, that's what kept replaying itself in my head like an endless loop tape, for an entire month of agony. So, if we have to separate again . . . I want you completely . . . mind, body, and soul, Water Oracle. Make a decision from what your own eyes see of me."

She found herself taking in shallow sips of air as this man—part lion, part mountain—held her stare and intensely gazed at her. He was a fire sign, core molten rock that she'd mistaken for earth energy, and he poured over her and burned her like lava, boiling her water until she nearly evaporated.

In a deft motion, he reached past her, pulled a tissue from the box on his nightstand, ditched the latex within it, and grabbed another foil package to begin opening it with his teeth again. There was something about the way he kept his line of vision trained on her while he did it. *Oh, yes . . . hunt me . . .* , her mind echoed, as he donned another layer of protection and pulled her in front of him, then reached under her belly and levered her until she was on all fours. Yes, she'd give him permission to eat her alive while she watched. . . .

"Hold on to to the edge of the bed, so you don't hurt yourself," he warned in a rush of air at the nape of her neck. "And . . . whatever you do," he whispered, "don't close your eyes. Promise me."

She lifted her head slowly and looked at the mirror in front of them, her hands clutching the foot of the sleigh as he came up behind her and kissed each vertebra of her spine. Her forearms trembled as his massive thighs parted hers, and his palms fused with her stomach and traveled up her torso to capture her breasts. She felt her head dropping from the sheer sensations that made her arch for him as she waited.

"Don't look away," he whispered through his teeth. "This is what you do to me. Total devastation," his said, he voice penetrating the skin of her back, mingling with her spinal fluid, and searing it as she lifted her head.

Then she watched him enter her—throwing his head back with his eyes closed and the way his Adam's apple moved in his throat under a heavy groan. The visual effect of his pleasure caused her eyes to go half-mast at the sight, sound, and feel of what he was doing to her.

The three-carat stone on her hand caught the soft candlelight and eclipsed the diamond around her neck that was once a lone star. The deep blues around it sent a prism into the mirror, as her hands held the dark wood, and her lion devoured her in heavy thrusts that almost made her parted legs give out.

"I can't keep watching," she whispered as her head dropped forward from the quake that was imminent.

She felt his arm brace the bed for her and his weight suddenly shift so that he was squatting on his heels. He'd gathered her against him, in a way that she could lean her head back on his shoulder, one muscled arm holding her waist in a vise, while his unencumbered hand ravished her torso. It felt like the pressure of his hold would burst her belly open, as his forearm held her tighter and pulled hard against the tender flesh. . . . But the way he rocked against her from behind, almost lifting her from each driven impact, she had to shut her eyes.

Teeth met her neck, and she cried out in pure pleasure, and her own hands became claws that grappled at his flanks, until her nails found anchor by digging into his thighs. She could not keep leaning back like this, as her spine required arching, and her hips needed more leverage to move of their own accord. . . .

That's when she shed all of her inhibitions, and she let go of his thighs, lurched herself forward onto her hands, her head touching the bed and her back dipping into a deep feline sway. And her voice became a throaty wail that brought him up to cover her, his hands alongside hers, his perspiration-slicked belly to her spine, his head craning back while he struggled for air, and she could barely watch him bring her down as jungle kill.

Eyes half shut, half open, she witnessed the hunt in the mirror as he thoroughly gorged himself on her body, and she felt herself begin to transform into something between human and animal as well. It began when her moan made him clutch her stomach; her nails gathered sheets and her breath escaped on an open pant. Immediately his voice rumbled, coming up from his depths, and he dropped his head forward, then threw it back hard and practically roared. She found herself following suit, matching his voice while her undulations became erratic, like his, and their thrusts became hard shutters, which became convulsions, which became tears, which became requests for mercy, which ended on her name.

Eighteen

Somewhere off in the distance, he heard the telephone ring. In the remote region of his consciousness, a parental knowledge made him reach out his weary, leaden arm and pick up the offending technology, half wanting to swat it away with the force of his heavy paw.

"Yeah," he growled to the intruder, still basking in the hold of his lover, who stirred slightly at the sound of his voice.

"Yo, dude," a distinctly British accent quipped. "You over your hiatus yet? Got a gig for you that will blow you away."

Instant clarity and terror fused in his intestines, and it propelled him to gently untangle himself from Corey's hold. "Yeah. Talk to me," he muttered, slipping out of the bed and grabbing his robe from the closet while glancing back at her sleeping form, then exiting the room and making his way down the hall with the cordless phone.

"This gig is off the hook, dude. Major contract—shoot is in Compton with a hot new group. How soon can you pack up and roll, man?"

"Not until after June," Trevor murmured cautiously. "But what's the format . . . I mean, I'm trying to get away from gangsta rap, go into message rap—positive music, and work on—"

"June? The opportunity is now! Be realistic, dude," the voice on the other end of the telephone warned.

"You've got the hot hand right now, and the industry is like a woman. Fickle. Don't start getting all metaphysical on us or you'll wind up starving. It's a jungle, and you know it. Don't tell me being home has made you go soft?"

"No, I haven't gone soft," Trevor countered in defense. "But I'm trying to change—"

"If it ain't broke, don't fix it," his buddy warned, growing serious. "What, all of a sudden you've had some religious experience, or something?"

"Yeah, sort of," Trevor admitted, looking down the hall at his son's room, then casting his gaze toward his bedroom, where Corey slept.

"Oh, for Christ's sake, dude. Fire up a blunt, get your head together, and get out here to L.A. so you can meet this new artist, and feel his vibe before we start shooting—"

"I don't know if I can do that, man," Trevor said slowly, sitting down on a kitchen chair and letting his head fall into his hands. "I cut my locks."

There was a silence that hovered on the line, and only intermittent static hissed to let him know the caller was still there.

"You did what?" the voice finally said, sounding appalled.

"I was goin' t'rough some changes, man, and trying to get my act together."

"Look, dude. Now I'm concerned. For real, for real."

"My son needs me, I'm gettin' married . . . I'm—"

"What? When did this happen?"

"Last night, and—"

"Get out of bed, take a cold shower, put on your clothes, and start packing for L.A. There's too much bank riding on this gig, and you can't let a woman get your head all messed up. I told you that monk shit was going to be your demise. Call me by Monday, and let me know what you're gonna do. I can stave them off, and say that I couldn't reach you over the weekend, 'cause you were hanging out. But I need an answer—or I've gotta get another photog and director. A decision, dude. This is serious capital, and could launch your career even into feature films. So don't be stupid."

The sick sludge of guilt made the acid in his stomach burn and come partway up his esophagus. Why hadn't he just told them while he had the conviction to do so? Why hadn't he made the clean and necessary break before the opportunity of a lifetime presented itself?

"I've gotta work some things out in my head, man," Trevor murmured, all previous satisfaction and calm draining from his being as he sat there.

"You know the old saying, 'you slow, you blow,'" his agent said coolly. "Don't mess this one up. All you've gotta do is one more hard-core video, because it's for a soundtrack for a major flick under development. The top brass in Hollywood is executive producing this, and they like your other work, and are thinking of giving you a shot at directing the flick to keep things stylistically and visually in sync."

The voice hesitated when Trevor didn't immediately respond, then rushed in again, presenting him with facts that made him ill.

"They want you on the West Coast for a meeting, and probably to slide a heavy video and film directing offer across the mahogany table to you, dude. You've been waiting for this all of your life!" the voice of temptation urged through the telephone line. "You screw this up, and they'll scratch you off their will-call list. Am I making an impact?"

"Yeah," Trevor whispered, glancing at the clock. Ten A.M. his time, seven A.M. his agent's time. Nobody in L.A. got up at this hour, unless it was serious business.

"When did you find out about it?" Trevor found himself asking against his own will.

"Last night at this gallery opening thing, and I tried

you by cell—check your messages. I must have left four or five. Then I had to dig up your home number, and I called till like midnight, but didn't get an answer so I didn't leave a message—figured you were somewhere hanging out, so why bother. Thought I'd try again after you dragged your ass home to crash and burn. My strategy worked, and I raised the dead."

"Yeah . . . it did. I heard you. I'll call you Monday. That's the most I can promise right now."

"Cool. I'll take that as a yes," the voice said, with a laugh. "Go get some more of her religious experience, and have your butt on a Monday flight. Talk to you in L.A. Peace."

"Peace," Trevor murmured, hitting the off button on the cordless and standing slowly.

As he walked down the hall, it felt like the walls were caving in on him. When he passed Miquel's room, he hesitated in the doorway and looked around. Guilt stripped the air from his lungs and siphoned moisture to his eyes as he moved toward the bathroom and stopped. Rose petals and abandoned champagne flutes littered the floor, and melted candle tallow had created rivulets of wax down the sides of the porcelain surfaces. He glanced at the small mirror that imitated the large one above it, and he drew a slow breath to steady his nerves. Moving past his bedroom, he went into the living room and sat down heavily on the sofa, allowing his gaze to sweep the once candlelit room. Then he hung his head in shame.

He wasn't sure how long he'd been sitting there when he glimpsed Corey's form in the entranceway. Swathed in a deep forest green bedsheet, she looked like an African goddess.

"What's wrong?" she whispered, sounding worried as her voice seemed to hover in the expanse between them. "Is everything all right with the kids? I heard the phone ring, then you were gone."

What could he say? How did he explain to the

woman who stood before him that he was in the middle of the biggest career crisis in his life, and he'd just proposed . . . talking about honor and commitment?

"The kids are all right," he murmured, and he watched her appear to relax slightly. Struggling with an opening to the truth, he kept his gaze on the floor.

"They want me to be in L.A. on Monday," he whispered, too afraid of what her eyes might contain even to face her.

"What about the project . . . ?" she whispered, her voice trailing off. "How long?"

"I honestly don't know," he replied, forcing himself to take in her stricken expression as he looked up.

Her hand went to her mouth and fresh tears glistened in her eyes. "The children," she whispered. "Oh, Trevor, you can't do that to them."

"I know," he admitted sadly. "This is . . . Oh, damn!" He allowed his body to fall back on the sofa and cast the telephone onto the coffee table. "Baby, I don't know what to do. . . . This is a gig tied to a feature-length film—the type of project and exposure that I've dreamed of all of my life."

"I thought you dreamed of *this* all of your life," she said, her voice becoming hoarse as she swept her arm before her. "One call and poof, it's gone?"

"No, baby," he argued, his voice now a plea for understanding as he tried to reason with her while his soul fractured. "If I don't go, the consequences can be irreparable. This—"

"If you go, leave on a moment's notice, with this project still hanging and these children believing in you, *those* consequences will be irreparable. Don't you understand that?"

"How am I going to transition into civilian life?" he asked her, hoping that his Water Oracle had the answer. "How am I going to keep the lights on over the long haul? How am I going to maintain this lifestyle, send children to college, and take care of a wife? How—"

"I'll finish the edit," she said coolly. "My heart's in this project. And you don't have to worry about taking care of a wife."

Silence sliced the atmosphere between them, and it punctured his lungs, making him bleed internally.

"I'll finish the edit," he said, standing to pace toward her as tears streamed down her face.

When he came near her she backed up and started taking the ring off her finger.

"No," he said fast and hard. "Not like this. I just need to think it out, okay? I just need some time to—"

"I trusted you," she whispered, her voice splintering him. "I thought you had taken the time to think this out before you ever gave me this," she added, holding out her hand. "And even though it all seemed so miraculously sudden, too good to be true, I believed you, Trevor, when you said that this—a family, a home, a harbor—was what you wanted. Now one call comes in, and all of that is brought into question? I'll give you time . . . as much time as you need."

Her ring was in his palm, making it go numb where it lay, and she'd swept away from him and gone into the bedroom, leaving him standing in the middle of the floor. Far off in the distance, he could hear her gathering her clothes, and in moments she reappeared, fully dressed, then she picked up her bag and scarf without a word.

"I'll take you home," he whispered, not having enough air in his system to speak above a murmur.

"Don't bother. I'm just around the corner, and I could use the walk," she replied, then slipped out the door.

He sat there for a long time staring at his fist that clenched the ring, then scanned the room to begin cleaning up before all of the children came home.

* * *

She stood in the middle of her classroom, not there, just a shell, going through the lessons by rote. Somehow, she couldn't bring herself to look at their bright expressions, and when they asked for Mr. Trevor, it was as if their questions had stabbed her in the center of her chest.

So she'd made excuses, and tried to force her face to smile, but the children sensed that there was something wrong, because they fidgeted and bickered all day and seemed to be palpably affected by the invisible change taking place.

Miquel's expression, however, drew her, and as the class broke for lunch, she held him back from the group to pursue what she saw.

"Hold up a minute," she said softly, touching the boy's arm as he tried to pass her. "What's up?"

He only offered her a shrug.

"You seem really down today," she noted, trying to coax the hurt out of him so that she might be able to help heal it.

Again, the child shrugged and cast his gaze to the floor.

"You used to tell me stuff . . . now I'm not your friend anymore?"

Miquel looked up at her, his innocence untainted. "This was a terrible weekend," he said flatly. "Ever since I had to go to Elliott's so Dad could take you to a fancy dinner."

Words caught in her throat and humiliation singed them there.

"I hate Elliott," Miquel muttered. "He says I'm always lying, and I wasn't."

"No, you weren't," she said softly, realizing that the child had probably bragged about his father and his teacher going out. "But don't hate Elliott," she said, trying to reason with Miquel as she touched his arm. "You're a bigger person than that."

"But why did Dad have to be so . . . I don't know . . . When I came home, he didn't even act like he was really glad to see me. Then he was on the telephone a lot, and yelled at me when I asked him was his dinner with you fun. And you look so sad. . . . He's going away again, isn't he? He got bored with us."

Her heart lurched with the child's questions, and she had to look away to fight back the tears in her eyes. She knew exactly what the eight-year-old was experiencing, and she'd wept all day Sunday, refusing to answer even Justine's calls.

"Sometimes . . ." she began, not knowing where to take the conversation. "Sometimes adults have things on their minds that make them sad, and they don't know what to do, so they take it out on the people around them," she murmured. "But your dad isn't bored with you." She wanted so badly to ask if he'd jumped a plane, and to ask the child whether he'd packed and gone to L.A. But she restrained herself, knowing that to open that wound in the school would be so unfair to Miquel, so she hugged him to transmit her deepest balm to him.

"Miss Hamilton," Corey heard a stern female voice intone, and she broke her hold on Miquel. "May I see you in my office?"

Both Corey and Miquel exchanged a look and, as if by telepathy, the child receded from her hug and ran down the hall toward the lunchroom.

Corey hesitated, then followed her principal. The carriage of the woman's back held the rigid authority of a military policeman escorting a felon to a court-martial. As they entered Mrs. Williams's office, the sight of Elliott's parents sitting there sent a low buzzing panic through her insides.

"Miss Hamilton," the principal began, "Mrs. Gates

is here with her husband as a matter of parental concern."

Corey's gaze darted among the members of the jury that already seemed to have come to a decision. The problem was that she wasn't aware of the charges against her.

"Over the weekend," Mrs. Gates said in perfect bourgeois diction, "one of your students, Miquel Winston, came over to our house."

Corey's gaze scanned the two upwardly mobile black professionals. Both were wearing suits, the father in navy pinstripes and the mother in a spring neutral with a Coach bag planted firmly in the middle of her lap. Corey's mind grasped the facts: okay, point one—whatever it was, it had obviously made them leave their very important jobs during a lunch hour.

"I don't know what a weekend visit between classmates has to do with the school." Corey responded nervously, surveying her principal's expression as her glance traveled between the parents and her boss.

"Normally, it wouldn't," her principal said, sighing, "but somehow the lines between our curriculum, your activities, and the project the children are working on have become a messy blur of events."

Corey could barely breathe as she looked at the faces that held contempt and judgment.

"Our son," Mrs. Gates began again, "is a solid student."

"We've never had any trouble with him at all," the immaculately dressed father chimed in. "Until he began hanging out with that child, Miquel Winston—who I understand has had some behavior and social issues."

"When his aunt called and wanted to know if the child could come over, we welcomed the attempt to bring the children together. We thought that some of their little skirmishes were boys being boys, and we took them out to a wonderful evening at an arcade."

Corey felt her insides knotting as the parents spoke

in perfect, polite cues, stopping and starting in courteous yields to the floor for each other to speak.

"That was a very nice gesture," Corey said weakly, suddenly feeling the need to sit down but not having it in her to move to find a chair.

"Sit down," her principal ordered on a heavy, disgusted sigh. "Under normal circumstances, that would make sense."

"Yes, well, as I was saying," Mrs. Gates said coolly. "I didn't realize that the reason our son was having an overnight guest was because you had a date with Miquel's father."

Stunned by sudden fury, Corey slowly found a chair.

"The boys were bickering about it all night at the arcade, and Miquel kept telling Elliott about how you were over his house all of the time working on the project in Trevor Winston's basement," the father intoned like an attorney, his gaze going to his wife's face to be sure that he'd opened the argument at the right seam.

"Yes," Mrs. Gates concurred. "I know we are all living in a so-called free society, but I have a problem with the fact that our child feels like Miquel has the unwarranted favor of you as a teacher—simply because of your goings-on with that boy's father."

"Wait a minute," Corey found her voice warning, "I have never singled out a child academically because of any external reason, and—"

"This is not the crux of what brought these people into my office," her principal warned, cutting off Corey's defense. "Mrs. Gates, would you produce what Miquel left at your house?"

Corey could feel her heart beating hard enough to crack a rib. Her mind sorted through every conceivable thing that the child could have found around his and Trevor's home—condoms . . . a copy of Trevor's videotape tribute to her—Dear God, what had Miquel taken over to the Gates's house in her name? As Mrs.

Gates thrust up her chin, opened her designer bag, reached in, and produced a little plastic bag, extending her palm to the principal, Corey blanched.

"Drugs, Miss Hamilton," her principal said in a hard voice. "Drugs. And a situation where we need to contact the parent whose house they came from."

"Our child would never participate in this sordid activity," Mrs. Gates announced, her voice tight with indignation. "And this Trevor Winston person, *an artist,* no less . . . who lives some type of free-form existence, per his son's own telling—who makes those awful videos—has been allowed to run rampant in our school, take our children over to a house where this abomination came from . . . and his very essence has been woven into our children's classroom instruction—because, my husband and I fear, you, Miss Hamilton, have permitted your personal involvement to allow it."

Seeming winded from the speech, Mrs. Gates sat back in her chair, and her husband grabbed her hand and patted it.

"What we are saying is this, Miss Hamilton. We cannot allow our Elliott to go over to the Winston household again, and at this late juncture in the semester, we don't feel like he should suffer the consequences of being academically and socially ostracized from this project, when the other children aren't—all because he has parents with values and structure." Mr. Gates ended his closing argument by smoothing the front of his suit and checking his Rolex watch.

She could only look at their faces. A thousand thoughts crammed into her brain and competed for an audience. Miquel? Drugs? Never! Trevor on drugs. . . . the thought made her worry. Scott? Her hands stayed at her mouth and let her insecurity at not being absolutely positive arrest her.

"This project . . . much as I hate to do it, must be dismissed—so that all the children feel the sting equally, and Elliott is not singled out. If they think that his parents were the ones who derailed what they have all worked so hard on, the child will never be able to fit in at this school—and that is not an acceptable option, Miss Hamilton."

Her principal's words had been brittle and to the point, but the woman's eyes betrayed a level of disappointment that she, too, well understood.

But Corey could not let this happen . . . no, not like this, and the courage and knowledge of the child she loved found her voice and sent air into her lungs.

"No matter what you may think of me, I can assure you that these drugs did not come from Miquel Winston," Corey said firmly, feeling rage and indignation coil within her as the Gateses haughtily surveyed her. "Or his father," she added, defending the Winston household's honor.

"Then where on earth would they come from?" Mrs. Gates shot back immediately. "Surely you are not suggesting that our Elliott would have—"

"I am saying that I *know* Miquel Winston, and that child did not bring drugs into your home!" Corey could feel blood hotly fill her cheeks and she was standing now, about ready to walk out when common sense prevailed.

"Vanessa, I told you this meeting would be fruitless," Mr. Gates said evenly to his wife. "She's involved with the man, and the school is going to protect one of its own, so we'll have to take this matter to the authorities who can handle it," he offered on a thinly veiled threat that made her principal go ashen.

"No, Mr. Gates," Mrs. Williams said in a rush. "We will handle this responsibly, and internally, within the school, and we will assure you," she added, her voice dropping to an octave of warning, "that we will not make allowances for anything this serious—all because of a personal issue that has inappropriately been visited upon this school."

On that note, Mrs. Williams rose to meet the couple as they stood, and she extended her hand as she silently passed sentence on the project and killed it. All of the life force felt like it was escaping Corey, and she folded her arms about herself and looked down at the floor, humiliation and anger making it blur as tears stung her eyes.

Hearing the door close, she looked up at her principal and could only stare at the woman.

"This is way out of line, way too inappropriate, and I am so disappointed that I don't even know what to say."

Corey stood there and took the charge stoically, her mind reeling and her arms aching to hold and protect Miquel . . . and then, there were all of the other children who would be devastated by this derailment—simply crushed beyond description. Yes, her principal was right. This was disappointing beyond Mrs. Williams's wildest imagination, so much so that she couldn't even offer the woman a reply.

Nineteen

Even the heavens seemed to mock him as he sat on the front steps of the duplex looking up at the flawless blue sky, praying for an answer. Crystal-blue expanse stretched out above him, while he remained dark, gathering into himself clouds of guilt and self-doubt.

His bags were all packed, and he kept telling himself that as soon as Miquel came home from school he'd explain the situation to his son. Scott would be home first, as would Janelle and Samantha . . . he could only hope that they'd take the news better than Gretchen would and Corey had.

No one seemed to understand that he wasn't leaving for good. What was worse, he had no credibility, it appeared, with anyone he'd ever cared for. None of his transformation mattered; all they remembered and held him to was the past. And that, coming from Corey, was possibly the most wounding blow of them all.

His plan was to go to L.A. for only a couple of days, to find out about the details of the gig and the contract, negotiate to begin shooting after the kids were out of school, then come home. Why was that so hard—and where was his family's compromise? He'd made up his mind about that on Sunday, as he'd polished off the final edit and made as many connections to ensure the project premiere would have the best venue—and have a run in the best-positioned place for festival options.

But a man had to do what a man had to do, he reasoned and argued silently to the sky. They hadn't watched him spend half the day Sunday, and most of today, making all the right connections by telephone to call in personal markers. They hadn't seen the tears ultimately stream down his face as he'd placed Corey's refused sacrament back in its case. Nor had they sat up with him all night completing work on the project. Sacrifice. Everybody was talking about sacrifice, as though he was a stranger to the concept.

As much as it had been an escape, his travels away from them, living alone, feeling no connection, bringing home the bacon without any of the close warmth of rooted pleasure, had been a sacrifice more than they'd ever know. Especially now. It felt like a heavy cross to bear, but they thought he was running away. He'd packed for only three days. Yet all they would see was his luggage, and then they'd turn away.

Deep within his soul, he knew that he owed his son an apology, one that words could not even describe, but Daddy had to go handle some business and would be back in a few days. He kept that mantra before him, as he thought of what he would tell Scott—who would probably take it worse than Miquel.

"Well, long time no see, stranger who cannot come next door to say hello to an old family friend but can sit on the steps and consider the sky."

Trevor looked up slowly, knowing who had addressed him before he did so. "My apologies, Miss Cleo," he said sullenly to the lady toting heavy bags. "Been rippin' and tearin' and the hour would get late—"

"Since you have so much hot air to make excuses wit, why not help a neighbor to her apartment, when she's bringing in groceries from da market?"

Instant memory coursed through him as he stood. Had his mother seen him slow to the get-up for an elder, she would have slapped the back of his head.

"I'm sorry, Miss Cleo," he murmured, walking

quickly to take up her parcels. "Just a little preoccupied, is all."

"No harm taken." She chuckled and gave him a broad smile as she managed the door locks. "I know you got a lot on your mind."

He let the comment pass as he hauled her bags up the stairs. She strutted before him like a vision from the Old World, her head wrapped in a bright fabric and her thick round body that belied its age swaying beneath a loose-fitting African print dress. Patiently waiting for her to open the inside lock at her unit, he wondered how long it would take for him to extricate himself from her formidable style of hospitality.

"Jus' set ev'ry thin' down in that kitchen," she ordered, leading him with a swishing behind as he heaved the parcels toward the room into which she sauntered.

"How'd you carry this all this way alone?" he asked as he released the weight and glimpsed around her old-fashioned environment, where religious ornaments hung or sat in every corner.

"You learn to make do when you don' have no help," she said with a wide grin.

"Yeah, but you've gotta be careful," he added, making room for the bags on her drain board. "Next time, let somebody help you, before you hurt yourself."

"I could say the same to you." She chuckled and gave him a wink.

Trevor knew that was his cue to leave. Not today, and not any day in the near future. He had too much on his mind to add the layer of complexity that Miss Cleo was angling for. This woman was *not* getting into his business!

"Well, Miss Cleo, this will have to be a short visit today," he said as humbly as he could. "I have to catch a plane later this—"

"What?" she said so quickly that it froze him midstep. "Oh, no, no, no. Not today. You don't get on a plane t'day, boy. Not with a storm comin'. I tol' dat to Gretchen already. She didn't tell you what I say?"

Trevor let his breath out hard and shook his head no. His sister hadn't told him about an approaching storm, just as he really hadn't gone into detail about his plans.

"There's no storm on the weather forecast, and—"

Miss Cleo waved her hand at him and sucked her teeth. "Don' act like you don' know what I mean."

Patience was ebbing away from him. While the last thing he wanted to do was to make his mother roll over in her grave—which she would do if she even thought he'd been disrespectful to one of her oldest friends—today, his nerves were frayed beyond the point of being able to tolerate parable or kitchen-table prognostication. He just wasn't having it, Miss Cleo's reputation for accuracy notwithstanding.

"Miss Cleo, I owe you an apology for not getting by here sooner. But there's been a lot on my—"

"Saw dat you cut off all your hair—asked Gretchen 'bout it. I see a lot from my window," she added with a wry smirk.

She was getting on his nerves.

"I have to go," Trevor said, turning to leave without more explanation.

"Seems the night you cut your hair, my pipe broke. Water was everywhere," she said, shaking her head and beginning to dig in her bags. "Came in my kitchen and it busted right under da sink. Knew it was a sign. Den da water hose in the laundry room in da basement. Water everywhere, but a lot in the basement. Storm's gonna hit there, after the kitchen."

He stopped and became very, very still. Water, and the sink . . . the way Corey washed over him at her kitchen sink. And something in the basement? Get out of here. . . .

"Got your attention, huh?" Miss Cleo said, giving him her back to consider as she put away her groceries.

"You got woman problems. Don't need a third eye to see dat much, though."

Okay, this time, for real, for real, he was outta there. "Miss Cleo—"

"One's hot water, the other one's ice—my hot water pipe went first, then the cold one—dats how I know."

"Okay," he finally said, his curiosity pulling at him. "I don't have two women, in fact, I don't have any women at the moment."

"Yes, you do," she said in stubborn opposition. "Both water, but one's got ice water running through her veins. Today's not a good day to travel."

"I'll take that under advisement," he muttered, again turning to leave. "I'll tell my sister you said hello."

"No need," Miss Cleo chuckled. "When I see her soon, I'll tell her myself."

Running into Miss Cleo had chased him into the house. The front steps were no longer a safe location for sitting while he contemplated his next move. But when he put his key in the door, that's when he heard it. The sound of his sister shrieking and Scott yelling, which made him bound up the stairs.

"How could you?!" Gretchen yelled, tears streaming down her face as she spun on her son.

"It wasn't mine, Mom." Scott panted, walking in a circle around his mother, who was in full-blown hysterics. "Hones' to God—"

Before Trevor could get to Gretchen, she had slapped Scott's face, and had the man-child cowed in the corner.

"Drugs?" she shrieked. "And a gun in your locker!"

She turned quickly as she saw Trevor, who tried to go to his sister to calm her. He knew that whatever had gone down, freaking like this would ensure that

Scott wouldn't talk to her. If they wanted to get to the bottom of this, Gretchen had to chill.

"What's happened?" he said as calmly as he could, standing between Scott and Gretchen.

"They called me on my job!" his sister wailed. "Told me that they opened my son's locker and he disgraced me with drugs and a gun. Heavenly Father, just take me up from where I stand," she sobbed, seeking Trevor's shoulder. "Not my son . . . please, Jesus, not my son involved in dat."

He petted his sister's head to him, and he scanned Scott with a warning. "Tell me that you are not breaking your mother's, my sister's, heart like this. Tell me to my face, man to man."

Trevor watched the hurt spread through Scott's expression as though he'd been punched. The sight of it gave him pause to consider that there might be a backstory. All of the sullen defiance had gone out of Scott's expression for a split second, then it hardened to mask the tears that had welled up in his adolescent eyes.

"Just like I told her!" he bellowed. "It wasn't mine, so why won't anybody believe me?"

Trevor held his sister away from him and blocked Scott's exit. "Downstairs with me," he ordered. "We need to talk man to man."

"I don't have to go nowhere wit you," Scott shot back, his voice cracking from the emotion. "Ain't like you my father or nuthin'!"

"Either go downstairs with me," Trevor repeated low in his throat, "or we can do this outside. Choose!"

"I had your back—and now you ain't got mine . . . so you might as well kick my butt right here. Why hide it from Mom, huh?"

Trevor shot his sister a visual warning not to move, not to speak, and to back off. There was something in the way the kid's voice fractured, and the way Scott's eyes searched his face, that made him know there was a deeper issue going on here. And there was sheer terror in the boy's expression—terror that had puffed itself up into teenage male posturing.

"You're right," Trevor said in a steady but firm voice. "You had my back, and I respect that. So you and me go downstairs to just talk, dig? To find out how all this happened, and your mom is going to let us discuss this like men. Cool?"

He could see the man-child's shoulders relax and drop two inches, and to her credit, his sister remained immobile to allow them to pass.

Although Scott didn't answer him, he did indeed head down the stairs toward the basement, and once they got to the studio, Scott flopped on the sofa hard. Trevor sat down slowly in the pilot's chair in front of the editing deck, spun it around to face the couch, and waited. He had been here himself, just moments ago, with a complex lacing of frustration, damaged ego, hurt, and the desire to make people understand, all poisoning his system to make every one of his words come out wrong.

"Look, man," Trevor began, not knowing how to suck out the poison from his wounded nephew, or how many hemorrhage points there were in the boy's bloodstream. "I'ma listen, and let you talk, 'cause I know what it's like when everybody thinks they know what's going on with you 'cause they make assumptions, but they don't. Cool?"

The kid who sat before him angrily leaned forward with his forearms on his knees and his hands folded between them, his head bent as though he were about to say a prayer.

"Been going through a lot of changes, Unc . . . for real, for real. Got a lotta stress on me. You know?"

"Yeah," Trevor murmured. "I can dig it. Talk to me."

Scott raised his head, and to Trevor's surprise, the kid had tears in his eyes.

"I messed up bad, man," the youth admitted. "But

I didn't deal with no drugs and no gun—that's some *other* added crazy drama that I just don't need right now in my life."

Trevor fought hard to process the information that was coming in cryptic teenage spurts. Realizing that Scott was more upset about something else, something worse than possibly getting expelled and sent to a juvenile detention center for possession. . . . This had to be bad. So he took in breaths and let them out slowly, and did all he could do, which was wait.

"She's *so* beautiful, man. . . ." Scott whispered, and returned his gaze to the floor. "Met her in November, around her birthday . . . she's fine—a Scorpio, she told me. Aw, man . . ."

"You didn't use anything, did you?" Trevor said, making an instant connection. The relief that washed through him was gratuitous—on the one hand, he was relieved that there wasn't a body in the trunk of a car stashed somewhere, or news that the kid had pulled some stupid robbery or something, but a high-impact bad situation was looming. Either way, his nephew was gonna do life.

"Saturday," he said flatly. "Seven months . . . we was just talkin', you know. Then, boom . . ." Scott murmured, then looked up like he was twelve years old. "How could she be late? I mean, one time, the only time . . . and she told me that the condom was probably old—'cause she didn't roll like that . . . it might have slipped, or had a hole . . . Unc, how could that just happen like that?"

Scott's bewildered gaze trained on him. It contained a plea for information and absolution all at once. He knew the feeling that produced Scott's pained expression well. It was the same one he had when he had to sit before his own father and explain about Miquel coming into the world.

"It only takes one time, boss," Trevor whispered to the youth. "Only one seal to break, one pinhole to be there . . ." Then he thought about Corey, and how he'd broken open packages with his teeth because he'd wanted her so badly. He remembered how at one point, he had to beg her to reach for the foil, since his mind wasn't functioning on anything but being in her—and he was not sixteen.

"What you both gonna do?" Trevor said in a quiet tone, allowing the question to hang in the air.

"Whatever I gotta do, man." Scott shrugged, then leaned back and let his breath out hard.

It was the kind of rhetorical answer that meant, "I'm scared to death, how the hell do I know, so please help me decide, 'cause I never thought I'd go out like this." Trevor shook his head. "What do you think you have to do?"

"I don't know . . . if she wants to keep it, den cool . . . you know, if she don't, I'll give her the money. It's her body."

"It's also your life, so you need to weigh in with a decision before too much time elapses. Feel me?" Trevor said sternly, not as an accusation, but to get the message to sink in.

Scott nodded, then looked away.

"What do you want to do after high school?" Trevor asked the youth, trying to put today in perspective.

"I don't know." Scott shrugged. "Was thinking about going to Temple, like you, at one point. . . . I like electronics, and working with the sound equipment. They got a good program, my counselor said, for radio, TV, and film. But all that's squashed now."

Trevor saw himself and let his breath out hard. "Regardless, you've gotta provide—so, better do somethin' you love. . . . Workin' at McDonalds ain't gonna keep no kid in Pampers, and you can't drop off no baby on my sister, especially if you can't even leave her no knot. She's paid her dues. We shoulda had this conversation a while ago. Coulda dropped some for real, for real knowledge on you—but dat's my fault."

"Ain't your fault, Unc. Saturday night, you ain't twist my arm . . . then, come Monday, she was late and all. Shit happens."

Something was not making sense. "You sure that's you?" Trevor asked against his better judgment, but the question needed to be asked. He'd seen too much in his day not to.

"What you tryin' to say, man? Tianisha ain't like dat."

Trevor nodded and took the defensive blow without judgment. He'd offended Scott's woman, and at any age, those were fighting words.

"Jus' tryin' to have your back," Trevor replied.

"Yeah, well, I 'ppreciate dat, but T ain't like dat."

"Okay," Trevor said calmly, letting the issue of paternity drop. "But if there was a breach in the hull on that condom, you need to go get tested."

"For what?" Scott exclaimed, now standing. "I told you it's mine, and I don't need a paternity—"

"AIDS, dude."

"Man, I told you she don't roll like dat!"

"What do people with AIDS roll like—or look like? Huh?" Trevor shook his head in disgust at the misinformation and ignorance among teens. And at the same time it broke his heart, because there was an era when you could learn and explore without having to die from trying.

"I don't know. But she ain't no skeezer," Scott defended.

Drawing his breath slowly, Trevor looked at Scott hard—the point had to sink in.

"You think I wouldn't knock you out if you talked about Corey Hamilton like that?"

The teenager stopped pacing and became very, very still.

"I'm mad crazy about her, Scott," he admitted, holding the teen in his gaze, "and even I used something with her . . . and if a condom busted, we'd both have to get tested. Dig?"

Somehow the admission made Scott edge toward a seat, as though stunned. The boy sat down without taking his eyes off his uncle—stun mixed with awe, as if Trevor had given him too much information at one time. It pained Trevor to watch the man-child trying to grapple with the fact that indeed Miss Hamilton had slept with him, and then try to process that even a woman of her pristine character could have contracted something horrific from someone before him. He hated to have to unveil his most cherished secret to a boy . . . but the boy was on the precipice of throwing away his life in a vain effort to define being a man.

"Unc," Scott whispered, "how soon can they tell? I mean, the baby ain't as bad as . . . possibly . . ."

"Yes, you could die," Trevor said plainly, "and you need to get tested annually—unless she was a virgin like you. . . . If not, I hope you dodged a bullet. Like I said, I gotchure back. But you need to say and think that out loud—*I could die*—so you don't roll like this again. Ever."

Scott nodded, and he wiped his damp face quickly and turned away. Trevor gave him a moment to collect himself, understanding that the youth had more emotions running through him than a raging sea.

"Talk to me about the gun and the drugs—since that's a known fact. The rest of what you just told me is pending information."

"Honest to God," Scott said quickly, holding his gaze. "I don't know how m'boy's stuff got in my locker, and I'm not gonna give up the tapes that it's m'boy Ice's stuff . . . we go back. Nobody has the combo but me and T . . . I wouldn't do that to Moms, for real—if nobody else does, you gotta believe me, man."

Trevor watched the tears well up in the eyes of what once looked like a street-hardened, six-foot-tall gang member who now slouched before him hanging on every word he had to say as though he were Miquel's age. This man was a mere boy, and this boy was also a man. L.A. would have to wait, and there was no way that he could make another gangster video now . . . not staring at the ripple effect of his images before him. Trevor rubbed his face and raked his fingers through his hair, and a dawning memory crept into his consciousness.

"Your boy had a gun and ran drugs?"

"Yeah," Scott said, letting his breath out hard with the confession. "He ain't never shoot nobody, but was always flashin' it around, you know. Ran reefer. Has his little cousin trying to be a hard guy now, too."

"Did I ever meet your boy? He been here?"

"Nah." Scott shrugged. "We used to hang out a lot, before we started working on this project . . . but he said this was bull 'cause we wasn't gettin' paid. Then he started actin' funny, and got new on me about a month ago—like he ain't have no time for me, since I wasn't rollin' like him . . . you know, you know."

Footsteps overhead made both Trevor and Scott look up, and Scott cast a nervous gaze in Trevor's direction. Then a key turned the locks, and he knew it was the kids.

"If it's Janelle or Sam, I'll tell them to go upstairs. The footsteps are too light to be your mom."

Scott only nodded and let his breath out hard, then rubbed his jaw nervously. "Cool. I just ain't ready to deal with them right now."

"I can dig it," Trevor said in earnest, listening to the first floor being crossed. "You're lucky they let you come home with your mom. They could have sent you right down to the precinct."

"They gave Mom twenty-four hours to bring me in," Scott whispered. "It's killing her." Fear flickered past the pain in his statement, and the youth looked away as his eyes filled again.

The sounds of footsteps on the basement stairs propelled Trevor from his chair to block the passage of any wanna-be studio editors coming down to intrude, and he stopped dead as he saw Miquel and Corey come into view. Miquel had obviously let her in, but now was not the time.

She didn't speak, but her eyes said it all as she led his son down the steps. For the third time today, Trevor held his breath.

"I'm down here with Scott," he warned. "This is not a good time."

"Before you get on that plane," she said in a low threat, "you'd better make time to listen to this."

When Miquel and Scott looked at him with hurt, anger shot through him. This was not how they were supposed to find out! He was going to sit down with them, talk it out . . . she'd just assumed . . .

"I said," he began again, his voice escalating beyond his will. "Scott and I have some import—"

"Eliott's parents found drugs in his room after Miquel was there, and they are blaming Miquel and are about to fire me. Turn off the edit decks. The project is dead."

Twenty

The quiet that engulfed the group hung over them like stagnant air. Trevor's gaze ricocheted around the stricken faces in the room, his fear and rage looking for a place to land. His focus settled on his son, then shot to Scott, then back to Corey as previous attempts to remain calm bled from his brain.

"What the hell is going on?!" he found himself bellowing, scanning first his nephew, then his son. "You take this boy with you and your boys, huh? Leave him in harm's way with a camera? Fill his pockets with—"

"No!" Scott hollered, and was on his feet in a flash. But the teenager was backed deep into the bowels of the basement, Trevor blocking his exit.

"I'll kill you!" Trevor yelled, advancing toward the youth—predatory, parental rage blocking wisdom. "My son, your cousin, is eight years old!"

"Is this how you intend to solve this, Trevor?" a female voice in the room cut through the chaos. "You can't talk, communicate, with anything other than a testosterone rush? Both of you!"

Spinning on her, Trevor felt his chest heaving, and he watched the trapped Scott from the corner of his eye—noting that the youth kept himself pressed to the wall. "Speak to me, and tell me what happened to my son."

The immediate silence was so loud that it could have shaken the artwork off the walls.

"That's why I walked Miquel home, when you didn't come," Corey said through her teeth, and she began to circle Trevor while the children hung back.

She would hunt him down and slay him and put his head on her desk as a trophy—if she ever got another job.

"Unlike you, I talked to Miquel while we walked. Figured you'd be off to L.A. by now, and it really doesn't matter anyway."

"Skip the editorial comment," Trevor warned, his chest still heaving with fury.

But she did notice he'd stopped following her circling motion with his eyes and she stood still. Scott, however, had not moved, and Miquel had gone to her side. *That's right, babies,* she said to herself, *he can roar, but I'll rip his heart out!* It was on . . .

"Today," she nearly hissed, "Mr. and Mrs. Gates came to the school, and said that over the weekend, while Miquel spent the night with Eliott, they discovered marijuana in their son's room—and Eliott said it was Miquel's . . . and that he got it from his older cousin, Scott."

"That's a lie!" Scott hollered, moving out of Trevor's swing range.

"I told Miss Hamilton that, too," Miquel offered in a loud defense of his cousin, "and she believed me, Dad. She lost her job because Eliott lied!"

Again, the room fell silent. Fatigue made Trevor's shoulders slump as the adrenaline spikes wore on him. But it was the tension of hearing that news while looking at her angry, hurt expression, and not knowing what to do, that took all of the fight out of him. What in heaven's name had happened?

"Okay, everybody calm down," Trevor said in a controlled tone, trying to restore the peace so that they could collectively gather the facts. "Let's take this from the top—"

"This is not a movie, Trevor!" she screamed, making

even the children back away from her as her fortitude snapped. "I have *lost my job* behind this. I quit, handed in my resignation this afternoon—because I was not about to allow them to pin a drug allegation on Miquel, and have it haunt his school career forever. And because they knew about my *relationship* with you, which they said clouded my ability to see straight—I have never been so professionally humiliated in my life. Where will I get another job teaching after this scandal? Huh?"

A full-blown hurricane came at him, just as Miss Cleo predicted, and he and the children stood in the basement huddled against some object to hold on to lest gale-force winds blow them away. The nosy old girl was right . . . this was definitely not the day to travel.

Angry tears coursed down Corey's face, and she swiped at them hard with the balls of her fists as she came up to him two inches from his face. "All because I would not kill this project that meant so much to these kids, even though you have probably booked yourself on the next thing smoking, and aren't thinking about this project. Well, I walked for it, and for Miquel! Go to hell, Trevor Winston, telling me to calm down."

He didn't know what else to do but reach for her—the pain she felt oddly becoming his own. He had to connect to her, to face this storm and step into the eye of it to find a calm place to get answers. His sister was running down the stairs, obviously coming toward the sound of a female voice gone out of control. And, in slow motion, everything collided when Corey hauled off and slapped him, then paced away.

Scott and Miquel's eyes widened, stunned. They didn't move. Gretchen gripped the basement banister as though she were keeping herself from falling over it. Corey turned her back, covered her face with her hands, and began to sob. Scott searched his fallen hero's eyes for redemption, his gaze asking the forbidden question—telepathically transmitting it—asking why a man would take what just happened from a woman. But it was Miquel who had the innocence of youth, the presence of mind to not allow anything but love to stand between him and the wounded member of their family.

Moving to her side slowly, he wrapped his arms around her waist and petted her. "Miss Hamilton, don't cry," the child crooned. "Scott didn't give me those drugs, and neither did my dad, I swear to you on my grandma's grave. Eliott gets them from his big cousin. Don't cry, Miss Hamilton, you're a really good teacher, everybody knows that . . . you'll get your old job back." Looking over at his father, the child's eyes begged for assistance. "Tell her, Dad. Tell her. She thinks you're gonna leave, but you gave us all your word that you wouldn't."

Corey's sobs escalated as she kissed the child's head and bent to hug him. Drawn to her and Miquel, Trevor wrapped them both in his arms and tried to get her to stop crying, kissing their hair, rubbing backs. Gretchen had her hands over her mouth as silent tears fell from her face. Scott swallowed hard as more footsteps overhead made their way down into the basement, and Janelle and Samantha turned into petrified wood where they stopped.

"Okay, okay, everybody . . ." Trevor said, trying to garner as much control in his voice as he could. "Multiple issues colliding here," he said with his arm still around Corey and Miquel. "People talk to me—one at a time."

"Miquel ain't running no drugs, Unc. Eliott is m'boy's little cousin, the one I told you about. His people live large up in Mount Airy, parents got phat jobs, but since his mom and pop got crazy work schedules, and the kid goes to the new charter school down here, his aunt—m'boy's mom—watches him down our way. The kid hangs with his cousin down here all the time, trying to act hard—and been jealous of Miquel from day one, den when we started making the movie, him and Miquel was always gettin' in it. So if his parents found somethin,' the little rat probably lied and blamed it on Miquel."

"Baby, why didn't you tell me you were always scrappin' wit dis chile?" Gretchen said, her voice growing soft as she came to Miquel's side.

"That's why I didn't wanna go over Eliott's house, even though you and Miss Peaches—his big cousin's Mom—are friends," Miquel said in a soft voice. "She's nice, but you wanted me to go to one of my school friends' houses, 'cause you always say you don't like what happens in Miss Peaches's house, Aunt Gret."

"God, forgive me," Gretchen whispered, pulling the child to her hard. "I thought because his parents had good jobs, and had class, it was a better place for you to be, honey. You have to talk to us." Gretchen's eyes searched the child's face, then she looked up to her son with an apology cast in her expression.

"I went because Scott told me not to be a baby, him and Ice were going to hang out, and he told me not to mess up this real important gift Dad had to give Miss Hamilton, and for real, I didn't want to spoil it for them 'cause I love them both."

Trevor couldn't even look at the boy as Corey gasped and went to his side with Gretchen, and Scott groaned as if he'd been stabbed.

"Aw, little man . . . this is all my fault," Scott said, leaning his head against the wall. "I didn't want you hangin' wit me and Ice, 'cause it had been a long time since we'd hung—dat was m'boy . . . den, since his mom don't care 'bout no time frame . . . you know, you know, I was gonna go by this house party, and hook up wit Tianisha. . . . This is all jacked up."

"Tianisha?" Janelle said, as Samantha gasped.

"You are not running with that hussy, are you? Oh, Scott." Samantha sighed.

"What?" Scott said defensively, glancing at Trevor for moral support.

"First she was with you, then been sneakin' around dealin' with Ice," Janelle said in a huff. "Said he kept her phat paid, because of his hustle, but she liked the fact that your uncle could get her into videos, so she been playin' you both with her pregnant self. Ice got her dat way early dis month, and she still walking around, trying to act like she ain't."

Trevor's gaze immediately went to Scott knowing that within moments, pain, betrayal, rage, hurt, relief, and humiliation would all gather slowly within the young man's chest and explode in his vocal cords in a sonic boom.

"What?!" Scott bellowed, pacing around the room. "That's a lie, Janelle! Y'all got it wrong!"

Trevor walked over, put an arm on the youth's shoulder, and held it firm. "Shake it off, man. Not in front of the women and kids. Later—we talk. Like I said, I got chure back. It ain't you. Not in twenty-four, I'm giving it to you straight."

Oddly, his sister hadn't flinched at her son's admission, appearing too fatigued. Corey held Miquel and now rubbed Gretchen's back. Samantha reached out and put her hand on Janelle's arm to stop a rebuttal, making Janelle seem to grasp for the first time that her brother was in distress in a way that was too fragile for sibling digs.

Mortally wounded, Scott whirred in a circle, then faced the wall. The room went silent and Gretchen looked up, searching her brother's face for answers he didn't have.

"Tomorrow, they want me to bring him down . . . they only let me take him home because they know me at the school, and Scott has turned the corner, and his counselor vouched for him. But what are we going to do about what they found in his locker?"

"I can prove it isn't Scott's gun," Miquel murmured. "It belongs to Ice, just like the drugs do."

All eyes turned to Miquel, except for Scott's, which were shut tight as his head remained against the wall.

"Thanks for tryin' to have my back, little man," Scott whispered on a heavy exhale. "I already got you in enough trouble."

"But I took pictures of it, just like I took pictures of Ice and Tianisha under the steps at school—when it was my turn to hold the camera."

"She used to carry his gun and some of his stuff all the time, tryin' to play the role like a gansta girlfriend, and showed it to us—that's how I knew . . . then she was bragging about her man getting her pregnant. She's ignorant, Scott—you deserve better than that. For real. Whenever there'd be a school sweep, like they had today, she'd always hide it somewhere, then give it back to her man. Bet she just opened Scott's locker and ditched it—to keep Ice out of trouble . . . and figured Uncle Trevor could buy Scott's way out. That's how the girl rolls," Janelle said in a quiet voice, looking at her brother with empathy. "I'm so sorry, Scott."

"It's true," Samantha concurred in a very sad voice, "Janelle told me all about it in April . . . just as a matter of girl talking about what was going on in the neighborhood. We just didn't know you were trying to be with Tianisha, or we would have told you, Scott."

"I'll be . . ." Trevor whispered, going to find the raw footage he'd marked. "Miss Cleo said there were two women of water . . . one with Ice in her veins. This is crazy," he murmured, finding the tape as Gretchen fled to his side.

"When did you see Cleo?" his sister asked in a rush. "What did she tell you?"

"Sittin' on the steps, minding my business today. I helped her in with her bags, and she said a pipe broke under her kitchen sink, the same day I cut my locks, then her basement flooded—she said that an underground storm was gathering, and it wasn't a good day to travel away from the house."

"Water? You know that brings messages?" Gretchen whispered as Trevor cued up Miquel's unedited sequences.

Corey listened and watched from a very remote place in her mind. It was like an out-of-body experience as she witnessed the family around her splinter, then pull together to save each of its vulnerable members from demise. And her heart lurched as she watched tears rise, then burn away quickly from Scott's hurt-filled eyes when the uncut version of the love of his life was captured on tape with his best friend.

Her heart ached for the young man, whose uncle supported him with no words, just touch, and she watched Scott sadly pat his younger cousin on the back in thanks, but then leave the group to be alone. Then she saw Miquel question his father, asking why if Scott was vindicated and this was a good thing, why did Scott still hurt so bad. And she watched Miquel's Aunt Gretchen tell the child that, hopefully one day, as a man, he wouldn't ever have to find out. And she watched Samantha put an arm around Janelle, and then caution her not to say a word to her brother. Somehow in that exchange the younger girl seemed to take in that some things were too painful, and privacy was in order . . . those gashes to the soul were not to be used in sibling taunts, and were to be edited for the school six o'clock girl news. Then she saw a man bend down and hug his son with his eyes closed as tears wet his lashes. And she saw the same man turn to his sister with care, and promise her what he'd said before, that he'd always be there for her, come what may—even if his trips were short ones these days. And that sister, out of abiding affection, escorted that child upstairs to allow his father room to restore another important aspect of his life.

Then she saw the storm pass, and leave love in its

wake, and lessons get learned, while family filed out of the space. And she was left there to consider the man who she'd just tried to flush out of her life.

"This came up so fast, and so hard, Corey," he whispered. "It could have been tragic—to epic proportions. It was like a tornado hit, and now we're standing dow' here pickin' up the pieces . . ."

"Yeah," she whispered. "It was absolute destruction. But I guess it's time to rebuild. A lot of lessons came out of all of this."

"What are you going to do 'bout your job?" he asked quietly. "After being so humiliated at my hand, and having to resign . . . baby, you should be back at that school."

"Oh, I'm going back," she said with a quiet chuckle. "I'm water, remember, and you can't keep me out of where I want to go. I'm marching right back in with a copy of this tape for my principal and those bourgeois Negroes—the Gateses—and I will explain to them how they need to stop making judgments, when their *own* son has a supplier in their family. Then I'm going to edit this film and let these children have something they worked so hard on."

"It's finished," he whispered. "I worked on it all day Sunday, and made the calls to set everything up, like I promised, with the intentions of only going to L.A. for a few days. My goal was to get the shoot pushed back until after the kids get out of school in June. But after all of this . . . I couldn't make that video the way they probably want it, anyway."

She just stared at him. "You were coming back to finish out the school year?"

"Yeah," he murmured. "I made a commitment. I just needed a little space to integrate the past career stuff into the future. But Corey, I was coming back for you, my son, and my family. Do you actually think I would just walk for the money? I was going out there to try to get some editorial control. I need to be able to write some of what I shoot, and put my slant on it. I can't do the hard-core stuff any more—not after you, and what I've learned."

His voice had dropped to a murmur, but his gaze held hers, as though trying to let her see into his spirit. "I was gonna go out there and give 'em a little drama, and come back here for, say, a few months of an adequate artistic snit—then you know, you know, shoot over the summer . . . after I came back from Martha's Vineyard."

"What . . . ?" she asked, her question trailing off into a very tiny voice.

"Thought you might come up there, after I had a few months to get you to take back my ring . . . figured standing on some cliffs, with the ocean spraying in our faces, as we put the project into the Flava Fest . . . I might be able to coax you into trusting me, then from there to come back to my room at the bed-and-breakfast . . . then maybe I'd slip the ring back on your finger, and let you watch again. . . . I don't know, it was just a thought."

Her laugh began deep down in her belly as he rubbed his face where she'd slapped it, then pointed to it for a kiss.

"This storm packed quite a whallop, but no casualties. It's all good."

"I am so sorry," she whispered. When she neared him to make up for the violation he pinned her against the wall.

"Water Oracle, you almost drowned me, slapped the livin' taste out of me mouth you was so mad at me."

"I am *so* sorry," she said, laughing tenderly, kissing his cheek.

"Cussed me out, stomped your feet, was gonna kick me butt, all in fronta all de children, you were . . . but I love a tempest woman, wit all her eccentricities. . . . Ruined my reputation in dis house as king of da jungle . . . beat me down in fronta me son."

"Ohhhh, baby, I thought . . . oh, I am so very sorry," she whispered as he chuckled, landing tiny kisses against his neck.

"Since you was standing up for my son's honor, however, I could be assuaged with an offer of contrition from the Water Oracle herself. Especially since she's now talkin' in my ear in the way that she knows makes me crazy."

"Tell me what would repair the damage I've done," she said on a husky breath even closer to his ear.

Trevor shut his eyes and smiled.

"Try the ring back on for size . . . although I have been married, I have never asked anyone to marry me before in my life. I meant this."

She looked at him and could only stare at him for a moment. The smile had gone out of his eyes and his gaze had become tender.

"Before, when I found out some disconcerting news about a baby on the way, the person and I just said, 'Okay, let's do this.' So we did, and it was a disaster. Lust led us to the altar but we weren't friends, and weren't soul mates. So I'm a virgin at askin' a woman to marry me," he said, chuckling, "and you stopped, dropped, and rolled me. . . . I know how Scott feels."

"Oh, my God . . ."

"Yeah, see, women make assumptions . . ."

His voice penetrated her navel as their bellies touched, and the scent of him filled her nose.

"Men love hard, Corey," he murmured against her hairline. "Once we fall, we don' see nuthin' else. Saturday night was my first time . . . and I wanted ev'rythin' to be perfect . . . and I wanted you to accept me, and I was inexperienced and shy, and scared, and didn't know what to do first, and I needed you to lead me, let me know ev'rythin' was all right. Dats why the next day I thought I was gonna lose it when you wouldn't even let me take you home."

"Oh, baby . . ." she crooned in his ear. "Had I

known it was your first time," she added with a deliciously wicked chuckle, "I would have been more gentle, taken my time . . ."

Her voice and the playfulness in it made him grin, and his groin ignited.

"You'd best to stop ohhh-babying me, and sounding like you're somethin' good to eat—Miss Cleo said there's water in my basement . . . a storm brewing down here underground," he murmured, nipping her neck. "And since the kids all know our business, as does half of West Philly, why don't you stay with me down here for a while? Everybody's upstairs."

She laughed as he moved against her, and she whispered into his ear. "Because down here there's always a chance of someone catching us while we're drowning. Since everyone knows you aren't leaving until later tonight . . . my kitchen has water, too . . . as well as leftover gourmet food."

"You'll stop in my room so I can give you back your ring before we go?"

"If you promise I'll get back out alive—since I know this lion has teeth."

"Can't promise, but I will try," he growled low near her ear.

Music going on and multiple feet heard overhead made them laugh and pull away from each other, and quickly kiss before they ran upstairs.

Epilogue

One year later . . .

"Why don't you come to bed, baby?" he whispered into her ear, leaning over to kiss her neck as she typed on the laptop. He breathed in a whiff of her light fragrance that summoned him as his cheek brushed her thick, soft tendrils at her nape. Her body had become so lush with its changing dimensions that the thought of being separated from it, even for a short time, made him shudder.

"I just have to finish this grant," she said, not looking up. "The production company needs some more equipment, and the children have a great idea to do some animation with clay. Plus, we need a second van, a fifteen-seater, just to accommodate our high school crew. How'd you and Scott make out with the move?"

"He's like a kid in a candy store. However, I thought Gretchen was gonna bust a gasket when her son took over my old unit. But, like I told her, come September, the boy's gonna be in college, so she has to respect his privacy if he's gonna stay close to home and commute up to Temple every day. Truth be told, Samantha needs her space, too. So the only way I could convince Gretchen to let him live down there was if Sam would be there with him, too. College cousins, sharing a dorm in unit one."

"Bet that went over like a lead brick." Corey chuckled, adjusting a pair of reading glasses on her nose and stretching.

"Yeah, but when I told her to formally draft Miss Cleo as her look-out agent, my sister gave in without a struggle. Da woman is like central intelligence, and could have ended the Cold War long ago—if the government had employed her."

Corey laughed, took off her spectacles, set them beside the laptop, and rubbed her belly . . . but continued typing. "I hear you," she said. "She called everything, didn't she?"

"Hmmm . . ." he murmured next to her shoulder. "Dat she did. Now she's on the lookout for Janelle, who has been home alone lately, now that Gretch has some personal business to attend to."

"But I bet Janelle is happy to have her own bedroom and the phone all to herself."

"I've gotta install another line over there soon, because the girl still doesn't know how to take a message, and Gretchen can't get in her caterin' client calls. Without Sam up there, things could blow. I tried to tell my sister to just have all her calls go to voice mail over at the restaurant—but you know my sister."

"Yes, I do," Corey replied with a smile. "But, I'm not about to take your side over my rice and peas and redfish supply. Oh, no, brother, let's be clear . . . Gretchen's coconut pound cake reigns supreme with me. You got tough competition. So don't bad-mouth her to me."

"I do have some competitive advantages, though. . . . I should still have some left, as we've just been married little over a year."

"Hmmm . . . maybe . . ."

Her voice was warm and joy-filled, and he loved it. He closed his eyes and let it flow over him, and again remembered that he would be gone from her for two weeks.

"Remember our anniversary . . ." he whispered.

"Oh, see, now you're trying to conjure images that will mess up my typing, huh?" She laughed and nipped his cheek.

"Remember our wedding?" he murmured, allowing his tongue to flick a tiny, soft section of her neck. "We stood under an arch of hibiscus and orchids that smell like you do now . . . and placed our parents' photos on the small altar . . . then the minister consecrated what we had together under a flawless blue sky. And you wore a white sheath, with tiny flowers in your upswept hair, and a long oblong sheer scarf caught the breeze and fluttered behind you like you were an angel standing on that cliff with wings . . . and you carried a tiny bouquet of blue and violet flowers . . . and my sister and Justine stood behind you in hues of blue, with Janelle and Sam . . . and you turned the side of a Jamaican cliff into paradise, and showed my son, nephew, niece, and cousins what a real Water Oracle looks like . . . and we ate a sumptuous meal with laughter and family all around . . . then you allowed me to take you away from the gala, and have you all to myself."

He noticed that she'd closed her eyes and had leaned back against him, and he watched the way her nostrils flared ever so slightly as he was whispering to her. She still had a wondrous effect on him, and he loved to slowly arouse her with images through her ear.

"Remember our honeymoon?" she murmured on a husky, sexy breath. "The waterfall in Ocho Rios . . . and the villa . . ."

"Don't go there, love, unless you are ready to turn off that laptop right now, and save your work. Taking me to the waterfall is unfair."

"And I wore pale blue for you and became your deepest ocean, with *nothing* between us, but skin . . ."

He shuddered hard and let his head fall onto the crook of her neck. "You don' play fair, woman," he murmured with a chuckle. "Come to bed."

"Payback—now let me do my work." She laughed amiably, reaching backward to touch his cheek before she leaned forward and began typing again.

"Yeah," he laughed deep in his throat, leaning over farther and wrapping his arms around her. He rested his chin on her shoulder and allowed his palms to cradle her extended belly. "You gonna be working much longer?"

"Why?" she giggled. "It's late, and you have to go to the airport in the morning."

"Because," he drawled out thickly in her ear, "it's late, which means Miquel is probably asleep, and I have to go to the airport in the morning."

"No, Miquel is not asleep," she said, giggling.

He let his breath out hard in defeat.

"He's over Justine's with her and her nephews . . . for the night."

"Really?" he asked, letting the relief come out on a hot shaft of air. "How did you arrange that?"

"Ever notice how coincidentally, the house is empty the night just before you go away?"

He hadn't put it together, in all honesty, but it was a lovely coincidence indeed. "You are clever, Water Oracle . . . insightful, if not psychic, to be sure. Miss Cleo has competition."

"I fill up my favor bank by taking turns with the other mothers while you are gone . . . and I call in my markers the day you return," she whispered on a lazy, sultry tone.

"You almost finished with that grant?" he urged, his hands traveling down her upper arms.

"Oh," she chuckled, still typing away. "Trying to get me back in that sleigh—which got me into this condition in the first place, 'eh?"

"You have misjudged my character and made assumptions," he whispered close to her ear.

"Really," she said, swatting his hands as they traveled up her torso and tenderly cradled her breasts. "Oh, my apologies," she said. "I guess I assumed that you would behave like you did when we went to all those festivals last summer, and when the documentary won awards . . . and since you're up for a new contract again, I wrongly assumed that you just wanted to work off some tension . . . like you always do before a contract . . . or festival . . . or premiere . . . or a screening . . . or after you've been riding your bike in Fairmount Park—collecting new images . . ."

"My character has been assailed, and this time the Water Oracle is incorrect."

"Ahhh," she crooned, leaning back to give him a peck on his lips. "Then the fact that you're breathing hard on me is just a special effect?"

"Yeah," he whispered hard at her hairline. "I just want to snuggle up to you and dissolve, very gentle effect, then fade to black."

"In that big old sleigh bed in front of the mirror?"

"Gurl, you are turning my intentions against me, and it isn't fair," he said, chuckling low in his throat. "I'll be very, very gentle . . . as you are carrying precious cargo."

"Ohhhh . . ." she said on a deep, sexy inhale. "Then maybe I'll have to shut off the computer and just talk to you in bed."

He noticed that she had pushed Save, and had closed the file she was working on.

"Yeah . . ." he said on a long breath. "Talk to me . . . and keep me company . . . while we cruise to nowhere in the open sea."

Dear Readers,

The underlying theme in LOVE LESSONS is about finding balance—learning to balance one's career aspirations with a family, responsibility with desire, and struggle with surrender. It is about learning to trust in the hidden plan of the cosmos, while also doing one's part to contribute to the hard work of shaping one's life. Most of all, it is about learning something positive from every experience and human interaction in a way that leaves you and your most unlikely teacher richer for the exchange.

I hope this book leaves you with something to think about, long after the story is finished. Who are your teachers, and what are you teaching? May we all teach and learn the most important subject matter of all: love.

ARABESQUE MAN
2000 AWARD-WINNER

Edman Reid steps from corporate life onto the cover of a romance novel

Edman Reid, a pharmaceutical sales representative from Philadelphia, is the Grand Prize Winner of the 2000 "Do You Know an Arabesque Man" contest. Reid will appear on the cover of the book LOVE LESSONS by Leslie Esdaile (also a Philadelphia resident), scheduled for release in September 2001. The contest was nationally promoted in Arabesque books and on the BET cable network, reaching sixty million households.

A corporate sales executive for a leading pharmaceutical company, Reid is far more comfortable in a suit and tie, meeting with medical professionals than at a New York City professional shoot designed to produce an alluring photograph. "It was exciting to step into the world of male models—if only for a day. Watching the professionals was inspiring, and it put me at ease. Once in front of the camera, I found it enticing. I won't quit my day job, but it was exciting and an outstanding opportunity," Reid says.

Reid, thirty-four, is an eligible bachelor, who is inspired by his parents, Herman and Edith Reid, to achieve success in both his personal and professional life. The youngest of seven children, raised in Pittsburg,

Reid has a commitment to the non-profit foundation NEED, which his father had led for more than thirty-six years. The foundation is geared to providing financial assistance and educational counseling to talented young African-Americans. "I'm inspired constantly by my father. In addition to raising all of us, he gave himself to the Pittsburg community with such a dynamic program. He is my role model and my friend," Reid says.

Being an effective professional and having a strong focus on family were only some of the reasons Peggy Smith, a colleague, nominated Reid for the contest. She stated, "As a five-year reader of Arabesque books, I knew that Edman exudes the confidence, integrity, and respect for women portrayed by the characters in the novels."

Reid has a strong sense of romance. His ideal first date would be "meeting a kind-hearted, fun-loving young woman over lunch, flowers in hand, and then spending the afternoon at an outdoor concert." He stated, "My best qualities are honesty in relationships and making sure I'm paying attention—lot's of it! I'm looking for someone special to build a lifetime partnership."

The future is bright for Reid, a business and finance graduate of the University of Pittsburgh, whose goals are to further his professional career into management and return to graduate school to earn an MBA. He holds in high esteem entrepreneurs, as well as corporate executives, with a proven track record of success. "My brother, a physician in Philadelphia, has been in private practice since the day he graduated from medical school. This is an accomplishment that keeps me focused on reaching my professional goals," Reid says. "Building wealth and financial independence takes discipline in life. I'm committed for myself, and through my father's foundation, to assisting others to achieve similar success."

Arabesque is proud to recognize Edman Reid as the 2000 Arabesque Man. For more information about the annual Arabesque Man contest visit our Web site at www.arabesquebooks.com.

ABOUT THE AUTHOR

Leslie Esdaile is a native Philadelphian and Dean's List graduate of the University of Pennsylvania, Wharton Undergraduate Program. Upon graduating in 1980, she embarked upon a career in corporate marketing and sales with Fortune 100 companies Xerox, Hewlett Packard, and ultimately, Digital Equipment Corporation.

With her daughter's near-fatal day care center accident in 1991, Leslie shifted gears and began an independent consulting career, assisting small businesses and economic development agencies with marketing, grantwriting, curriculum development and workshop facilitation. Also a filmmaker, she recently returned to school, successfully graduating from Temple University's Master of Fine Arts Program.

Blending her understanding of business with her creative force, Leslie develops the basis of her novels and screenplays from her entrepreneurial and life experiences. She currently works as the Director of Competitive Initiatives for Ben Franklin Technology Partners of Southeastern PA and lives in Philadelphia with her new husband, WHYY Engineer Al Banks, and their blended family of four young children.

To contact Leslie, please e-mail her at:
WriterLE@aol.com
or visit her Web site at:
http://www.paintedrock.com/authors/esdaile.htm.